PRAISE FOR MAX BYRD

"Max Byrd is an expert at mingling real historical
figures with his invented characters."
—*THE NEW YORK TIMES*

"Lock Byrd's cage and throw away the key—until he slips out
a few more thrillers."
—*THE PHILADELPHIA ENQUIRER*

"Max Byrd's plots, like his wit, are sinister and charming."
— DIANE JOHNSON,
bestselling author of *The Shadow Knows*

"Max Byrd is a fine and forceful writer."
—LAWRENCE BLOCK, bestselling author of
Eight Million Ways to Die

"Max Byrd is in the first division of American crime writing."
—*THE NEW YORK TIMES*

"Sharp writing . . . exciting . . . fulfills the promise of its title."
—*PUBLISHERS WEEKLY,* for *California Thriller*

FINDERS
WEEPERS

FINDERS WEEPERS

MAX BYRD

TURNER

Turner Publishing Company
200 4th Avenue North • Suite 950 Nashville, Tennessee 37219
445 Park Avenue • 9th Floor New York, NY 10022

www.turnerpublishing.com

Finders Weepers

Cover design: Glen Edelstein
Book design: Kym Whitley

Cover image: Masterfile

Library of Congress Cataloging-in-Publication Data

Byrd, Max.
 Finders weepers / Max Byrd.
     p. cm.
 "A Mike Haller mystery."
 ISBN 978-1-61858-027-6
 1. Private investigators--California--San Francisco--Fiction. I. Title.
 PS3552.Y675F56 2012
 813'.54--dc23
                              2012022560

Printed in the United States of America
12 13 14 15 16 17 18—0 9 8 7 6 5 4 3 2 1

"I'm looking for Muriel Contreras," I started to say, and she jumped the chair back from the table and came to her feet.

"You're the cop!"

I stood up too and shook my head, about to speak.

"You shot her old man. You're the cop's been chasing her. You're the one she was going to see south of Market and you shot her old man."

I wanted to lunge for her wrists and hold her down to listen, but I shook my head slowly so the reassuring expression wouldn't fall off and tried to speak again.

"I didn't do it," I began.

"What the hell's going on here?" the bouncer growled, materializing at my elbow. A flush spread from Christie's face to the tops of her breasts and she looked first at the bouncer and then at me.

"I didn't do it," I told her. "You're making a mistake."

"This guy bothering you, kid?" the bouncer asked Christie. "You want me to toss him out?" He turned his big, flat face toward me like a rusty turret revolving. Christie chewed her lower lip and looked unhappy. "The owners don't like tough guys with the broads," he said. "You wanta be a tough guy, you gotta start with me."

CHAPTER 1

IF I WALKED UP TO CHICK GANNETT'S DOOR AND knocked, I thought, the Doberman would probably answer.

I relaxed my stranglehold on the steering wheel and used one finger to stab the cigarette lighter into the dash. Then I turned off the engine and stared down the street, away from the house, trying to move my mind from Chick's front door.

Richmond, California. Ten square miles of asphalt and oil refinery on the northeast corner of San Francisco Bay. An elegant old Confederate name buckled across a piece of Sunbelt suburbia. The California they televise in nineteen-inch color squares may be all palm trees and rolling surf and pickup trucks full of lite beer drinkers, but Grande Street in Richmond begins under a freeway and ends in a mud flat, in a dingy clutter of cinderblock shopping centers and auto parts stores and strips of cheap forgotten houses like the one I was staring at again. I spat tobacco off my lip and rolled down the window.

It was a two-story wooden house about fifty years old that Chick had rented, with a porch that sagged like a belly and a jaundiced yellow paint job flaking around the windows. In front of the house an exhausted scrap of brown lawn had stretched out to die. In back would be the fenced-in yard where the pup could run.

The lighter popped and I held up its red tongue. A few streets away clouds of gray fog peeked over a line of roofs. Half a block down the sidewalk two burly teenagers strutted toward me, one of them carrying a radio the size of a trashcan next to his ear. At the brown lawn they slowed down, looked me over first and decided I was too big. Then they looked the car over and decided it was too old. They had it backwards. The car was a 1958 Mercedes 190SL, 200,000 miles young, just entering its prime. I, on the other hand, was an aging and abruptly unemployed p.i. whose future had just come to a dead end and whose stomach was clenching and unclenching like a fist.

Stay away from him, Yetta had warned. Stay away and stay cool. The fog swirled and nodded on the horizon. Frank Yetta was a professional hard guy, one of those tough cops who spit-shines his billy club and flosses his teeth with barbed wire. But Yetta wouldn't risk his lieutenant's bars on perjury. I looked at the cigarette as if I had never seen it before and then flipped it out the window. Yetta believed Chick. But Chick should have known better. He had had an hour's start on me from Sacramento, but he should have known better. I got out of the car, and the fog crept in on little rats' feet.

There was a U-Haul truck in the driveway. I stopped and felt the warm hood with one flat palm, wondering. Then I walked slowly, half in a crouch, toward the detached garage, keeping the truck between me and the house. From somewhere far in the back of the house drifted a woman's voice. Nearer, close to the side door, Chick's voice answered her.

I stopped at the end of the truck. The garage door was up, showing the open trunk of Chick's olive green Plymouth, a toothless reptilian mouth. Inside the trunk were two rows of liquor boxes taped shut and clothes on hangers draped over the boxes. The rest of the garage was empty, stripped. More boxes and suitcases littered the walkway to the house, almost obscuring the battered redwood fence that blocked off the back yard. Smells of dog hair, motor oil, fog.

I rubbed my palms against my trouser legs, and the screen door of the house jumped open with a bang as Chick staggered toward the truck, carrying three more liquor boxes piled on top of each other. While he brought the boxes around and grunted them onto the floor of the truck, I stepped back into the shadows. "Moving day, Chick?" I finally said.

He spun toward me making a foolish yelping sound, then fell back a step.

"You get out of here, Haller. Yetta told me he was going to warn you off. You get out or there'll be big trouble."

"That'll make two of us in trouble then, Chick." I circled him carefully, watching his muddy brown eyes slide nervously back and forth between the house and me. His left hand inched along the truck floor toward the handle of a ball peen hammer that lay beside the stack of boxes.

"Go for it, Chick," I hissed. "Go for the hammer and I'll break you into matchsticks." The hand slid back to his side and I took half a yard of his shirt in each fist and jerked them together under his chin.

Chick swallowed hard and made his Adam's apple jump six inches. "You been warned, Haller," he whispered.

"Why did you do it, Chick? Did Yetta put you up to it?" He kept on swallowing. My fists rode higher, pushing his chin to a jaunty angle. His skin felt like cold, damp sand against my fingers. I wanted to shred him open and look for my lost license, my lost job.

"Did Leo Matz?" I pressed him. "But Leo's an old man," I said, shaking my head for him when he didn't answer. "Leo's seventy years old. He's got no interest in flim-flam games. Leo doesn't care about anything except his pieces of paper and his arthritis. Why did you do it, Chick?"

He pumped his knee up toward my crotch, just the way I had expected, and I turned my right hip to deflect it, then turned again as he tried to squirm free and hit him twice on the side of the face, clumsy, glancing punches that snapped his head but didn't hurt him.

"Bastard!" he screamed and tried the other knee.

I grabbed his shirt again with both hands and slammed him high against the metal panel of the truck. He gasped and started to skid toward the ground and I hit him again, another glancing punch that caught the back of his left ear. My breath was jumping in crazy starts, my vision had gone red and cloudy. I was doing what I didn't want to do, losing control and shaking with anger. I swung again and missed and Chick scrambled under my arm on his hands and knees and lurched toward the house, still screaming.

Two steps before he reached the screen door I yanked him up by the shoulders like a rag doll and hauled him around to face me.

"I'll kill you, you bastard!" he screamed, swinging wildly.

The screen door exploded and a black shape with a growl like a diesel locomotive hurtled toward us—teeth slashing the gray air inches from my shoulder—and then the shape was flung backward in a tangle of legs and paws, dragged by a woman whose white arms strained and quivered in a tug of war with the Doberman's leash.

"Hold her, Jeanette!" Chick yelled and staggered away from me. "Hold still, Poppy. Good dog, good dog. Hold still, baby, hold still." The dog sprang half a foot in the air and fell back, sprang and fell back, ear-shaking barks slowly winding down, its great teeth clattering like a drawerful of kitchen knives and its breath hot and foamy in my face. I was only inches from the end of the leash. I stood as still as a house.

"All right, Haller," Chick said, straightening up from the dog and trying to fit a crooked grin in between wheezes of breath. "All right, you can get your ass off my property right now, before I let her have a taste of you."

"Is that him?" the woman asked. She was as tall as Chick and heavy-set, wearing a purple tank top and black toreador pants a size too small. "Is that Haller?"

"Shut up, Jeanette."

"You've got a hell of a nerve," she said. The dog was growing calmer now, resting on its haunches at Chick's feet and growling intermittently as he stroked its ears. Jeanette took a step toward me, and I could see that her hair had been dyed the color of lemons and that her mascara was running in sweaty rivulets over her cheeks. She took another step and I saw twin rolls of baby fat bulging over the waist of the toreador pants. Wish they all could be California girls.

"What the hell do you mean coming here and attacking my husband?" she said in a shrill voice.

"Your husband owes me a couple of explanations, Mrs. Gannett. He just cost me my job today."

"He's getting out of your rotten business," she told me, angrier and angrier now that the action was over, beginning to shout over the dog's growl. "We're moving to Phoenix and getting out of this dump of a state. We've had enough of this nickel and dime hustle."

I pulled out my handkerchief and wiped my forehead. Poppy's growl shifted gears.

"We'll talk again, Chick," I said. "You'll tell me why you lied to Yetta."

Jeanette took another step and slapped me hard on the left cheek, her pudgy face blood red with excitement.

"Take that back!" she screamed. "My husband's no liar!"

I wiped the handkerchief against my stinging cheek. "Your husband would sell us both for five dollars," I said childishly.

"Not five," she gloated, stepping back from me and swinging her hands to her hips. "Five thous . . . "

"Jeanette!"

Her voice trailed away and a little girl look of utter dismay replaced the triumphant she-mate expression of a moment before.

"Jeanette, for God's sake!"

"Who paid you five thousand dollars, Chick?" I said.

"More money than you ever saw in your *life!*" she cried, trying to recover.

"Get in the house, Jeanette!" Chick shouted fiercely, and she swung her moon-shaped face first to me, then to him. Then she ran into the house and slammed the door.

Chick stood in the deepening shadows with both hands wrapped tightly around Poppy's leash. Motionless, I watched him tie and untie the leather loop at the end of the leash. Poppy didn't take her small black eyes off the jugular vein that was twanging like a wire in my throat.

"I should of let her loose on you," Chick said. "I still will if you don't get your ass off my property right now."

"Who paid you, Chick?"

He almost turned away, almost took his dog and ended the scene. But the urge to crow was too strong. His lips twisted in a smirk like Yetta's and he spat on the black pavement beside my shoes.

"You got friends all over, Haller," he said, letting the smirk widen.

"Who, Chick? Yetta?"

He shook his head from side to side and Poppy gave a low growl, about 3.5 on the Richter scale.

"Matz?"

Another shake. "You and Matz think you're such smart shits," he said. "Paying me shit for doing all the legwork and letting you two assholes collect the bread. Nobody pays me shit for working that hard."

I stared at his pasty face, my mind stumbling from one

name to another, rejecting them all. Stay cool, Haller, I thought. Remember the psychology of the individual, like Hercule Poirot. Remember that the dog's teeth can strip you to soup bones. Then the penny dropped.

"You don't know," I said. The smirk wavered. "You don't know who it was. What happened, Chick? Did the check and a letter come in the mail? Did the phone ring last week?" He stopped and rubbed one hand along the muscles of Poppy's sleek, powerful neck, and the other hand started to unwind the leash.

"Get the hell out of here, Haller," he said.

I began to back away, along the side of the U-Haul truck and toward the street. At the sidewalk I turned, fighting the impulse to sprint like a maniac for my car, and then, stomach quivering, turned back again.

"Did you get paid yet, Chick? Did you get paid all your money?"

But the only answer was a cannonade of savage barks.

CHAPTER 2

"YOU WENT TO BOSTON LATIN HIGH SCHOOL when they still taught Latin, didn't you, Mike?"

"And men were men," I said. "Arma virumque cano." I took an ice tray from the refrigerator. "Illigitmus non carborundum." I slapped two cubes of ice into an old-fashioned glass and poured three fingers of Laphroaig single malt scotch over them. "Don't let the bastards wear you down," I translated.

"So do you know Greek too?"

Dinah Farrell appeared in the kitchen doorway and leaned against the jamb, red hair glowing in the reflected light from my living room lamps.

"I'm OK, you're OK."

"No, really."

"I can piece together a few words," I said and took my glass over to her. I had drunk three-fourths of a bottle of cheap Barbera with our hamburgers and two scotches before this one and I still didn't feel a thing. Dinah held out a thin white paperback and I took it. She put one arm around my waist and pointed with her free hand to a word that had been rubbed over with transparent yellow ink. I looked at the tiny Greek characters and then looked down and kissed the top of her head. She nudged me with her hip and pointed to the word.

"Strategos," I read very slowly. "Strategos means general," I said. "Strategy. Congratulations, you picked one of the five Greek words I know. What's the book?" I turned over the cover and saw that it was Freud's *The Problem of Anxiety.* "I didn't think you guys were permitted to read him anymore," I said, handing it back.

Dinah works as a staff psychiatrist at the Washington General Hospital, training medical students and seeing patients. Her fellow psychiatrists couldn't cross the street together safely, but they all agree that she's throwing herself away on a semi-macho misfit with no degrees, no class, no credit rating. And no license. A defrocked detective. I undraped her arm and walked into the living room.

"There's a guerilla movement afoot," she said, and followed me in. "The interns this year want to read Freud and discuss him at lunchtime. They took a vote. It was a runoff between him and Kurt Vonnegut." Her glass of Barbera still stood on the arm of the couch. "You should be glad," she said, reaching for it. "You're always saying that Freud was the first great detective."

"He made it easy for himself," I said. "He just decided everybody was guilty."

She laughed and sipped wine, standing three feet away from me a little awkwardly. I looked down and discovered that my old-fashioned glass was already empty.

"I'm sorry, Mike," she said. "I'm really sorry."

"Want to hear a record before you go?" I asked. I had drunk the two scotches at a cocktail party thrown by one of Dinah's medical colleagues, a burly neurosurgeon from the

V.A. Hospital who had already learned about my license from the afternoon paper. It was like being disbarred, wasn't it? he had asked pointedly. You must feel as if you've lost your whole identity, his well-meaning wife had wondered. The other docs had drifted warily away for the rest of the party, as if I had been caught campaigning for socialized medicine or profit-sharing.

"Something to suit the occasion?" I went over to the wall of the walnut bookshelves that I had built two summers ago and rummaged through the records. "What do you think?" I said, and held up the jacket of *The Beggar's Opera.*

Dinah came over and knelt beside me, soft and warm against my hard shoulder.

"Isn't there anything you can do?" she asked. "Isn't there any way to get the stupid license back?"

"Sure, I can go to the pet store and buy a jar of Pooch-Be-Gone for the Chihuahua and beat Chick senseless with Jeanette's mascara wand," I said. "I don't know. I feel like shoving my fist through the wall. How would you feel if you had lost your license to practice?"

"I know," she said.

"Gone just like that," I said, standing up. "The whole potato." Dinah got up too and walked over to the big French doors that open onto a balcony two feet wide. Beyond the balcony stretched the long black horizon of San Francisco Bay, sprinkled like a fairground with strings of colored buoys. Fog was reaching through the Golden Gate in long gray fingers now, spreading toward the city and gobbling up the lights. "I have the problem of anxiety," I said.

When they license a private detective in California they turn him upside down and shake out his pockets for the dirt: written and oral examinations, two-month wait, six-month probation. When they take away the license they hold a one-hour hearing in Sacramento.

The man who had held my hearing was named, improbably, Henry Sampson.

Sampson the strong man, as half the people dragged into his airless green cubicle must have thought. A dumpy, nondescript little bureaucrat with a face like an eggshell and a brown toupee that fit his head like a Frisbee.

"You've read the D.A.'s report?" Yetta had asked when Sampson had finished his preliminary questions and patted all his folders into a neat square. Sampson bobbed his head, making the toupee fringes shake, and Yetta stood up and ran a finger around his collar. Like me, he had forgotten that September could be a warm month anywhere outside of San Francisco. And in downtown Sacramento, where the Board of Collection and Investigative Services has its office, the September sun could raise a blister on a curbstone.

"Then you know that Haller has a record of violence," Yetta said. "The Department has had its eye on him for more than a year, ever since that episode out here in the Valley."

"There's no earlier charge against him in these documents," Sampson said mildly. "Just a letter of reprimand three years old from a former District Attorney."

"All right, all right, there's nothing formal," Yetta grumbled. He looked at Sampson's prim face, grimaced, and decided to loosen his tie anyway.

A big man, swarthy and sour-faced, with a military crew-cut that stood up like the bristles on a hair brush and a nose that could open a beer can. Eighteen years on the force, goose-stepping his way straight up the ladder from patrolman to lieutenant. If he did well on this, I thought, if he nailed me to the wall the way the new law-and-order D.A. wanted, he could retire in two years as a captain. On the other hand, I thought, he had about as much chance of making the charge stick as the governor had of making up his mind.

"There's a personal letter in there from the District Attorney," Yetta said, taking his seat again, "about the high incidence of shootings of civilians in the last couple of years by the police and by p.i.'s. He's taking a hard line with the police and he wants to bring that to your attention."

"All right, lieutenant," Sampson said. "You don't have to wave the flag at me. I'll make my decision on the facts."

That was what worried Yetta. He shook another mentholated cigarette from his pack and glowered at it. Reasonable. You can get the same rich taste by lighting up a deodorant stick.

"The report shows you what the D.A. means," Yetta said, wagging a match under the cigarette.

What the report showed, in fact, was that I had been hired two weeks ago by a harmless old gumball named Leo Matz to find a missing woman. Matz is an heir-hunter, an offbeat kind of sub-specialist in the private investigation business who does nothing but look for people who don't know they've inherited money. You find a few like him in most big cities, p.i.'s who drop out of the divorce, child-custody, commercial security loops and use their experience instead to read funny wills in the probate court and unearth the guy who's never heard about the legacy from his long-lost Uncle Eddie or about the trust fund that benefits anybody in Tucson named Sowash or about the estate of the father who deserted his family forty years ago but remembers the kids in a deathbed codicil. Nuts and crackers, Matz calls them. In 1982, with liberation for all, you begin to see a few deserting mothers in the files, but the deserting, repentant father is still by far the most common kind of case.

I lit my own cigarette and looked over Sampson's shoulder to the open window, half-expecting the governor to come levitating past. Instead I saw the gold dome of the state capitol, a dusty green park, and heat waves rippling up like shiny fish to a chrome-colored sky.

When Matz actually tracks down potential heirs—and he bats about .050—he charges them a percentage of the inheritance as a finder's fee, forty percent if he can get it, ten percent if he has to. And when he gets a job with special problems, he sometimes takes on temporary help to do the legwork. Which was how I came to be looking for Muriel Contreras.

"The folder indicates that you yourself specialize in missing persons, Mr. Haller," Sampson was saying. "And rather successfully. I don't understand your connection with Leo Matz."

"Leo's an old friend," I said, straightening my back against the chair and paying attention. "And an old man. The kid he'd hired to help out was running into problems and he called me."

"The woman was unusually difficult to find?"

I shrugged. "She's a topless dancer, a taxi girl. She was working the whole Bay Area and up as far as Sonoma, and she kept moving, the way they all do. Two weeks in the same bar is a career for a dancer. This one is also in the books for two felony drug possessions in Los Angeles, which made her leery of meeting anybody with a badge of any kind."

Sampson nodded. I didn't have to explain to him that while the first two can be on the house, a third felony conviction in California means mandatory time in state prison. "The kid and I spent a lot of time in bars and sex clubs looking for her." I let my cigarette smoke drift in Yetta's general direction. "She just didn't want to be found."

"Nonetheless," Sampson said, flicking each syllable with his tongue.

"Nonetheless," I said, trying hard not to sound like him, "she got herself a new pimp who liked the idea of her coming into some money, and he arranged the meeting."

"Do you know how much money was involved?"

I shook my head. "Matz doesn't tell. I don't even know who left her the money or why. If he told his helpers the details, Matz figures, they'd make their own deals with the heirs and shut him out."

"All right." Sampson scratched a note to himself with a government issue blue ballpoint. Then he blinked solemnly at me a couple of times and started the hard part.

"Why did you take a gun?"

Yetta ground out his cigarette and leaned forward, big hands spread palms down on each thigh as if he were going to jump.

"The pimp wanted to meet us at a place south of Market and Castro," I said. "He was going to bring the girl along to talk. The address he gave us used to be part of a stables, so both the kid and I took guns."

"What's a stables?" Sampson asked.

Yetta coughed impatiently and shoved his oar in. "A gay bondage place," he said, then twisted his mouth to one side as if "gay bondage" needed a little explaining outside the city limits of San Francisco. "They're sets of buildings, abandoned buildings, where homosexuals discipline each other. They tie each other up and, ah, use leather and chains and so forth."

Sampson blinked back to me. "That still doesn't explain the gun."

"Stables can be dangerous," I said. "Sometimes people are left there overnight or heavily drugged. Sometimes rape gangs go prowling. There've been knifings. Two years ago a San Francisco cop was shot to death in one of those stables."

Yetta rubbed his cigarette ash back and forth on the edge of Sampson's ashtray and didn't say anything.

"And so was this pimp," Sampson said in a sharper voice, tapping his pen on the pile of folders. "What was his name? Neal Eglee? Shot to death in a crossfire, wasn't he, Haller?"

"Not by me." I jammed my cigarette butt into the ashtray and flopped back in my chair. The "mister" had vanished with a tap of the pen, I noticed. My partner Fred had told me to bring a lawyer, but I hadn't seen the point. "The ballistics report in that folder," I said, "shows plainly that Eglee was killed by somebody else's gun. And it shows plainly that I fired only twice. When the cops arrived, I handed over my pistol just the way the law says, they trotted it down to Bryant Street for testing right away, and they still have it there in a cage. I fired twice in the air as a warning when all the hoo-ha started. I didn't aim at anybody. I didn't shoot anybody." I lit another cigarette and tossed the match into Sampson's beanbag ashtray, which had started to look like a desk model Mt. St. Helens. "This hearing is a farce."

Sampson boxed and reboxed his folders into the neat square and shook his toupee fringes. "Nobody is accusing you of shooting Eglee," he said, looking at Yetta and not at me. "Do you want to bring him in now?"

Yetta lifted himself quickly out of the chair and padded to the office door. When he opened it and said something into the hallway, he stood back. Through the door, dressed in chinos, a cowboy shirt, and a blue polyester sport coat with sequins outlining the lapels and cuffs, strolled Leo Matz's new staffer, my old bar buddy, Chick Gannett. A thin, cocky kid adrift somewhere in his twenties and still affecting the Grand Ole Opry style that distorts half the vowels in California, turning grown men who've never been south of Disneyland into Merle

Haggard clones, twanging and chawing as if they'd just crawled out of a cracker barrel. Truckers carry the unspeakable accent, Dinah claims, the way rats and fleas carry the bubonic plague; and the army passes along the C & W taste in clothes, fringes on the pockets and brass studs on the crotch. Olive drab meets redneck. From where I sat suddenly bolt upright in my chair Chick looked like about five feet ten of stringy blond sideburns and pimpled chin. From the grin on Yetta's face, about five feet ten of trouble.

"You know each other," Sampson said and Chick sat down in one of the narrow armless chairs.

"Chick," I said. He nodded once at me, looked at Yetta, looked at Sampson.

"This is a formal administrative hearing, Mr. Gannett," Sampson recited, reading from a card on his desk. "You're not under legal oath, but willful or deliberate misrepresentation of facts or omission of pertinent facts can affect your own license as a probationary investigator." When Chick didn't say anything, Sampson put down the card, picked up his ballpoint pen again and pressed the blunt end hard against one fat white cheek as if he wanted to puncture it.

"Do you want to tell us what happened when you and Haller arrived at the stables to meet Muriel Contreras?" Sampson asked.

"Sure." Chick slid a few inches forward on the chair and his right hand started turning a gold-plated link bracelet around his left wrist. "Me and Haller go to the stables about eight-thirty, the night of August 25th, like I told the lieutenant. The pimp was supposed to meet us in this apartment upstairs, just over an alley, at nine o'clock sharp, but Haller wanted to be there early. He said he likes to look a place over before he meets somebody. So we leave the car in the alley and go upstairs to the apartment, and Haller knocks a couple of times pretty good.

Nobody answers, so he looks around a little and then pulls out his charge card and jimmies the door."

"Breaks in?" Sampson asked, his voice rising a little.

"Sure. He jimmies it and tells me to come on in with him and I do."

"What did you find?" Sampson asked. He had stuck the ballpoint under his desk blotter and was leaning forward on both elbows.

"You wouldn't believe it," Chick said. "Sir," he added with a quick sly grin at Yetta. "There's chains hanging all over one wall, like snow chains at a hardware store. There's whips in some kind of wooden rack, twenty or thirty whips all sizes, some of them with knots every couple inches, some of them made out of silk. On the floor there's a stack of steel ankle bracelets and a cardboard box full of handcuffs and leather jackets with belts all around them, like strait jackets. There's a mattress in one corner and two wet suits on it, surfers' suits, you know, like they wear surfing. And a pile of dirty lace shirts, dress shirts like for tuxedos, and doilies with stains on them that they must use for handkerchiefs. And one whole wall is clear of stuff except for some handcuffs nailed up high, and that whole wall is unbelievably filthy, if you know what I mean. The whole wall is just smeared with dried shit and it smells like an outhouse. I mean it was unreal."

I inhaled and felt my cigarette smoke warming a hollow place deep in my lungs, as if my belly were smouldering. Sampson had a gleam in one small bureaucratic eye. He liked Chick's description of the stables, I thought. Chick had taken a long look around. I dragged more smoke down. It was a pretty good description, in fact; the room had looked like the home of a perverted Victorian scuba diver. But Sampson didn't like the breaking and entering part at all.

He cleared his throat. "What did you do then?"

"There wasn't anybody there, and Haller said he didn't want to hang around in all that garbage, so we went back to the car and waited for our people."

"And they came when?"

"In about five minutes." He slid the sly grin over his shoulder to Yetta again. "I guess they like to get to a meeting early too, like Haller." He paused and looked doubtfully at Sampson. "What happened next," he said with an apologetic wave of one sequined cuff, "went pretty fast."

"Just take your time," Yetta said and dealt him a cigarette from the crumpled pack. Chick accepted the light and lifted his chin high so he could blow smoke in twin gray lines down his nostrils. Merle Haggard by way of Gary Grant. He had an Adam's apple the size of a doorknob.

"Well, down one alley—you know it's a pretty confusing area, sir, south of Market—lots of old buildings that used to be factories and then got turned into rooming houses and apartments and stuff. Down one alley to our left comes a man and a girl, walking up from the street and going toward the doorlight for the apartments. That was the pimp and the Contreras. And Haller and me start to get out of the car. And then from the other end of the alley two or three guys start shooting. They were in the shadows and I never did see how many there were. But the pimp starts yelling and shooting back, of course, and Contreras is gone before you know it, just rabbiting out of there like a bitch, but all of a sudden Haller is shooting too and I'm crouching behind the car door, holding my ears and then the pimp is laying there dead, and the two or three perps are long gone again. They must have been waiting over in the other corner even before we got there. But Eglee the pimp was over by the stairs up to the stables with about half his face shot off. I heard later he took a couple of .357 magnums in the neck, was how he died."

"Haller couldn't have shot him," Sampson said. "The ballistics tests prove that conclusively. He says he was only firing warning shots."

Chick looked at Yetta once more, no grin this time, and twisted his gold-plated bracelet another revolution. "I don't know about ballistics tests," he said after a moment. "But I don't think they could have been much good as warning shots. Haller's pistol had a silencer on it big enough to stifle a cannon."

"What did your lawyer say?" Dinah asked me now from the French doors of my apartment.

"He said he felt a beep coming on and would I please leave a message."

"Do you think he can help?"

"I doubt it. Besides, an appeal could take three years to go through the courts." I picked up my glass and swirled the scotch, making the ice cubes crack. "I haven't got an idea in the world who did it," I said. "Somebody paid Chick to set me up, I'm not guessing about that. Somebody called him or wrote him or suckered him, and Chick's just young enough and greedy enough and half-assed enough to fall for it. But who and why . . . ?" I rattled scotch and ice against my teeth.

"How could somebody fix the silencer at the police lab?" Dinah asked after a moment.

"Police labs are run by people," I said. "People have mortgages and dentists' bills and brakes to reline. You give me five thousand dollars to fool around with and I can come up with a lab report that makes you the Boston Strangler."

And you could probably get a discount, I thought, if you wanted a report that would sap a p.i. There are a few private detectives that the regular police get along with, mostly ex-cops themselves, good old boys who retired early and set up shop or who got fired for acceptably macho reasons like drinking on the job or bashing the clientele too often and too publicly. Even the law and order fanatic who quits because the force isn't tough enough on the scumballs will get a fair shake and more from his ex-colleagues. But in the policeman's eye all the others are losers, the guys who couldn't make it into the fraternity— the wimp who was too short and light for the physical or too dumb to pass the civil service test, the law student who fails the bar three times and starts to scavenge, the ex-M.P. who spent his time in the service directing traffic. To Yetta and most cops like him it didn't matter that after I had dropped out of college I had served my two years as a grunt in John Kennedy's army and later worked the crime desk for newspapers in England and L.A. I had committed the cardinal sin of drifting into the business without the right credentials, bringing the pseudo-liberal, pseudo-intellectual world of the ex-reporter down onto the mean streets of real life.

"I can't show my face in Yetta's lab," I said, finishing the drink. "I'll have to get Fred to ask around."

Dinah put down the wine glass and slung her tote bag over her shoulder. Short, plump, perfect. An Elaine Powers dropout she had once called herself. She walked across the rug and put her arms around my neck.

"I'm sorry I have to go now. Mendelsohn wants the meeting to start exactly at ten p.m. so the night shift can hear her speech too." She nuzzled my neck with her lips and I let my hands roam up from her waist. Shirley Mendelsohn is chief of psychiatry at the hospital and a militant feminist, dedicated this year to the elimination of gender in English. The title of her speech tonight was "The Pregnant Person."

"Do you want me to come back later?" Dinah asked after a moment.

I felt about as sexy as a lamp base. "I've got to get up early," I said. "I'm going to see Leo Matz."

She nodded solemnly, kissed me again and said, "Call me."

When she was gone, I went into the kitchen and moved the dirty dishes around in the sink for a few minutes. Then I built myself a bigger drink and walked back to the living room to see if the fog had reached Green Street yet. Five minutes later I punched my fist through the flimsy apartment wall, shredding the cheap plasterboard as if it were tissue.

CHAPTER 3

YOU CAN'T DROWN YOUR TROUBLES.

But marinate them maybe, I had decided halfway through a second bottle of Barbera last night. Or stew in them.

I wheeled the ancient Mercedes into a parking lot on the corner of Columbus Avenue and Washington Square and sat very still for five minutes while my hangover jumped up and down on my bumpers and kicked my tires. Then when the wise guy attendant asked if the car got Senior Citizen rates, I took my ticket and stood blinking in irritation at the bright September morning.

I had swatted Chick Gannett halfway across the little cubicle.

"Sit down, Haller, goddammit!" Yetta had roared and spun me around and punched me two steps backward with his big palms on my chest.

"That's assault," Chick whimpered to the room in general. "You seen him assault me." He shook out the collar of his striped shirt so that Sampson could see how I had assaulted him. Sampson sat unmoving in his chair, pen in hand, cheeks full of nuts for the winter, and watched the show.

"I hope you've got something better than Gannett here for this charade, Yetta," I said while Chick slipped into his chair again. I bent and retrieved my cigarette from Sampson's government gray carpet and took a long, poisonous drag. "I have never owned or fired a gun with a silencer in the state of California," I said slowly and deliberately, something I should have done in the first place instead of yanking young Chick up by his Adam's apple. "Silencers are illegal in California for every kind of firearm except air guns," I went on. Sampson nodded. "I carry a Smith and Wesson .38 that fires the standard 158 grain Police Service Round. The gun's with Yetta's ballistics boffins right now. Gannett has made a mistake, and you can check out how bad a mistake by reading the D.A.'s report right there on your desk."

Sampson nodded again. One plump hand rustled in the stack of papers like a white mouse, and he pulled out two sheets stapled at the corner.

"Lieutenant Yetta brought a supplementary report this morning," he said. "Just finished yesterday. His ballistics laboratory does have a silencer for a .38 Smith & Wesson, and the rifling marks on the two barrels and on test bullets show that the silencer was used on your gun." He lifted one page and read something to himself. "Was used on your gun within the last two weeks." He snapped the top sheet down again. "They can't be more accurate about the date unless they have the original bullets too. Unfortunately, those are somewhere south of Market."

I sat back and stared. The skin on my face was starched and dry. In the quiet of the office Yetta scratched one big paw loudly across his thigh. "Where did they come up with a silencer?" I asked finally, groping for the right questions. "I didn't give anybody a silencer when the cops came for Eglee." An unauthorized silencer was normally a misdemeanor in California, although it could be turned into a felony if death or injury resulted from its use. Fred had told me to bring a lawyer.

"Gannett gave us the pillow, Haller." Yetta was close to smirking now. "Two days ago he brought it to us, but we were going to haul you up here anyway. That just tied it."

"Haller denies knowing about this silencer," Sampson said in his small voice. "Why did you wait so long before bringing it to the police, Mr. Gannett?"

Chick rolled his shoulders slightly under the sportscoat and fingered the bracelet again. His face was still the color of dish water, but he swallowed once and spoke right up.

"Like you said, sir, I'm still a probationary p.i. I mean, I've only had the license for a couple of months. At first I didn't say anything because, well, what the hell. I didn't really know all that much about what goes on, like out in the field. In the army I was just an M.P. Spec Two. But then I got to thinking about the probation, and me and my wife talked it over and just thought I should go downtown."

Sampson nodded and swivelled his stomach an inch in my direction. "And you still deny any knowledge of all this, Haller?"

"Absolutely." My tongue rubbed like a towel against the roof of my mouth. A lawyer would have known questions to ask, motions to make. A lawyer would have understood how to punch holes in Chick's story and then rip it to shreds.

"I have a question," I heard myself asking.

"Go ahead."

"How did you get it, Chick? Did I just hand it over without a word and say run tell Yetta?"

"Good question," Sampson said and flicked the small eyes toward him. "How did you get the silencer?"

"He pulled it off the gun when the shooting stopped and we heard the sirens coming," Chick said without hesitation. "He was standing by the car, on the driver's side even though it was my car, and he just wrapped a handkerchief around the barrel because it was still hot and flipped the pillow through the window. I was on the other side and I sort of automatically knocked it up into the little, like, Kleenex rack under the glove compartment. Next morning I remembered and picked it up and kept it."

"Haller didn't ask for it later or mention it?"

"See, you can only use one of those big asbestos silencers a couple of times and it loses all its, you know, power. Then the gun sounds so loud you might just as well not have it on. So I figured Haller wanted me to dump it for him and keep my mouth shut."

He was right about cheap silencers. He sounded right about everything. He sounded coached down to the last comma. I licked my lips and tried to think of a question.

"Do you carry a plastic-coated credit card that you use as a jimmy, Haller?" Sampson asked suddenly.

"I have a Visa card that I use to charge submachine guns and machetes, Sampson. What's the point in talking about that? You can jimmy most locks in California with a matchbook. Yetta here could do your office door with a get-well card."

"May I see your card?" Sampson asked quietly. His eyes had gone hard over the flat button nose and he held his plump hand toward me over the desk.

I licked my lips again. They tasted like sandpaper. Sampson's white hand hung steadily in the air by the side of his desk, palm up, fingers aimed at my chest. A guy in a North Beach hardware store had laminated the card in my wallet with Herculon to make it as tough and flexible as an airplane wing. He had done the same thing for half the cops in San Francisco, but Sampson's hand wasn't pointed at them.

"I think I had better talk to a lawyer first," I said at last. The hand snapped back and vanished into the stack of official papers.

"You have every right to discuss this with an attorney," Sampson said as he flipped the pages of a three-ring binder notebook. "But this is not a legal hearing. This is purely a regulatory matter. My decisions are not open to appeals. To alter them would require a civil lawsuit against the Attorney General."

"Nobody's won a case like that in ten years," Yetta said. Sampson glanced at him and returned to his notebook. I didn't say anything. Chick didn't say anything. Didn't say anything and didn't meet my eyes. Yetta offered him another cigarette, which he took and lit with a bright plastic red lighter that looked like a Christmas tree ornament. Outside Sampson's window the golden afternoon slowly began to die.

"I'm looking for the revised paragraph 7551," Sampson said, still flipping pages. There were no personal touches in Sampson's office that I had noticed, no plastic cube with pictures of the family, no funny cards that said I'd rather be fishing, no Shriner's hat or college pennant or paperweight shaped like Dolly Parton. There was just Sampson and his regulatory manuals. A soft little man swivelling thoughtfully in his chair as he read, his back to us. From where I sat it was impossible to tell if he was enjoying his demonstration of power.

"This is it," he said, coming around to face me. "Subsection h of paragraph 7551. It concerns revocation of license for conviction of a felony or violence against other persons, including especially 'assault, battery, or kidnapping.'" He turned his pale face toward Yetta. "We added kidnapping last year because so many child custody cases these days involve parents kidnapping their children from each other." Yetta looked attentive and interested. Sampson turned back to me. I looked attentive and interested, too, and clenched my left fist in my jacket pocket until my knuckles felt the size of golfballs.

"I have the authority in these cases," Sampson said, "to impose a fine up to five hundred dollars, if in my judgment that better suits the situation."

A frown dug its way across Yetta's brow.

"Now using a credit card jimmy," Sampson went on in his small, tight voice, "is illegal, but it hardly falls under the category of violence against a person. And in candor we do overlook some of the things our people do that just skirt the law. But the silencer," he said and leaned toward me, tapping the ballpoint on his desk blotter for emphasis. "The silencer is extremely serious. It is not a felony charge, since no one can prove that you fired it at the man who was killed. Indeed, no one can prove that you even fired it on precisely that night. But the police laboratory has proved that it fits your gun, a witness has testified to that, and the District Attorney has made a special request, which under the circumstances I am obliged to weigh carefully."

He tilted back in his chair as if there were great weights on his shoulders and exhaled in a loud sigh.

"I'm revoking your license, Haller. Effective right now. For a minimum period of three years."

Along the border of Columbus and Green Street, for a space of a dozen or so square blocks, Chinatown and Little Italy back and eddy into each other's currents like parallel rivers. In this part of the city you can find a salami factory next to an acupuncture clinic, a glass and chromium espresso bar next to a bleak doorway filled with serious, big-eyed children or impassive old men reading Cantonese newspapers. I turned left on the short stretch of Green that is still all Italian and made my way past a Sicilian coffee house decorated from floor to ceiling in orange and white tiles and golden sparkles and called the "Caffe Sport," past two rival Italian bakeries side by side, Guelfs and Ghibellines, past Gino and Carlo's no-name bar, jammed as always with argumentative, unshaven long-shoremen, and finally stopped at a dead-end alley about sixty feet long that the city fathers had mysteriously named Cadell Place. On one side halfway down stood the back door of an adult fortune cookie store, on the other side an occult book-shop with a purple half moon in the window and, just beyond it, a rickety outside stairway two stories high.

At the top of the stairway on the right a tattoo parlor had hung a poster of designs to choose from and a cheery hand-lettered sign—"Come in and browse"—and on the left was Leo Matz's office door. I knocked and went in.

Leo was on the telephone, as usual, and as usual he waved the cigar stump in his hand toward the cups and cream and sugar while he went on talking. I squeezed by a bookshelf and tilted the antique silver-plated samovar he keeps on the cor-ner of his desk, pouring a stream of black Russian tea into an orange cup from the Caffe Sport. Then I shoved a stack of telephone books to one side and sat down in the free space I had made on his couch.

"So see if you can find out his address, I'll wait," Leo said into the mouthpiece and to me whispered, "Milton what's-his-name at the courthouse, he's losing his mind."

I nodded and crossed my legs. The tea always tasted so strong and thick and black at Leo's that I wondered if the Russians pump the stuff out of the ground like oil and ship it in tankers. Besides the desk and the samovar and a window with a view of a brick wall, Leo's office had a bathroom and a hot plate and a couple of hundred thousand manila folders stuffed with papers, folders cascading out of drawers and filing cabinets, stacks of folders growing out of the floor like square stalagmites, folders sprawling across the couch and across the books in the shelves like giant decks of mis-shuffled yellow cards, folders for every potential heir and unprobated will in Northern California. Leo belched into the telephone and said in his thick Russian accent, "Sure I'm still waiting. What do you think, I've got all day?"

The accent was genuine. His parents had been political refugees, émigrés, and until their deaths three years ago never spoke to Leo or each other in anything but Russian. His father, Leo once told me, had been a general in the "White" Army that fought so long and so badly against the "Red" Army of the Revolution—the most quarrelsome army in history, Leo said, except they quarrelled mostly with each other. When the White Russians were finally defeated, Leo's family had lost everything—house, fortune, and thousands of acres of land—and had just managed to hop a boat from Vladivostok to Anchorage with the Red Army baying at their heels. For as long as I could remember the only decorations on his office walls had been a photograph of another White Russian general named P. N. Wrangel, wearing a high starched collar and looking like the headmaster at Eton, and a photograph of Nixon looking like a customer sneaking out of a tattoo parlor. People don't really get swept away by ruling passions, Dinah tells me, unless they're institutionalized obsessive-compulsives; they always have conflicting drives to stall their neuroses, distractions, murky backwaters to their psyches. But she hadn't met Leo. Leo had no family except his folders, no future except his work. He lived for the paper chase and nothing else, like some moony character in a Chekhov play, alive only in his office and smacking his lips in fascination at the thought of all those other heirs like himself and all of those other lost fortunes. And of course like every Russian he had managed to turn it all into exquisite paranoia—the melodramatic, pennyante secrecy, the intense conspiratorial conversations with courthouse clerks about funny wills, the endless fear that the same courthouse clerks had been bribed by some other heir-hunter who was already three steps ahead of him in getting to the money. If Leo ever lost his license, I thought, it would kill him.

He swivelled in his chair abruptly, showing me his back, and adjusted his green eyeshade. Then he started muttering into the telephone in a low voice that I couldn't follow. A big bald jelly-roll of a man. He almost never went out into the field anymore, partly because he could keep in touch with his army of contacts more easily by phone, partly because he had grown too old and fat. Seventy-four last month, he had told me, and looked twenty years older than that. From the front, flesh seemed to spill down his neck in wider and wider undulations, like a waterfall of fat, billowing in soft rolls under his shabby green Shetland sweater. He still had three or four teeth, yellowish with black tips, like pencil stubs left in his mouth, and he had his hearing, but his eyes were growing weaker. From the back—my angle at the moment—he looked like a cantaloupe wearing a visor.

He scribbled something on a memo pad and swivelled around to me, hanging up the phone with a bang that hurt my eyes.

"I heard about Sacramento, Mike," he said after he had worried the dead cigar with his gums for a minute. "Guy I know in the State Probate there called me up long distance. What the hell you take a silencer along for? You think this Contreras shiksa's going to gun you down like the movies?"

and he pantomimed firing his forefinger rapidly at the brick wall. "You're supposed to be a smart guy, Mike."

"I didn't do it, Leo."

"Yeah." He put down the cigar and sipped tea from his own orange cup. "Yeah, that's what I heard, you said that." He slurped and slid the cup into an open drawer along with some balls of string and a tuna can full of paper clips. "I can't pay you, Mike, if that's what you come for. You lost your license, I can't even hire you to answer the phone. You know that. And me with all this"—he waved a surprisingly thin and graceful hand at the rat's nest around us. "First time in six months I've got extra work to hand out, and then you go, and now the kid."

"He quit?"

"Yeah. Gandy, Gannett, whatever the hell his name is, he called this morning first thing and says he's moving to Arizona and to forward his check. What the hell, he didn't lose his license. So you're giving him a hard time, maybe, Mike? The guy in Probate says you slugged him with a chair."

"Maybe he came into some money, Leo." The tea got smoother as it cooled, but it still tasted like Valvoline.

"So maybe I can give you a little for expenses," he sighed when I didn't say anything else. "For old times' sake. What do you need, a hundred, two hundred? Tide you over, rent money?"

"Tell me about the girl, Leo. About Muriel Contreras."

He leaned forward as far as his belly would permit and tilted more tea into his cup. Then he looked at the ancient black telephone in front of him, as if hoping it would ring. And then he wiped his gray lips with a crumpled paper napkin and shook his head.

"I can't do that, Mike. That's a rule. Sometimes when you're not busy I hire you to do a little business, to help us both out, but you know the rule. The will is top secret. The will is how I stay in business. If you know about the will and the money and how to get it for her, what do you need me?" He shook his head slowly and sipped more tea. Then from the litter on his desk he picked up the one photograph of Muriel Contreras that I had ever seen, a black and white publicity still from a night club in Hayward showing her dressed in a bikini with more sparkles than the Caffe Sport and less fabric than a Pamper and arching both hands above her head like a belly dancer.

"She's Mexican," he said after a while. In the photograph her shapeless black hair looked like spilled ink and her long, horsey face looked sad and shopworn. Big breasts, stringy arms and legs. The photographer's spotlight had brought out the shadows of her ribcage as well as her cleavage.

"Half Chicano, half white," I said. I knew that much from talks in bars across half of San Francisco. I also knew that she had grown up in East L.A. with her aunts because her mother had very early on driven out to the La Brea city dump and taken a mouthful of Clorox mixed with shoe polish, which turned out to make bargain basement cyanide. Muriel talked about her mother's suicide with her tricks, with girlfriends, with bartenders and pimps. Everybody agreed that she was a nervous person, heavily dependent on drugs, skittish as a colt.

"Who's leaving her money, Leo?"

He kept shaking his head, lips pursed just over the tea cup, eyeshade slipping lower as he frowned. I tilted the samovar and filled my cup again, feeding the hangover. Outside the window two women began shouting in Italian about a man named Guido. Leo looked at my newly filled cup and shook his head again.

I sipped tea. My knuckles hurt and my brain had dried up like the great Gobi desert. What was I supposed to do? Grab the old man's precious files out of his hands and search them? Lash him with his Medicare card? Chick Gannett was gone, too stupid to know why he had framed me, too stupid to be worth following. I warmed my sore knuckles against the tea cup. Leo didn't have a Doberman. I could sit here all day, bullying him, taking it out on the old man. Sipping tea until my bladder had swollen to the size of a volleyball. Why would Muriel Contreras have anything to do with my license? She was just another of Leo's nuts and crackers, somebody who stood to inherit a few thousand dollars from one of her aunts or a sentimental ex-boyfriend. But I had no place else to start, no better place.

"Who's the lawyer at least, Leo? Give me a break."

He looked out the window and moved his gray lips soundlessly. In the pale light reflected from the window I could see white bristles of beard on his cheek where the razor had skipped. You can find out a lot in a courthouse if you know how to look and if you have Leo's rabbinical patience. You can find out if somebody owns property. You can find out if somebody is registered to vote. You can find out if somebody has ever filed a lawsuit or been sued. You can even find out if somebody has signed a petition for a political cause like Save the Redwoods or Nuke the Gay Whales. And in every one of those cases the state of California records the person's name, address, and zip code. That was how Leo made his living. Zip, unzip. But you can't find out if a person is the beneficiary of a will. Wills are filed according to the name of testator only, by date of probate only. I could spend the next six months in the basement of Civic Center and not know who had left Muriel Contreras money or how much or why.

"Where was she born, Leo?"

He slurped more tea, eyes hidden under the visor, head turned toward the window.

"Her mother's dead, Leo. I heard that from two bargirls in Redwood City who know her. The mother killed herself a long time ago."

"I can go four hundred, tops, Mike," he said, still staring at the window. "I can lend you that much from the bank down on Columbus."

"Who's leaving the money to her, Leo? Father, sister, boyfriend?" He shook his head harder, jaw clenched.

"Just tell me who the lawyer is, Leo. I don't want to run you out of the inheritance. Give me a paper to sign. I just want to get my license back."

"You," he said, voice quivering, turning away from the window and leaning over the desk toward me, so that I saw for the first time that morning the pale blue eyes under the visor. "Things happen to you. You're a young guy and you push people too hard. You'll find her and there'll be trouble and no matter what you say the money'll be gone and I won't have it." His lips went black with an old man's miserable, petulant anger. "I don't *want* you to find Muriel Contreras," he wailed.

It occurred to me for the first time that he wasn't the only one.

CHAPTER 4

"IT COULD BE TWENTY GUYS," FRED SAID IN disgust. "It could be a hundred." My eyes were two aspirins bobbing in an ocean of Leo's tea, but the hangover had receded, so I gripped each side of the hamburger and took another bite. Fred tugged at the brim of his porkpie hat and slouched uncomfortably in his chair.

"You've sent guys away, Mike, remember that," he said. "But you sent them away and the state of California tosses them right back on the street like goddam tennis balls. A lot of those guys are loose now, and there's got to be more than one kook who spent his time inside thinking about how to pull off your wings once he got out. What about the doctor down in Hillsborough? The one with the runaway daughter and the fistful of amphetamines he's scattering around like Johnny goddam Appleseed? He's got to be out of Lompoc now. And the guy was using his place at Tahoe to store all his friends' cars till the theft insurance paid off?"

He scowled at what was left of his burger and got up to deposit it in the trash can by my desk. I kept chewing mine, even though it tasted like shirtboard with special sauce, while he brushed off his sports jacket with both hands. A man without an income suddenly starts eating at McDonald's and liking it.

"You missed some special sauce," I said.

Fred sighted down his belly and shrugged. "Goes with the plaid," he said and gave one more half-hearted swipe. Then he began to pat himself down, looking for a cigar. He had retired four years ago from the San Francisco Police Department, after he had done twenty years and change, as he said. But I had been able to talk him into taking me on as a retirement project, him to be part-time personal assistant, gadfly, and grandfather figure, me to keep him busy roaming the streets of the only city he had ever lived in. A lot of cops grab their twenty year pension and retreat to a worm farm in Utah, swearing never to look again at anything more dishonest than a small-mouthed bass. Some of them take desk jobs with the security firms that are springing up all over California or else become patrolmen in a senior citizens compound and chase down speeding golf carts. But a few of them, like Fred, are married to the streets. Even working for a misfit p.i. and looking for runaway kids in the pot holes of Berkeley and Oakland didn't depress him as much as the thought of his four walls in the Sunset apartment and afternoon game shows on TV. It was possible that my lost license hurt him more than me.

"So how do you like the new sandals?" he asked, pointing at his feet with the cigar he had found, a black panatela so big that it would fit in a gun rack. I looked over the edge of the old wooden desk and saw a pair of light brown crepe soles, Fred's black socks, and shiny tan leather straps.

"You look like you're standing on a pair of fig newtons," I said.

"They're podiatric," he said. "The doctor said they support my arches better than shoes."

I took another bite and waited for the lecture to resume.

"Muriel Contreras has got nothing to do with it, Mike," he said in a moment, after the cigar was smoking. "That old fart Leo Matz just picks up scraps from courthouse clerks that nobody else will bother with. Where's he going to run into somebody that pays a hood like Chick Gannett five thou?"

"Nobody paid Gannett five thou," I said through shredded lettuce and beef. "Somebody paid him something—maybe one or two thousand—and promised him the rest when I was dumped. That's how I'd do it. That's how you'd do it."

Fred looked at the ash at the end of the cigar, then turned and waddled back to the chair in his podiatric sandals. Dinah says Fred looks like a California sea-lion when he takes off the porkpie hat and lets you see his small head and narrow shoulders swelling to a sleek, pear-shaped middle. But since he started losing hair he won't take the hat off even in the shower.

"I think you got to start with the lab," he said. "I think you got to start with the pillow you're supposed to have flipped to Gannett and you got to see who signed it into the evidence room, who tested it, who supervised the report." He exhaled smoke and I got out my own pack of cigarettes in self-defense. "You didn't use a silencer, did you, Mike?" he asked abruptly.

I paused with the lighter hallway to my mouth and stared.

"All right, all right," he said, angry at something, angry at the air. "I had to ask."

He got out of the chair again and walked to the window on the other side of the room, opposite my desk, and looked out at the street. From the window behind me afternoon shadows swam across the ceiling and swooped down in long ripples toward his hat. The office is just one big room in a building near the Southern Pacific depot and the docks, a reconverted building given over to struggling architects' offices, some artists' studios, one accountant, one guy in souvenir imports from Taiwan, and me, Mr. Trace, Keener Than Most Persons. From his window Fred could look out on an ordinary city street that had the tail end of a park at one end and, half a block in the other direction, a police precinct station, which didn't seem to take away as much of my business as it should. From my window, if I had turned to look, I could have seen part of the long gray arch of the Bay Bridge and below it the China Basin wharves. When the weather is gray and foggy and the sky has fallen down like a damp flannel blanket, the view out my window reminds me of Boston. Boston and its red eyes and sallow white Irish skin and its nose-pinching, eye-glazing cold. Boston and its gritty, exhaust-blackened winters and its crooked dark streets that turn on themselves, snarling, between Back Bay and the Combat Zone. Home. When the weather is bright from corner to corner with luminous western sunshine, it reminds me that I had left Boston like everybody else because California was supposed to be paved with gold.

"It makes as much sense as you sitting there feeling sorry for yourself and talking about some 'feeling' you got that it's mixed up with Contreras," Fred grumbled from his window. "'Feeling.' You drink that old fraud's goddam Russian tea for half an hour and you come back sounding like some kid with a Ph.D. from est. 'Feeling.' Cops don't have 'feelings.' You got to go after whoever's mad at you. You got to go to the lab."

"I can't go to the police lab, Fred. I can't even talk to the janitor there. Yetta would have me carried out in pieces."

"That's another thing," he said, still grumbling. "You and your mouth. I know one or two working cops wouldn't mind seeing you eat a little humble crow. You cracked altogether too wise a couple of times with them." He cleared his throat with a hawk and watched something moving down the street. "Jerks," he said.

"I'm not cracking wise now, Fred."

"No." He looked down at the huge cigar. From where I sat it looked as if he were smoking the Sunday *Chronicle*. "No, you're not cracking wise." He walked over to the chair and sat down carefully, holding his lower back stiffly. "It must hurt," he said. "It must be like having the rug pulled out. One day you're working at what you're good at, the next minute you're on the sidewalk, and they don't let you work anymore, they don't let you do what you're good at." He tilted the brim of the hat back and glanced around the office. I had a six-foot wooden case of books to reassure the clients, a couple of dusty olive-drab filing cabinets that must have seen duty in the Spanish-American War, and a framed five-foot-square map of Northern California. No picture of Trotsky. Next to the map hung a poster of a painting by Matisse, a portrait of his wife done entirely in grays and blues, that I had bought when the DeYoung Museum had put on a special exhibit. "His austere period," Dinah had said, looking doubtful. In the painting Madame Matisse seemed to be leaning forward like a ghost passing through a wall, her pale face floating above the colors. They can't revoke artistic license.

"How long you going to keep this open?" Fred asked after a moment.

"The rent's paid through the end of the month."

He nodded his head in and out of a cloud of smoke, looking more ghostly than Madame Matisse. "You got enough money?" he asked gruffly.

"Twenty-three hundred dollars in the Christmas Club," I said. He raised one eyebrow to show he was impressed. "I've been saving to go to college."

"So you don't want those twirls to break into the Wells Far-go," he said, aiming his cigar at the chromium-colored strips of metal sitting on my desk blotter next to the hamburger wrapper. The strips were actually made of gun metal, tempered and plated and riddled on all sides with tiny indentations as if they'd been chewed by a bionic gopher. They were church keys from Uncle Fred's cop kit, a set of jimmies and picks that would open any door or safe or cookie jar this side of San Quentin. Fred had traded a junkie in Dolores Heights a few years of free time for the set, back when balloons of heroin could send you to prison instead of to a social worker. The junkie claimed they were stolen FBI keys, but Fred said Hoover had never asked for them back.

"Not me," I said. "While you go give your pals in the police lab the third degree about illegal silencers, I'm going to hang around here and study the psychology of the individual."

He tapped a foot of ash into the trash can. "You mean you're going to break into Matz's office and find the will," he said.

"Same thing," I said.

CHAPTER 5

MOST OF THE GLASSES HAVE "MODESTO'S Famous Tavern" embossed in white letters around the side. For some reason mine had "Golden Gate Saloon" and a decal of a seagull and a cable car. While I drained it, the bartender held up the Bushmill's bottle and looked expectantly at Fred.

"Give my uncle another one too," Fred said with a nod in my direction. The bartender, who was as old as Fred, glanced at me and made an adenoidal snorting sound. Then he turned around and started rooting in the bottles under the cash register for the Laphroaig malt scotch I like to drink there. At the end of the long bar, over the white curve of his back and through the plate glass window, we could see the midnight singles swinging up and down the pickup strip of Union Street, the Maginot Line of heterosexuality in San Francisco. Breeder bars, the gays call them.

Fred followed my gaze. "In the last five minutes," he said, "I seen enough stewardesses go by to staff Pan Am."

I turned back to the bar and flipped through my stack of papers again while the bartender poured.

"You find her and I'll marry her," Fred said.

"You'd have to pay the inheritance taxes."

"On eight hundred thousand dollars I'll pay taxes." He slid the photo of Muriel Contreras out of the pile of papers and grimaced. "She looks like a horse," he said, snapping one finger against her glossy breasts. "I tell you what. You marry her and just give me a raise." He handed me the photo and picked up his Irish whiskey again. "You figure this guy Maranian was some kind of sugar daddy and just sprinkled a little extra sugar in the will?"

"For a taxi girl at a topless joint?"

"So he goes for sleaze," Fred said. "He's not the first rich old goat that's got a taste for the junkyard. When I worked Vice twenty years ago I got to know the best-paid call girl in San Francisco, Marianne something. I forget her name. A girl that was collecting a thousand dollars a night in 1960. You know what she looked like? You think she looked like Hedy Lamarr? She looked like a whore. She wore makeup thicker than a pie crust and mascara that looked like ivy growing on her eyes, and she wore those wide plastic belts she bought at Woolworth's and skirts so short you could count her moles when the wind blew. Sure, she had bazooms like she was shot in the back with rockets, but she had peroxide hair she had to part with a hammer and chisel, she sprayed so much gunk on it, and she looked exactly like an Eddy Street whore. I asked her one day, I said, why don't you dress up nice in $300 outfits and put on decent lipstick and spend some of that money on your looks? I mean, she was making more money than the president of General Motors. And she says she dresses that way because her customers want her to look like a whore. They're all already married to broads who dress nice and look like ladies. They come to see her because they want to strip and get down on all fours in a plastic raincoat and go woof,

woof, and chase her around the floor. She said those guys want paid sex to look like paid sex. And the executive type also likes to bang the merchandise around a little bit, no pun intended. You got somebody that looks like Grace Kelly, you kiss her hand, madame. You got somebody that looks like Muriel here, you slap her silly and screw her any way you want to."

"The bequest to Contreras is in a codicil," I said, reading the top sheet. "It was added six months before the will was probated, so that must have been just before Maranian died. The personal property goes to his beloved wife Margot. The 'residue and remainder' is to be divided into three equal parts and given to his son Taghi Maranian, Contreras, and Margot."

"So how do you know a part is worth eight hundred thou?" Fred asked. "I don't see any numbers on the stuff you got there, just lawyer mumbo jumbo."

"It's here," I said and pulled out another set of papers from the bottom of the stack. "There was an inventory of property in the same folder in Leo's office, but it's dated thirty days after the will. Leo must have had one of his clerk buddies Xerox it and pass it on—the lawyer wouldn't have any reason to give it to him. It lists ten thousand shares of IBM, a side order of Gulf & Western, some Sony, some CD's—Leo went through the newspaper and wrote die value of each stock in the margins. The residuary property checks out at just under two and a half million. The personal property includes a house in Pacific Heights that comes in at seven hundred thousand."

"It would have been simpler if he had just told you," Fred said.

"Leo doesn't split heirs," I said, and Fred winced. "He had written down the address of the son in his own handwriting—a place called GreenGenes, Inc., down on the peninsula."

"That's a kid's TV show," Fred said. "GreenGenes. My granddaughter watches that."

"And the last thing he had is what bothers me most. The business card of the lawyer who did the will." I passed the card to Fred and read it again over his shoulder while he twisted slightly to get better light. Edward Asbery III. Tinkham, Asbery and Fulton. Attorneys at Law. 350 California Street. San Francisco.

"So he's got a lawyer in the financial district," Fred said. "So what?"

"That's the Bank of America headquarters building," I said, taking back the card and putting it in my jacket pocket where the gun used to go. "They've got vice-presidents to run the elevators there and door guards dressed in more gold braid than a fleet admiral. Lawyers line up for years to get office space in that building. Leo doesn't deal with people like that. Leo's a half-crazy old coot who talks on the telephone all day with file clerks. Why's a lawyer who charges $120 an hour going to come to Leo to find a missing heir?"

Fred shrugged. "There's not that many heir-hunters," he said.

"He could have used a bureau, a regular service."

"So he's an incompetent lawyer. Leo's in the phone book. Don't go making up problems, Mike. You got enough already."

I absorbed another inch of scotch, like a thirsty houseplant, and thought that was true. On the black and white Motorola in the corner of the bar a group of voices bigger than the Mormon Tabernacle Choir was singing about antacid. Twenty-three hundred dollars was not going to buy a hell of a lot of antacid tablets. If I found Muriel Contreras and still didn't find out who had framed me for my license, I would have to will the office furniture to Fred and get a job to pay my bills. Dental hygienist by day, crimebuster by night. A spare-time sleuth.

"You want me to go down to the station tomorrow and see if there's a book on Maranian?" Fred asked.

"Yeah. And check the morgue at the *Constitution* too. See if any of the reporters kept a file on him."

"You thought about asking your pal Carlton Hand to let you do some writing for the paper? To keep up the old cash flow?"

I watched two ice cubes wrestle each other down to the bottom of the glass and say woof, woof. Carlton Hand was the editor of the *San Francisco Constitution*. About a generation ago we had started out together as cub reporters on the L.A. *Times,* but I had dropped out of the newspaper business, coming north to try to find myself—the original missing person, as Dinah never tired of telling me—and Hand had stayed in the race. People who have to find themselves are losers, my father had said.

"He wouldn't give me a paper route now, Fred. You know that."

He shrugged and rubbed one hand around his dewlap. "There wasn't anybody I knew at the lab this afternoon," he said apologetically. "The Civil Service biddie wouldn't even let me see the report. 'You're retired, you know,' she says. You'll have to wait until I lieutenant Rubenstein comes back from vacation.' I used to change Lieutenant Rubenstein's diapers. Did you have any trouble with the church keys?"

I reached automatically into a side pocket and handed Fred his set of tools. Down at the other end of the bar, where he was permanently polishing glasses, the owner of Modesto's, a white-haired Chinaman in a black and orange Giants sweat-shirt, looked up at the flash of metal and then back at the glasses. For all his nervousness, Leo actually kept his office about as secure as a shoe box, probably because a real alarm system would have cost him a year's profits. On the door a chain lock, a thumb lock, a Kwik-Set deadbolt. Standard tab locks on the desk and all the drawers of the filing cabinets. Half the two year olds in North Beach could have opened it up with a spoon. I had broken in, Xeroxed the papers two blocks down the street, and returned them in half an hour.

"I thought Leo might have it booby-trapped," Fred said. "Like an exploding samovar. You want another one for the road?"

I shook my head. Walking slowly down from the end of the bar was an aging blond youth named Jack who worked for drinks as Modesto's bouncer. When he reached us he leaned in against the bar, turning his back to Fred and showing me a pair of forearms the size of drainpipes. Ex-boxers make good bouncers. Jack wore his hair long to cover the scar tissue around his eyes—Golden Gloves hurt—and the lumpy gristle that used to be his ears. But I would have known what he was anyway because he was wearing a black clip-on tie with his white shirt. On Union Street you can't even date a Greyhound hostess unless the gold chain around your neck lights up and spells "Gucci," but bouncers in bars like Modesto's are the last guys in the world who wear clip-on ties. A gesture of respectability, they would say, a touch of class. And of course it slips right off when the first drunk of the night tries to hoist you on your own Windsor knot.

Jack put one paw on my drink and pushed it a few inches away.

"You're Haller," he said.

"We've met before, Jack."

"The thing is, Haller," he said, rotating his big head to

see if the owner was watching. "The cops come in this afternoon about how you lost your private license." Fred started to say something and Jack's voice rode right over him. "Now Sammy don't care how you make your living, but the cops said you also lost your gun license. They said they know you come in here sometimes and if Sammy lets you in with a piece, then Sammy's an accessory."

"Bullshit," Fred said from behind Jack's shoulder.

"So Sammy sees you passing some kind of metal to pops here, and he gets nervous." Jack straightened up and cast a shadow halfway to the sidewalk.

"That goddam Yetta," Fred muttered.

"There's some nice bars down the block," Jack said, pushing my glass away another inch. He flexed the drainpipes again. For an instant I wondered if I could take him or if he could just stand there with his ten years and thirty pounds and hammer me into gumbo. When I didn't do anything Jack let a tiny contemptuous smile crawl out of the corners of his mouth. "Sammy don't want to make a federal case out of it," he said.

"I can take him in Scrabble," I said outside. A woman sauntered by, stopped five feet away, and looked me over. She wore an ebony leather skirt and a pink tee-shirt that had the words "I AM BABY SOFT" printed from nipple to nipple.

"You can take him anyway. He's big, but he's got a belly like a mashed potato. What's the matter with you, Mike? I've seen you when you'd stand a twerp like that on his head in the corner."

"Maturity," I said. "Self-control. Moderation." The tee-shirt hesitated, then bobbed off.

He hauled out one of his big cigars and studied my face while he peeled the cellophane away. "You got to watch yourself, Mike.

This license thing is walking all over you. One minute you're panicking out of control, playing a game of pepper with Gannett's head against the side of a truck, the next minute you're meeker than Mary's goddam little lamb. You're going up and down like a yo-yo." He found a match and ignited the panatela.

"I'm a panic-depressive," I said.

He sighed. "Come on, I'll give you a ride home in the Terrorist."

Fred's Buick Terrorist as he calls it—"What kind of cop would drive a Rabbit?"—dropped me at the corner of Green and Buchanan and roared off into the night. I lifted the collar of my jacket against the chill and started to walk the half block down Green to my building, listening to my heels tapping the black concrete in a slow, disembodied rhythm. I wasn't even sure I could take him in Scrabble. From the sidewalk where I paused out of habit—Haller likes to look a place over, Chick had said—I could see the light in my kitchen window that meant Dinah had let herself in. And from the stairway she heard my steps and swung open the door.

"Where have you been, Sherlock?" she smiled, crooking her arm in mine and leading me down the hallway to the living room. Out of the two big speakers on the wall of bookcases floated Papageno's first solo in *The Magic Flute*. "It's almost eleven," she said. "I skipped out early on Mendelsohn's seminar just to bake you chocolate chip cookies and cheer you up, and no you." She rose on her toes and kissed me lightly. "Scotch," she accused, licking her lips.

"I've been in one of those classy bars on Union Street," I said. "The guy at the next table sent back a bottle of Perrier."

"You've been to Modesto's," she said, "on which the Board of Health has long had its eye."

"I'm going to see Matz's lawyer in the morning," I said, and I was about to tell her about my visits to Leo when two loud knocks rattled the door and drowned out Mozart. I disengaged myself carefully and walked down the hall.

"I'm going to personally wreck your ass, Haller," Yetta said, pushing past me and into the living room. Behind him hustled another cop, younger than Yetta, wearing a tan raincoat and a dark suit. Yetta stopped at the center of the room and smacked a pair of pigskin gloves against his palm to look commanding. The kid strode to the window and leaned around the curtain, checking the balcony.

"Who's this?" Yetta said, pointing his gloves at Dinah. The kid reached over and turned down the volume knob of the phonograph.

"This is Dinah Farrell," I said, coming around him and stopping three feet away. Outside the bridge, cotton puffs of fog were gathering, peering our way to see if the fun had started.

"Blow," Yetta said to Dinah.

Dinah turned around, went to the couch, and sat down with her arms folded.

"You might need her help sometime, Yetta," I said. "Dinah is a psychiatrist." I dragged a cigarette out of my pocket and used both hands to light it. Otherwise I would have used them to correct his manners. Maturity, I told myself. Moderation. You couldn't correct Yetta's manners with a two-by-four.

The kid had pulled his head back in from the balcony and now stood by the wall of bookshelves, sneering. In the full light of the room his black hair looked as if it had been blown dry with a bellows and patted down with Crisco, and his tan raincoat was so new and crisp that he seemed to be standing in a taco shell. Mod Squad.

"Lieutenant Yetta is a policeman, Dinah," I said. "He's out of uniform, but he's a cop. You can tell by the way he keeps disciplining his gloves. Downtown they say he's the manliest man's man since Attila the Hun. I don't know who the cocker spaniel is or I'd introduce him."

"You through, Haller?"

"If you're on the way to your constitutional law class, Yetta, don't let us keep you."

"You went after Chick Gannett when I told you to stay away, Haller." He took two steps and planted himself in front of me, so close that I could smell the sweet leather of his new gloves as he slapped them against his palm again, the menthol filter of his last cigarette. Two boys standing chin to chin in the schoolyard. "You went after him in Richmond and assaulted him," he said. Up close the hooked nose was cratered by old bouts of acne and the swarthy complexion was peppered by new bristles of beard. Up close the clenched fists looked as big as ham hocks. "His wife called me this morning," Yetta said, "and told me how you came to the house and if she hadn't had the dog you were going to drop kick Gannett into the basement and bust up his car."

"Did she sign a complaint?" Dinah asked from the couch.

The kid cop curled his lip and put two hard-looking hands on his hips, gunslinger style. If Dinah hadn't been there the new gloves would have been on Yetta's hands and the kid would have been helping me off the carpet with a full nelson.

Yetta gave her a look intended to freeze blood and Dinah said, "Well, did she?"

"I heard that Chick was moving to Arizona today," I said, taking a step back before I lost control and actually hit him. Starting with calm, bureaucratic Henry Sampson I had wanted to hit everybody I had met for two days.

Yetta transferred the glower to me.

"Ask him what happened to his hand, lieutenant," the kid said with a nod at my bandaged knuckles. He was running his own hands over my records shelved next to the books, the two hundred or so opera records that I started collecting years ago. Opera was the first theatre of the absurd, Dinah had said after reading a plot summary of *La Traviata*. But I had been introduced to it a long time ago by a man in England, now dead. And I didn't like people touching the records.

"Get the kid away from my stuff, Yetta," I said. "I don't think he's housebroken."

Yetta looked over at him, back at me, trying to think of a way to change the game plan. You can't wreck asses in front of medical witnesses and be promoted to captain. "You've lost your license, Haller," he said. "I don't want you trying to find Contreras for Matz on the sly. I don't want you trying to find anybody. You're out of the goddam business." He folded the gloves over and stuffed them in his suit coat pocket. "And I don't want you around guns. I don't want you even to dream about a slingshot while your yellow slip is out. The bouncer down at Modesto's told me he had to eighty-six you tonight. I find something in here I don't like, I'll take you down to Bryant Street and lose you."

"Did you bring a search warrant, lieutenant?" Dinah asked.

"What are you, toots, a doctor or a lawyer?" the kid snarled.

"Out," I said, both hands trembling now, on the far side of moderation. "Out, Yetta. If you don't have a piece of paper you're just another uninvited guest. Go kick sand in somebody else's face."

The kid picked up the plastic dust cover of the phonograph and pulled the record off. Then with another sneer he brought it down against his raised knee and snapped it in half with a sound like a wrist bone popping. The turntable kept on spinning, making whispers of static in the speakers.

"It must of had a crack in it," the kid said.

Yetta looked at him in disgust and turned around. In a moment, uncertainty slowly rising on his face to replace the sneer, the kid walked after him and the hallway door banged shut.

CHAPTER 6

I HAD PICTURED THE INSIDE OF THE
Bank of America building as something like Scrooge
McDuck's vault, with vice-presidents in three-piece suits diving in and out of forty-two stories of coins. Instead, Tinkham,
Asbery and Fulton had a corridor of offices like any other in
the city—blond wooden chairs upholstered in rough fabrics,
indirect lighting only, a dark blue carpet criss-crossed by a
pattern of faint orange lines. In the modern fashion there
was no sign at all of what they did in the backrooms to make
their money. No statuettes of Justice weighing her scales,
no Daumier prints of pettifogging lawyers and judges. Not
even law books. Just a coffee table stacked with bulletins
from the various embattled fronts of capitalism: slick new
copies of *Business Week, Fortune, The Wall Street Journal,* and
Barron's, fanned out in a semi-circle like a deck of cards at
Reno. For all the room told me I could have been calling on
a chiropractor or a successful bookie as easily as on one of
San Francisco's premier law firms.

The big mahogany door whispered shut behind me and

I walked over to the receptionist's desk, where behind a tilted desk sign that said Ms. L. Fromsett sat a young man wearing a coral pink shirt and a blue tie and a spot of rouge on each cheek. Bending over him was a woman who pointed to a lighted button on the telephone console and said, "Answer 'Tinkham, Asbery Fulton good morning' and connect them to the partner they ask for, except for Mr. Shipman." The man gave a little wriggle of pleasure in his chair and reached for the telephone.

"May I help you?" She was about my age, I thought, and weathering it nicely, sensibly dressed in a Kelly green business suit, a black four-in-hand tie, no rouge. Somebody's wife, somebody's mother. Somebody in control. She looked at me with clear, healthy eyes. She hadn't spent the night burgling offices or backhanding cops or drinking scotch until her backbone turned to Ipana. I looked back with eyes that felt like manhole covers.

"Mr. Asbery, please."

She read the card I handed her while the man on the telephone glanced up and said, "Personal call, Lois—of course I can see you, Derek. On Tuesday night or Wednesday. But you have to make up your mind *which*."

"You don't have an appointment?" the woman asked doubtfully, and I wondered for a moment if I should have given her the other card, the one Dinah had had printed up last Christmas with a trench coat rampant and tommy gun gules.

I shook my head. "It's on business," I said. "There's a note on the back of the card." Like a well-trained secretary she didn't flip it over to see.

"It's not possible to be that impossible," the man on the telephone said.

She flicked the card against her thumbnail. "I'll give it to him, but I can't make any promises. He has a very heavy morning." She glanced at the clock above the desk. Nine-ten. "You can wait over there."

Asbery took the better part of an hour to fit me into his schedule. While I waited I smoked too many cigarettes and overheard too many personal calls. I also learned that *U.S. News* thought high interest rates weren't so bad if they taught us all a moral lesson and that *Fortune* thought business leaders should major in English. *Barron's* had a feature article on pork belly futures, and I was still trying to imagine what the hell people did with pork bellies when Lois Fromsett returned.

"You can see him now," she said, gesturing with one hand toward an inner hallway. "But he only has five minutes."

It could have taken five minutes to cross his office. When she closed the door I found myself looking across half an acre of Oriental rug toward a low frame desk and a picture window that deserved the name. In its precise center, out of the pastel tangle of roofs on Telegraph Hill, rose the white bulb of Coit Tower, Lillie Coit's eccentric tribute to the firemen whose trucks she used to chase, sometimes in drag, across the old city. Beyond the tower I could see the orange flanks of the Golden Gate Bridge, veiled in cobwebs of fog, and under the great pyramid of Mt. Tamalpais the brown northward curve of the Marin coast. From the thirty-sixth floor the great bay at its feet looked as manageable and sedate as a bathtub, and the tankers and naval cruisers so small that you wanted to reach out and push them with a stick. An illusion of power that vaguely annoyed me. Lawyers have enough illusions of power in the course of things.

"Come in, Mr.—" the man behind the desk paused and glanced down at the card in his hand. "Haller," he finished smoothly.

I waded over the rug and shook hands with Edward Asbery III. He read the message on my card again while he indicated with a peremptory nod a leather chair by the corner of his desk.

Peremptory. The lawyers I usually deal with are criminal defense specialists, a flamboyant breed largely given to hard liquor, loud clothes, and louder arguments. The few estate and trust specialists I had ever worked for had tended to be higher caste, stylishly Ivy League in dress, smoothly respectable if not actually Social Register themselves, authoritative and remote. "After two minutes you'll feel like de-icing his wings," my own lawyer had said earlier in the morning—the lawyer I should have seen three weeks ago. "But he's about as sharp an estate lawyer as you can find on the West Coast, and probably one of the five or six best legal minds in the city. What he'll tell you about a confidential matter," my lawyer had added, "you'll be able to fold in an airmail stamp."

Asbery was just leaning forward to say something when his telephone buzzed and he swivelled in his Eames chair to a speaker box beside it. What should I call him? Edward? Ed? III? On the wall just above his head were framed diplomas from Harvard College and Harvard Law School. To their left, over high bookcases and a military parade of law manuals dressed in brown and gold, hung an engraving of Harvard Yard in springtime, or maybe winter—modern art and Massachusetts weather can leave you guessing—and beside it a colorful print of Beacon Hill and the Statehouse dome in Boston. I craned my head and saw an autographed photo of Archibald Cox standing in front of the Harvard Law School entrance and wrapping one arm cordially around Asbery's shoulder. "To Ed Asbery—come back, all is forgiven. Archie."

He clicked the speaker off and swivelled back to me with a

squeak of polished leather. "I'm sorry for the interruption," he said. "I'm expecting a client very shortly. You wanted to see me?"

"Yeah. Is it true that Harvard has had more All-American football players than any other school?" I asked.

He released a smile the way you might release a balloon and picked up a pipe from the desktop clutter. "My wife says I overdo it too," he said. An urbane shrug. "As a matter of fact, yes. But they all date from the time when only six or eight teams in the country played football."

A top contender in a Graham Greene look-alike contest, my lawyer had said, indulging his literary turn: soulful but not saintly. Women love his eyes. He can be amazingly charming if he takes the trouble, and if you have an estate big enough to hold his interest. With you, he had said with a grin, he will probably be patronizingly offensive. I dug out a cigarette and watched him start the pipe. Dark black eyes that somebody might call masterful, thin-lidded, no glasses. The silver-gray hair led down to a square, cleanshaven face that looked a few years either way of sixty, down to a lantern jaw and wide, strong shoulders on a mesomorph's chest. The very opposite of Leo Matz's body. The body of a halfback buttoned into a sharkskin suit and larded over with urbanity. He crinkled the corners of his eyes in concentration and spoke with the pipe stem still in his mouth and the wooden match flickering over the bowl.

"I'm sure Mr. Matz didn't send you to me to talk football, Mr. Haller. Do you have a legal problem?"

I liked his voice, though most people wouldn't. I liked the stiff civility and the hint of New England frost in it. Why would a guy like Asbery, who probably had "Veritas" embroidered on his Doctor Dentons, pick up his Harvard chair and move west? I glanced at the Oriental rug and its bright design of the Persian Tree of Life. Because California was paved with gold.

"Leo didn't send me, Mr. Asbery," I said. Since visiting Henry Sampson I was getting good at sitting in other men's offices and speaking with unnatural politeness. Getting practice at, I corrected myself. Not getting good. "I put that on the card to get past your secretary. Until two days ago I was working for Leo on your case, looking for Muriel Contreras."

His desk telephone buzzed and without looking away he extended one hand and flicked it off. "I didn't know that Mr. Matz employed other people," he said, moving the frost right up to the front of his voice. His eyes travelled down my wardrobe, estimating in the straightforward manner of the financial district, where clothes still make the man. He would size up my blue jacket as off the rack at Macy's, the brown tie as domestic polyester. I should have worn crimson.

"Sometimes, when he's busy." I didn't see any reason to explain that Leo Matz needed young legs and arms more than I needed his money. That I took an interest in Leo. People in offices like Asbery's think of charity as something you deduct, not give.

"I see." He leaned forward, elbows on teak, pipe at present arms. "I dealt only with Mr. Matz on the telephone. I assumed he did his own work." Puff of smoke. "I also assumed that the terms of the will I sent over were confidential."

"Leo didn't give me the will, Mr. Asbery. He didn't discuss it. He refused to discuss it, in fact. But it's a probated will, in the public records, and I've read it. What I need to know now is what isn't in the public records."

Puff of smoke. Bland silence.

"Like, how a seventy-year-old businessman with a Pacific Heights address ends up leaving nearly a million dollars to a Tenderloin hooker," I said rudely.

Asbery inspected the back of his hands as carefully as he

had inspected my clothes. He liked them better. They had deferential manners, they brought him pipe tobacco and debentures, they had been to Harvard.

"The family history could not be of any possible use to you, Mr. Haller," he said frigidly. "You have a specific job to do, nothing more. A job in any case you apparently stopped doing two days ago.—Come in, Margot!"

He was on his feet before I could turn around in the chair. Miss Fromsett, smoothing her skirt self-consciously, had stepped to one side of the door to make way for another woman.

She wasn't fat, I thought as she crossed the rug, but there was too much of her. Too much pneumatic figure packed into a frame not much over five feet. Too much round, middle-aged face sandwiched between thick fringes of blonde hair that swayed like drapery when she walked. Too much rouged cheek and lip, packed close together like wax apples in a fruit bowl, too much nervous intensity in the smile she gave Asbery. But there was no mistaking the ingratiating way he had jumped up, the solicitous hand at her elbow. The client can always take a walk in estate planning, my lawyer had said, so estate lawyers, especially estate lawyers for the very rich, tend to be a cross between Dink Stover and Uriah Heep, unless of course they're very rich themselves.

"Margot," Asbery said, coming around the desk and escorting her protectively to the chair opposite mine. Miss Fromsett closed the door with excessive gentleness, as if it were a sickroom, and Margot sat down, thanking Asbery. Her chin lifted toward me in a polite question, and Asbery made the introductions walking back to his desk.

"Michael . . . Haller, this is Mrs. Margot Maranian."

I stopped halfway down to my chair and stared.

"Mrs. Maranian is the widow of Aram Maranian," Asbery said, picking up his pipe again. His voice was casual and mild. "I handle the affairs of the estate for her, of course. Today is one of our regular appointments. I thought you wouldn't mind if she sat in on our discussion."

I heard myself saying I didn't mind at all.

Margot leaned toward Asbery and smiled. Her dress was expensive, a Burgundy-colored designfrom one of the Magnins, and her silk blouse had a brightly colored floral pattern topped by a gigantic silk bow that stood out straight like the wings of a butterfly. She would be in her late forties, I thought, trying to get myself past the shock of Asbery's little bombshell; still attractive, still interested in being attractive. A fine womanly figure, as my father liked to say, even though much of it looked as if it had been pumped up at the local gas station, like the cartoon man in the Michelin ads. A young widow, dressed to kill. She rotated the smile and said she was glad to meet me and I said likewise and she let the smile die away slowly into her powder and lipstick. Asbery stoked up the pipe again and watched us settle into uncomfortable silence.

"Haller is the private detective we hired to find Muriel Contreras," he said finally.

Margot jerked her head and her purse slid from her lap to her knees. "I thought his name was—" She looked at me, looked at Asbery, swung her round face back to me again with no smile at all. A cruel game, I thought, and perfectly timed, like the flick of a whip. Under Asbery's urbane expression you could imagine a secret grimace of pleasure at Margot's confusion, at my shock. Uriah Heep's servility had disguised a lot of hate.

"You haven't found her?" she asked, not attempting to hide

the anxiety in her voice. From her point of view I was eight hundred thousand dollars' worth of bad news.

I shook my head. "Not yet."

"Thank God," she said, deflating back into the chair. "I thought sure the man's name was something else."

"Haller works for the man the office hired," Asbery said, resuming the solicitous manner. "As a kind of subcontractor. But he was dismissed from the job two days ago without finding her. To tell you the truth, Margot, I don't really understand why he's here now."

"Because I'm still looking for her," I said. And as concisely as I could I told him about my license, the shooting and the frameup.

When I had finished he tilted back in the Eames chair and watched the pipe smoke drift up to Harvard Yard. "You don't give any real reason for connecting my work with your misfortune," he said patronizingly. "You don't give me any kind of reason." Behind his crewcut a kid's boat loaded with half a million tons of Sacramento rice rounded Alcatraz Island and swung its prow toward Japan. "You had barely begun the job," he said. "It could have been anyone, anyone from your past with a grudge. Private detectives step on toes, Mr. Haller. I've worked with my share of them. Any lawyer has. And you seem to be the kind who would step rather hard. From the tone of your voice you think it could have even been someone unfriendly in the police. My connection, as you call it, is just a wild guess." The telephone buzzed again and he looked at a digital clock beside it before flipping the switch off.

"It certainly seems farfetched to me," Margot said emphatically. She glanced at Asbery. "He doesn't even have a license to work. If there's no other reason, I don't think . . . "

Asbery shook his head gently, making a wreath of smoke.

I held on. "You develop instincts in my business, Mr. Asbery. Feelings. It might have been an ex-con with a grudge, sure. But the ex-cons I know don't rate high on subtlety. They don't think about psychological revenge. They'd stop me in the Tenderloin one night and take batting practice on my knee-caps, not work out an elaborate frame with the Board of Collection and Investigative Services. Whichever way I turn this it always comes out the same. The net effect was to stop me from finding Muriel Contreras."

He glanced at the clock. "It doesn't seem to have stopped you, however. And I assume Matz has hired someone else by now. In any case, I can't help you." The telephone buzzed and he tapped the hold button briskly and stood up. "Confidentiality," he said. "Simple confidentiality. I can't discuss the contents of a will with a third party, or the background. Matz knows that. You should know that. I'm surprised he even told you I handled it. Unless Margot feels that she wants to—" He looked at Margot and she shook her head once, a jerky motion that made the blonde sideburns sway again. "No," he said. "That's right. I don't advise it, Margot."

"Wait a minute," I said, standing up too. "We're not talking about a dog license, Mr. Asbery. We're talking about my life, how I make a living."

"You were given a hearing, Mr. Haller. If you want to appeal it, I can recommend a public interest attorney. Good day." He started to come around the corner of the desk to show me the door. Margot swung her plump knees to one side in an elegant huddle. I stood on the roots of the Tree of Life and blocked his way.

"We're talking about the equivalent of disbarment," I said. I was three inches taller and twenty years younger and he stopped and scowled, pumping a flush into the sleek jowls.

"There's nothing confidential about a probated will," I said. "It's awkward and you're making it more awkward, but I need to know why Mrs. Maranian's husband left the money to somebody like Contreras. I need that relationship explained. I need to know more about her. Otherwise I've got no lever when I find her, no way to work on her, no way to bring out whoever took my license."

"I hired Leo Matz to find her," Asbery said. "Not you." He turned around and walked his beautifully tailored suit to his telephone, pressed a button. "Mr. Haller is leaving now, Lois," he told the talk box. "Have Sidney show him out."

Sidney would be a piece of hamburger in a security uniform, one of the bank's centurions. Good job, Haller. Push the haughty lawyer into a corner and make him mad. Frighten the widow. Cut off your best chance for breaking out of the frame. Asbery turned from the telephone and stared at me, big jaw tight, square face pink. But not frightened, not out of control. Not like me.

I turned around and walked out of the office, down the hallway, into the reception area. The big mahogany door was just swinging shut with a disapproving sigh as a chunky, middle-aged man in a Burns uniform hurried past me. I crossed the blue carpet and reached for the door handle.

"Love your shoes," called the guy at the desk.

CHAPTER 7

O N THE MORNING OF THE 1906 EARTHQUAKE Enrico Caruso is supposed to have wrapped a hotel towel around his throat and run down Market Street carrying only a picture of Teddy Roosevelt under his arm.

I stood at the corner of Market and Montgomery, five blocks from Asbery's office, and inhaled my own cigarette smoke and whatever hydrocarbons the passing Muni bus had to spare. I knew how Caruso had felt. Blind panic. I stepped in the striped crosswalk and made my way over to Second Street. No job, no income, no prospects. My fingers came up with an empty matchbook from my jacket pocket and I saw a sketch of a good-looking curly-haired man and the caption "High School Graduates—Learn a Trade." I wadded up the empty cover and dropped it into a gutter before I actually hauled out my ballpoint and a stamp and sent off for Mechanical Drawing Made Simple or Raise Your Own Minks. Then I crossed Second, walked another block east under the big clock of the Criterion Hotel that said 10:45, entered something dark and quiet called the After Hours and ordered my first martini of the morning.

Early drinkers are nothing special south of Market, where most of the bars open up at 6 a.m. and most of the customers are ready long before that. A few places near the Southern Pacific depot even sell highballs in plastic cups, to go. With one eye still on his folded newspaper, the bartender of the After Hours bounced an olive into a glass of gin, shook vermouth from an empty bottle, and slid it down the bar. I stared out the window and wondered again how a Harvard lawyer in five hundred dollar suits ended up calling a small-time specimen like Leo Matz to do his job. Why not Burns? or Pinkerton? or Haller? And with the buxom widow Maranian on the scene, what did it mean to handle the affairs of the estate?

"What do you think of a black guy named Murphy?"

I turned my head in surprise and breathed in a cloud of stale beer and dentures. An old man was pointing one unsteady finger toward the television set where the Oakland A's were playing somebody back east. The camera shifted as I looked. Boston. "What do you think?" he wheezed, hitching thin shoulders under a collarless overcoat and a shabby cardigan. "Murphy's an Irish name. Don't it bother you that a Murphy's black?"

"It doesn't even bother me that our governor's Brown," I told him. He had a face like a crumpled paper bag. He rubbed one dirty hand across the lower half of it and stood looking puzzled.

"Buy him a beer," the bartender said from his newspaper. "He'll leave you alone."

I shoved another buck across the damp bar and watched the old man hobble back to his stool at the other end. Overhead Murphy made a diving catch to end the inning and the camera rolled back to show the Boston skyline beyond Fenway

Park, five square new skyscrapers with the architectural charm of Tupperware, then the noble old John Hancock building still standing sentry over Copley Square. You never smell the ocean in San Francisco, I thought. Only its ghost, the fog. In Boston I had taken it in with almost every breath, in every corner of the city, a bleak, sudsy Atlantic smell of too much salt and too many bones and too much rotting timber. When we were very young. I ordered another martini and watched the traffic. Outside the window a pimpmobile drifted to the curb and stopped, a Cadillac convertible as crimson as Edward Asbery's Harvard pajamas. Out of the passenger side stepped a tall Hispanic man wearing a black moustache, a white suit, a white shirt, a white vest, white shoes, and a white floppy ten-gallon hat. He posed there for a moment, both hands tugging the points of his vest, and looked up and down the sidewalk to see if anybody noticed.

When nobody did, he turned and strutted across the street, patting the rump of a matronly Volvo that had braked for him. Then he disappeared into a building that six months ago had been a mangy porno theatre called the House of Paradise, featuring live strip shows between movies and nickel bags of heroin in the men's room. And if the bag turned out to hold Oxydol instead of heroin, you could always grab a stripper between shows and cross the street to the Hotel Criterion. Blazing saddles, Fred called the girls south of Market. Now the building was an arcade for electronic video games and the House of Paradise had moved to a place on the Embarcadero near China Basin, not all that far from my office. Chick and I had even spent an instructive couple of hours there looking for Muriel Contreras. Trying to give her $800,000. I finished the martini in one swallow. It was too soon for people to start buying me beers. And too late to expect any help from Edward Asbery. I walked to the back of the room and dropped a dime in the telephone.

"Your friend Grab left a message," Fred said. "Hold on." I started a cigarette and watched Murphy run to center field while Fred made assorted clunking sounds at the other end of the line. "I wrote it down," he said, coming back. "He's going to be outside the office at one sharp. If you don't show, tough darts. Now that school's started he's probably got to hustle Quads at recess." Grab is a black man who spends most of his time sitting in the backroom of a delicatessen on Eddy Street and collecting money in envelopes. When Fred thought Grab was just a pimp and a numbers organizer, he liked him. But he draws the line at pushers. As far as I knew, Grab didn't draw the line at anything.

"Did Bryant Street have a book on Aram Maranian?"

"I never got there, Mike. I went to the dentist again. I'm going over now, and then to the *Constitution*. You coming back here for lunch?"

"I'm having some olives where I am. Forget the *Constitution*. I'll go over myself."

"What did the fancy lawyer tell you?"

"He told me a lawyer's confidentiality is a sacred thing." I dragged more smoke down to ballast my lungs against the martinis. "My own lawyer told me nobody has ever beat one of Henry Sampson's decisions. He said it takes six months just to file an appeal."

"So what are you going to do?"

"I'm going to find Muriel Contreras. After that, I'm a modern scientific snoop. I'm going to let Newton's third law take over."

"What the hell is Newton's third law?" he said.

"For every action there's an equal and opposite reaction," I said.

On the television screen somebody swung at a curve ball and the bat broke into two pieces with a loud, bloodless snap.

When I pulled up to a meter at quarter to one, Grab was already there, leaning against the haunch of an enormous white Cadillac and drumming his hands to the beat of the radio. In the front passenger seat an elegant black woman in a pink leotard and a white fur coat was doing her nails, her back to Grab. Facing him across the sidewalk, arms crossed like the Punjabi in *Little Orphan Annie,* stood a black man with a shaved head, muddy yellow eyes, and a torso the size of a two-car garage.

Grab winked at him when he saw me coming.

"They's Batman," he said, drumming his hands faster, "and Spiderman, and here comes"—slow roll, pause, crescendo—"Waspman!" And he rolled back and forth against the Cadillac, laughing and hugging himself with delight.

I walked up and leaned against the roof of the car with one elbow and shook out a cigarette with my free hand.

"Dressed for church as usual, Grab," I said.

With both hands he spread out the long points of his yellow silk shirt and looked down at them. Below the shirt he could see luminous purple trousers and white ostrich skin boots with a red feather running up each ankle. Cuddled around his thin neck were a couple of pounds of gold chain hooked to a polished ruby as big as my thumb. Fred says Grab dresses like a man from Mars.

"Shit, man," he said, still spreading out the collar for me to admire. "What you *show* is what they *know.*" He reached into my pocket and took one of the cigarettes. "How long it take you to button down that collar? You think somebody gone rip it off, you got to button it down?" He stuck the cigarette between beautiful capped teeth and grinned. I struck a paper match and lit his, then mine. Thomas Jefferson Randall was his full name, a man in his early forties with a soft brown complexion and a shortish prison record by Eddy Street standards. But everybody who did business with him called him Grab.

"I hear you love-life took a dive, Sherlock. I hear you want a date with a little hooker named Muriel Contreras."

I took a long drag of the cigarette and watched the bald bodyguard refold his arms and glower down the street, where a cop had just come out of a coffee shop. The cop waved at Grab with a rueful smile and Grab gave a mock salute in return.

"One of your clients, Grab?"

"Hell no, Sherlock. I just love The Man."

"You're not mad at The Woman either."

He looked over his shoulder at the woman in his car. "She a nun, man. She a soul sister!" And he laughed uproariously again, banging his palms against the car. The woman didn't look up. The bodyguard followed the cop down the street with his eyes.

"You know where she is, Grab?"

"I know where you can find out. You go over to the Club Eden on Turk Street tonight, you ask for Christie, white chick. She use to be roomie with you girlfriend. But nobody around seen her, man, not since her sweet daddy got offed down south of Market. You ask for Christie, say Grab sent you." He blew smoke from his nostrils in two evil streams. "You should of asked me in the first place, man."

I pulled away from the Cadillac and shook the circulation back into my arm. I should have asked him, but I had thought I would do it by the book that time, do it by the book and maybe show my apprentice Chick Gannett a thing or two. "How much does that cost me, Grab?" I asked, as everybody did with him sooner or later.

"On the house, man. No charge."

I took my hand off my wallet. "Now there's a switch. Since when do you turn down money?"

He clasped his hands behind his head and leaned all the way back, as comfortable as if he were sitting in Edward Asbery's custom-made chair. "I don't need the money, man, and that's the truth. I like to have people owing me, too. Next time one of you friends got something heavy comin' down Eddy Street, I like to know you owe me."

I thought of my dwindling pile of savings and nodded.

"I don't work for money, you know, man. Not just for money. Dude works just for money ain't got no soul." He reached one lazy hand over and fingered my blue Macy's jacket. "You sure as hell don't work for money, Haller."

I pushed the hand away, not gently. "I don't work for you either, Grab."

The bodyguard grunted and Grab's eyes narrowed and went suddenly yellow, and for a moment I could glimpse the hard, calculating self that he kept hidden under all the jive. Then he smiled again.

"Shit, man. You ninety percent mouth."

"And ten percent soul."

He liked it. He whooped and slapped the side of the Cadillac until even the soul sister forgot to be cool and looked around curiously at me. Grab danced and laughed around the front of the car and grinned at me across the roof while the bodyguard unpropped himself from my office building and got in the back.

"Actually, man," he said, holding the car door open, "you ninety percent ice."

CHAPTER 8

THE LAST MARTINI OF A LONG DAY WAS STILL walking around my belly in warm circles, like a pup making himself comfortable, when I reached the Club Eden.

Eight-thirty, my wrist watch said. I stood on the sidewalk outside the entrance and looked up at the big flashing neon apple with a bite taken out of one side. Underneath it **"C-L-U-B E-D-E-N,"** two bulbs missing from the D. Zero from my afternoon of reading obituaries and files at the *Constitution*. Zero likewise from two thirsty reporters in the city room at the *Chronicle*. Aram Maranian, aged seventy-one at death, wealthy owner of Maranian Carpets and Rugs near Market and Powell, in poor health for years, generous contributor to Armenian charities, especially St. Gregory's Armenian Church near Golden Gate Park. Reclusive, uneducated old man. Married a young wife fifteen, twenty years ago, but not a whiff of scandal, not a word in or out of the papers' gossip files. Zero, zero, zero. Eight-thirty-three.

"You wanna check it out, big guy? Best action in San Francisco, man, all moving parts. Whadya say?"

I ignored the barker and glanced up Turk Street. Twenty feet away, leaning against the door frame of a darkened coffee shop, a pale woman in a bright palomino wig and a red velvet dress smiled at me and said something in a low voice. The dress was much smaller and much tighter than the wig. I smiled back and shook my head. Turk Street, the corner sign said, one block south of Eddy, one block north of Market. The heart of the Tenderloin, if I had the anatomy right. San Francisco's Disneyland of Decadence. Most Johns, their convention badges and wedding rings in their hip pockets, would have looked automatically at the pale woman's spectacular, pneumatic cleavage. I looked at the calves instead, checking for muscle and hair, because these days half the street whores on Turk Street are actually men in drag. And about half the Johns are acutely surprised, disappointed, and mugged.

"Hey, big guy, check it out," the barker chanted, crooking his finger at me. A thin kid in his early twenties, with fluffy black hair and shoulders the width of a sawhorse. He could be working his way through Stanford. He could also be selling filthy Easter eggs.

I took a drag on my cigarette and looked the other way down Turk Street. I like red light districts sometimes. I had liked Soho and Pigalle when I was a college dropout, defying my father and fancying myself a Bohemian with poetic sensibilities and advanced morals. I still like North Beach, where you can find unpretentious bookstores and coffee houses in the very shadow of Carol Doda's silicone peaks. And I like the name Tenderloin, promising vice as cuddly and innocent as a pair of kittens on a featherbed. In the Boston of my youth they had roped it off with squad cars and called it the Combat Zone. But Turk Street is what slinks into a wide-open city. Turk Street has all the innocence of a Tijuana brothel and all the poetry of a septic tank. Twenty feet the other way a man in his late fifties, wearing a dirty khaki shirt and khaki trousers, sat on the curbstone under a streetlight and stared at me with a face wiped clean of expression. Beside him an empty jug of Boone's Farm wine rolled back and forth on the sidewalk, in slow time to the breeze. The one brown shoe I could see had only half a sole. The toes peeking out like a family of mice were gray and bloody.

"Come on in, big guy," the barker whined again, holding to one side the heavy red curtain that served as the door to Club Eden. Pedestrians churned past me on the sidewalk, in a hurry. "Strictly hard core here, strictly live sex acts. Come on in! You from out of town? You won't see nothin' like this in Topeka, big guy."

But you will see maybe twenty or thirty places like the Club Eden in downtown San Francisco, to the delight and shock of the tourists, who never expect a big city to be so morally compact, never expect to step straight out of the Hilton lobby into a string of dives that would have brought blushes on the Barbary Coast. "The City That Waits to Die," the newspapers call it in their periodic stories about the famous earthquake. From the window of his well-carpeted office six or eight blocks away, I thought, Edward Asbery III could almost have tossed his Harvard chair into Eden. If he had really been looking for her, he could almost have tossed Muriel Contreras her $800,000 in plain brown packets.

A dive takes you to the bottom. I would write aphorisms for fortune cookies if I didn't get my license back. I flipped my cigarette toward the street, its sparks making a brilliant orange arc against the night, and plunged in. As I took my first step the derelict began to crawl toward the butt.

The outer room was a brightly lit sex shoppe like any one of the thousands that sprang up in American cities during the late sixties, sometime between Esther Williams' last movie and Linda Lovelace's first talkie. Deep Splash. "Bun boutiques," Fred calls places like the Club Eden: half a dozen metal racks of books and magazines for the literate clubman and giving off the peculiar green, unscrubbed odor of a bus station floor. To my left, like the display case in an X-rated delicatessen, stood a long glass cabinet jammed with fleshy rubber artifacts: sleek white vibrators that ran off AC-DC current, naturally, and had adaptors for European voltage, pink Brobdingnagian dildoes, batteries not included, two life-size rubber dolls named Mandy and Mindy who were lonely, and dozens of kinds of playing cards, statuesque candles, and multi-colored prophylactics—the avant garde, of the sexual revolution. Mandy was full-blown, stretching half the length of the case and realistic, as the placard said, in every detail. Mindy, uninflated, had been left folded in a sad little flesh-colored square that would slip easily into a raincoat pocket.

Behind the display counter lounged a woman in her early twenties who wore only gold pasties over her nipples and a bikini bottom the size of a watchband. Just above her head hung a framed copy of the First Amendment printed in the seventy-two-point newspaper type they used to announce Pearl Harbor, and next to that a quotation from Thomas Jefferson about freedom of speech.

"You got to sign this," she said and poked a clipboard in my direction. While I read a mimeographed statement that said I was over twenty-one and understood that acts of a sexual nature were shown in the club, she chewed gum and tapped her foot to the hard rock music that filtered out of a cheap speaker overhead. The six names above mine on the membership sheet all said "John Smith." I wrote "Frank Yetta" in my space and gave her the ten dollar bill that made me a member.

"For another five you can have a private booth at the show," she said. "Talk to the girls in private."

"Is Christie working here tonight?"

She shrugged and the right pasty tumbled onto the top of the glass counter. Still chewing the gum, she began to roll the exposed nipple between two fingers while her other hand retrieved the pasty.

"Who knows names?" she said.

I twisted past a rack of illustrated magazines devoted to recreational leathercraft and followed the ambiguous hand-lettered sign for the show: "Live Acts of Love—Members Only." Then I entered a long, wide hallway that must have been used for office space once or storage and, still following signs, pushed deeper and deeper into the building.

Before love, drinks. The last part of the hall had been half-heartedly remodeled into a bar and decorated with a big papier-mâché apple minus a bite. Somebody had slapped wrinkled *Playboy* centerfolds where the plaster was peeling and added twenty feet of ornately framed mirrors at shoulder height along one wall. Behind a plywood bar on the other side another bikini clad woman, this time with a fluffy hairdo like Margot Maranian's, polished glasses with a towel. On my left, three kids with blazers were counting their money at one of the tables, and at the end of the room, perched on a barstool by another red curtain, a bouncer about my age was counting his knuckles. He didn't wear a clip-on bow tie like Jack at Modesto's, just gray slacks and a green polo shirt that made his biceps squeeze out from the sleeves like apples in a boa constrictor. On the edge of his jaw was an old ribbed scar the color of bad hamburger.

When I reached the curtain he stood up and held out a warning palm.

"You want to see the show, it's another five bucks," he said.

"I already paid ten dollars upstairs for a membership."

"We just raised the dues. You wanta see what you get?" He swept the curtain to one side, exposing a half-darkened room and a spotlighted stage. Around the stage, on rows of fold-up chairs, sat fifteen or twenty men, ranging in dress from business suits like Edward Asbery's to work shirts and Levi's. On the stage, sweating under the spotlight, a tall, heavy-set blonde, completely naked except for crusts of mascara and lipstick, was shuffling her feet in time to the loud recorded music, staring over the customers' heads into the faceless blackness of the ceiling. On one side of the stage I could see the gauzy clothing she had stripped off and, scattered around it, dozens of crumpled dollar bills.

While I watched, one of the men in business suits stood up and tossed another dollar bill at her feet. The blonde began dancing toward him, rubbing her shiny breasts with both hands as if she were kneading dough. As she moved she arched her back until her face disappeared and her hair almost swept the stage floor. Somebody in the audience shouted and the businessman moved closer. The record player needle hit a scratch and jumped from "Goldfinger" halfway into "Love to Love You, Baby" as the blonde woman reached the edge of the stage and, still swaying rhythmically to the boom of the music, arched completely back like a girl in a gymnastics class, so that both hands were straight down on the floor and her knees straddled the businessman's face. Somebody else threw a dollar bill on the stage and stood up. The businessman put one hand on each of her thighs and leaned forward.

"Five bucks," the bouncer said, dropping the curtain.

"I'm saving to buy a club tie," I said. "I wanted to see Christie or Muriel."

He reperched on the stool and jerked his scar toward the tables and chairs under the mirrors. From behind the curtain came disconnected gunshots of applause.

"So buy a drink, champ," he said, waving a paw to the woman tending bar. "And they'll send one of them out."

Welcome to Eden. I sat down and lit a cigarette and hunched my shoulders against the music pounding away in brutal rhythm to acts of love behind the curtain. Strictly hard-core, the kid outside had promised, you won't see nothin' like it in Topeka. Or Boston. I had learned about sex from P. G. Wodehouse novels and from a second-string blonde soprano in Paris when I was nineteen and supposed to be on my way back to college. She had been gentle, cynical, and mercenary, and I had been enthusiastic and confused, a situation that hadn't changed much in twenty years. But looking for Muriel Contreras in swinging San Francisco had made me begin to feel like Bertie Wooster at a Rolling Stones concert. Everybody's favorite city, the tourist posters said. There were days when I thought San Francisco's wide-open style was fun too, days when I expected to run across an adult carwash on Turk Street or a topless production of *The Mousetrap*. There were also days when I thought my Puritan ancestors had diagnosed human nature just right, days when I thought what San Francisco needed was an iron-cold, flinthearted New England winter to clean it out, a bleak season of repression after its long, squalid binge of toleration. But most days either way, I noticed, nobody asked my opinion.

"Twenty dollars for champagne," the bikinied bar girl with the bowl of hair said, popping gum in the corner of her mouth. "That's all we sell. Christie'll be here in a minute."

I gave her another bill from my Christmas Club fund while she deposited a bottle and two glasses on the table. Then she bent over to take a swipe at the ashtray with her bar towel, and the movement made her heavy breasts shake like two bags of water. She grinned at me, straightened, and undulated back to a flip-up door in the bar.

When I was sixteen, I thought, the sight of naked breasts that close would have short-circuited my optical nerves. When I was sixteen, I put on two jock straps to go out on a date and spent half my daylight hours in front of the bathroom mirror wondering why adolescence had brought my complexion to a boil. But now, rounding the curve on forty, I had told Dinah, there were only a few things left that I didn't understand. Make a list, she had said. Sex. Violence. Money.

"I'm Christie."

She sat down quickly as if I might change my mind, a tall leggy peroxide blonde wearing only a lacy black slip and a pair of slippers, smiled professionally, and poured champagne from the bottle into two clear plastic cups. I didn't see where she had appeared from, and in the dim light I could just make out that her hair had been cut pixie fashion and that dark layers showed up beneath the blonde. Her face, heart-shaped and pleasant, was lined with makeup and fatigue, but she looked up with a clear-eyed, intelligent expression that strangely enough reminded me of Dinah.

"Mike," I said. The champagne tasted like Seven-Up and soap and I turned the bottle to look at the label. There wasn't one.

"Do I know you?" she asked with the same poised directness.

"A guy named Grab gave me your name."

"I don't work for him," Christie said with a slight frown and crossed her legs. "I work inside."

I nodded. Like most big cities, San Francisco has a strict division of labor in prostitution. Street hookers almost always work for black pimps. The inside girls work for whites—in fact, about a quarter of them are supposed to work for two white brothers named Slam and Dunk who own a chain of adult clubs like the Club Eden, some artistic porno theatres, and a couple of massage parlors with clever names like "The Rubdown." They used to play semi-pro basketball, but their nicknames apparently came from their sex lives.

"I'm looking for Muriel Contreras," I started to say, and she jumped the chair back from the table and came to her feet.

"You're the cop!"

I stood up too and shook my head, about to speak.

"You shot her old man. You're the cop's been chasing her. You're the one she was going to see south of Market and you shot her old man."

I wanted to lunge for her wrists and hold her down to listen, but I shook my head slowly so the reassuring expression wouldn't fall off and tried to speak again.

"I didn't do it," I began.

"What the hell's going on here?" the bouncer growled, materializing at my elbow. A flush spread from Christie's face to the tops of her breasts and she looked first at the bouncer and then at me.

"I didn't do it," I told her. "You're making a mistake."

"This guy bothering you, kid?" the bouncer asked Christie. "You want me to toss him out?" He turned his big, flat face toward me like a rusty turret revolving. Christie chewed her lower lip and looked unhappy. "The owners don't like tough guys with the broads," he said. "You wanta be a tough guy, you gotta start with me."

"You told her old man something about money," Christie

said and hesitated. "A lot of money. That's why she went to meet you."

"That's right," I said, concentrating on her face, not bothering to glance at the bouncer, who was puffing his chest and flexing his muscles like Muhammad Ali. Body language. If I got tough he was supposed to fold me in his wallet and drop me in the alley off Turk Street. But if he actually touched me just then, I thought, breathing like a sprinter, I would pound him into sandwich spread.

"She stands to inherit a lot of money," I said to Christie, who had taken one hand off the back of the chair and begun to straighten a strap. "And that's why I'm trying to find her. I had nothing to do with her old man, that's the truth."

"Did you hear what I said, champ?" the bouncer was looking from Christie to me with a puzzled frown.

Christie stared a moment longer. The flush on her pale skin had faded as fast as it had appeared and she hitched her shoulders square so that the small high breasts settled again into the slip.

"It's OK, Tony," she said finally. I let out my breath. She moved the chair back to the table, sat down and wrapped both hands around her cup of champagne. "Just a misunderstanding, Tony."

The loudspeakers in the next room abruptly switched from disco to reggae. Tony gave me a semi-pro hard look and made his biceps jump once more, like galvanized frogs. Then he let his chest drop six inches toward his belly and swaggered back to the barstool, muttering.

"Muriel said a white man shot him," Christie said. "A big guy that sounded like you." I shook my head. She sighed and looked down at the chains of carbonated bubbles trying to climb out of the cup. "Muriel could be wrong," she said.

"Muriel could be wrong about whether it's day or night." She lifted her eyes and spoke with half a smile tugging apologetically at one corner of her mouth. "She's been, like, hiding, ever since that happened. Not working here or anyplace else. She's a very nervous girl, a very nervous screwed-up girl, and when her old man got shot that was about the last straw. She thinks she kills everybody she loves."

"I didn't shoot him."

"Like her mother," Christie said. "Or this other old man down in L.A. before she came north. She heard a cop was looking for her and she thought you were from L.A."

"I'm just a private cop," I said. "Lawyers sometimes hire private investigators to find heirs, people who don't know they've inherited property. The lawyer takes a cut and the p.i. takes a cut. But you've got to find the person first. Muriel stands to inherit a lot of money, but she's got to claim it first, and that's why I've been looking for her."

Christie studied my face with the same cautious frown she had worn when I had given her Grab's name. I kept my eyes up and tried to look trustworthy, loyal, and kind, not unconscious all the time of the smooth curve of her breasts in the nests of black lace, the hard bulge of nipples pressed like fingertips against the fabric. Beneath the fatigue and the mascara, she had the comfortable, intelligent face of a college girl, and the elegant body of a dancer. Not the kind of hooker Fred thought would make a bundle of money. Not the kind of face or body I would have picked for the role at all, and one way or another I had spent the last three weeks in dumps like the Club Eden looking at women's bodies, looking for Muriel Contreras.

"Who would leave Muriel money?" she was asking. The music in the next room thundered to a climax and more applause pattered in its wake. "She's got no family except a couple of old aunts in East L.A. and they couldn't leave her busfare."

Two men in dark business suits came out of the auditorium and walked quickly past us, eyes on the floor. Christie watched as they left the bar and the expression on her face changed from comfortable intelligence to winter.

"Can you tell me where she is?" I said. She brought the cold expression back to me and I reached in my pocket. I didn't want to make the same mistake I had made with Asbery and the widow, I told myself. I didn't want to push so hard that I pushed her out of my corner.

"If you don't want to tell me," I said after a moment, "will you just give her my card? She can telephone me. Or you can. Or just leave a message on the machine."

She took the plain business card and read it. Then she scraped back her chair and stood up. "I'm on for the next show," she said. "I'll think about it. Maybe I'll tell her." I stood up and watched my shadow cover her shoulders. "Or maybe I won't," she said, half turning away. "She's not staying with me anyway, so don't get any ideas about following me home."

"Not for Muriel anyway," I said without thinking and felt myself suddenly blush like a schoolboy. In martinibus Veritas.

She turned all the way back to me and held my card between two fingers. The cold expression had melted into something like amusement, like big girl, little boy. "You know what, detective?" she asked. I shook my head, still blushing. Goddammit, did Sam Spade ever blush? Did Philip Marlowe flirt? Sampson was right to lift my license. "If I do tell her," she said, "it'll be because you have an OK face. You don't have a"—her tongue searched for the word—"judgmental face."

"I'm way behind on my judgments," I said lamely.

"Like those creeps that just left," she went on. The music

began to thump again in the next room, but she still stood, amused. "You didn't even ask what's a girl like me doing in a place like this."

"What's a girl like you doing in a place like this?"

"I wanted to be a dancer, a ballerina," she said. "Muriel did too. Even hookers were little girls. We both met at a night school ballet class, not in this place." The smile flattened. "You going in for the show, detective?"

I shook my head again.

She nodded and turned to go dancing.

"So thanks for the drink," she said over her shoulder.

CHAPTER 9

HOW DOES SHE REMIND YOU OF ME?" Dinah said.

"Well . . ." I stood to one side to let an orderly or an intern or a five-star surgeon push some sort of medical cart by.

"How tall was she?

"About five eight or nine."

"I'm five four. What color was her hair?"

"Blonde, at present."

"You may have noticed over the last four years that my hair is red."

I touched a tuft of red hair on the nape of her neck and attempted to nibble her ear. "The light was bad," I said.

"Letch," she said. "Brute. Animal. Man. Mother was right. Mendelsohn was right."

"We could double date," I said. "Just the three of us."

"Let go," Dinah said. "And stop doing that. You can't do that in the lobby of the Washington General Hospital. Besides, I want my nails free so I can scratch your eyes out."

"Sublimation," I said. "You're repressing your attraction to me."

"I'm repressing my urge to drive my spiked heels through your heart, you macho vampire. What's with you, Haller? Ten o'clock at night and you're as high as some of my patients. Was finding this Christie girl that much of a break?"

I pulled my arms away from her and reached for a cigarette. Dinah looked at her watch. Around us flowed a steady stream of doctors, nurses, visitors, the hospital's lifeblood endlessly circulating. Except for the expressions on the faces, the room looked like the lobby of any big building in California—cheerlessly pastel, decorated with pots of plastic flowers and detached rows of plastic chairs that looked as if they'd fallen from a passing jet. All as eccentric and individual as the counter at McDonald's. Upstairs the impersonality continued, of course, in the rows of beds and the shiny machines that rolled from ward to ward and the loudspeakers that mumbled a litany of doctors' names in every corridor and closet. I had tracked down a missing doctor once, a young guy not long out of medical school who had walked out on his internship and his wife and baby daughter and ended up in La Jolla, tending bar. When I had caught up with him, he had shaken his head and said he just couldn't stand to be around sick people. And when I had laughed, he had said a lot of doctors were like that.

"She's not much of a break," I admitted. "But she knows Muriel Contreras. She can find her. I feel like a human being again, or at least a detective."

"I've got to go back to the ward," Dinah said. "I get off in another hour. Why don't you go back to Green Street and open a bottle of wine and tell me about it from the start when I get there?"

I kissed her and watched her hurry back upstairs to the psychiatric receiving ward. Then I rescued the Mercedes from its parking place outside the door, where it had been waiting like somebody's faithful iron dog, and I pointed it north on Van Ness, over the spine of hills that make up Pacific Heights and on through the fog to Green Street.

The wind can carry a knife in San Francisco, even in September. I pulled up my collar and closed the garage door. Then I snapped the combination lock and tested it twice before I stepped back to face the slanting sidewalk and the uphill walk. The streets were momentarily empty in every direction, as they often are in a big American city when the cars have gone off to sulk somewhere and the people are inside twirling their dials. Lonely puddles of watery light gleamed at black intervals under street lamps. Thin fingers of gray fog, colder than a bar girl's hands, were reaching out of alleys and over low pointed roofs, clutching the gables of the restored Victorian house on the corner, now a museum, formerly a brothel. A block away somebody's heels clicked against the damp pavement.

I shoved my hands in my pockets and started down Green. Sometimes, I thought, all of San Francisco seems like a set for a Victor McLaglen movie. The wind sawed away at my neck with a low whistle and tugged at my jacket buttons, and out on the restless water a foghorn groaned like a tomcat basso profiindo. Before old William Hall had built Golden Gate Park at the turn of the century, almost all of San Francisco south of my block had been sand dunes, raked by these same cold westerly winds and as bare of vegetation as the Sahara. New arrivals used to drive down in mule wagons from Nob Hill just to look at the "Outside Lands" and the desolate beach below the Cliff House. Now I can drive across them from Dinah's hospital in ten minutes, from desert to asphalt jungle.

I stopped at the corner of the building out of habit and looked up for signs of life. Dead space, two lights on in the apartment above mine, a few more on the top floor. Most of the building's windows were black, except for the occasional pale glow of a television set, which Dinah denies is a sign of life. Turn on, tune in, drop out. Even the hallway bulb just at the entrance had burned out again, leaving the front steps in total blackness. I fit my key into the lock, swung the door open and stepped in.

"You . . ."

Something hard thumped the side of my head and grazed my ear. I staggered a step and swung wildly, hitting loose cloth. Took another step and swung again, losing my fist in somebody's big belly. Swung my left at nothing, at shadows. Somebody slumped down with a loud cry and flopped against my feet. I shouted for help, kicked wildly loose, and stumbled backward in the dark. The man at my feet cried out again and I knocked over a bicycle propped against a wall.

"Who's down there?" A man's voice carried down from the first landing, a detached hand poked a pocket flashlight through the shadows.

"Get some light down here!" I shouted.

"Who's that?"

"Haller, goddammit!" I was on my knees shoving the figure upright, feeling blindly for the face. No mugger ever collapsed after a glancing punch like the one I had thrown. No mugger smelled of Russian tea and tobacco and warm, salty blood.

The man with the flashlight had stopped halfway down the stairs and was waving the flashlight beam in my eyes.

"Mister Haller?"

"Turn on the big light, dammit, the one over the stairs. This man's hurt!"

He rustled and probed. I patted my fingers against sticky wet flesh and heard another groan and then the big two-hundred-watt stairwell light came on, killing the shadows instantly. Leo Matz groaned again and his open mouth filled with blood like a cup. Streams of blood trickled over the stumps of teeth in his jaw. He blinked against the glare and tried to speak, spilling more blood down his chin and across my hands and wrists. Blood splashed everywhere, on his shirt, his trousers, his arms, but no wound showed, only the spillway of his wide red mouth.

"Oh my god—did you kill him?" My neighbor stood just behind me and pulled back the skirts of his bathrobe with one hand, still pointing the useless flashlight.

"Call an ambulance," I said. "Call the police."

"There's no wound," he said. "He's just spewing blood out of his mouth."

"He's hemorrhaging," I snarled. "Call the police." I propped Leo's head against the flat row of tenants' mailboxes and held him upright to prevent his choking. With one hand I tried to stanch the blood, but in a second my white handkerchief looked like a bandanna. "Hurry, goddammit!" I shouted at his vanishing back.

"Mike," Leo whispered and began to choke. I tilted his head forward, pouring out blood. My rough, clumsy fingers seemed to squeeze it out of his old body like a sponge.

"Don't talk, Leo. Take it easy. You'll be OK."

"Two men, Mike," he whispered, gagging on every word. "Some kind of ball—what do you call it?"

I had undone his sweater and started to rip the shirt open. Something had to be puncturing the lungs to drive out so much blood—a knife, a bullet. He winced and cried out again as I yanked the sopping cloth apart. All across his blubbery chest stretched long red welts, starting to go black-green already, the size and shape of a man's forearm. They had played baseball on Leo, the way they do in the Tenderloin these days, beat him with a bat like a carpet hanging on a line. Broken ribs must have punctured the lungs. And they must have wrapped the bat in cloth, a jacket or a towel, to prevent bruises. In three days there would be no mark on his body at all.

In three minutes he was dead.

CHAPTER 10

YOU'RE DRUNK, HALLER."

I gripped the doorframe harder with one hand and hunched my shoulders against the chilly wind at my back.

"Leo Matz is dead," I said.

Edward Asbery III stiffened and stood patrician straight. His hands dug farther into the purple pockets of his bathrobe and he looked at me without expression. Behind him down the brightly lit hallway I could see a lacquered antique sideboard holding hats and gloves, next to it the brass pendulum of a grandfather clock and a pale white face registering a couple of minutes before one. While he stared at me a woman's voice called something from the recesses of the hallway and he turned his head.

"It's all right, Dorothy. I'll handle it. Go back to bed."

"He was murdered," I said. "Tonight."

Asbery turned his square face back to me. "All right, you'd better come in," he said finally, stepping aside and holding the door. I crossed the threshold into the bright light and he gasped. "You're covered with blood! Are you hurt? Where are you hurt?"

I shook my head. In the oval vanity mirror over the sideboard I could see my own pale face and my jacket and shirt splashed dark red, in broad swathes as if somebody had painted me with a brush.

"Go into my study," he said, and I followed his gesture down the hallway to a small room, heavily draped and carpeted, that overlooked the street. Asbery closed the door and crossed to a bar built into a white wall of bookcases, glancing back with a shadow of apprehension as if he were worried that the blood would drip from my jacket onto the carpet. What the hell. He liked to decorate in crimson.

"That's Matz's blood on you," he said, coming back with two snifters of brandy. I didn't say anything and he looked me over again, this time as coolly as if I had spilled taco sauce on my tie, the self-controlled lawyer taking over the human being, the iron mask coming down. I was sick of self-control. I was sick of New England flintiness transplanted to Babylon on the Bay, my own included. The first swallow of brandy glissaded down my throat and went off in my belly like a bomb. I sat down in a brown leather club chair and found myself facing yet another print of the goddam Harvard Yard.

"Did you call the police?" He was still standing over me, holding his drink at present arms and turning it automatically between his fingers. I nodded.

"All right," he said and turned and walked to the other club chair in the room, planted with geometric accuracy between a polished mahogany desk and a bell-shaped reading lamp. "Tell me what happened."

"Somebody played knick-knack, paddy-whack on Leo's chest with a baseball bat or a club," I said brutally. "It's a form of psychological revenge in some parts of town. The Tenderloin, for instance, where your friend Muriel Contreras works. I came home tonight and found him on my front steps, bleeding to death." Asbery crossed his legs, crisp white pajamas swinging under the purple robe, and said nothing. I reached in my shirt pocket for my pack of cigarettes and pulled my fingers back abruptly when they touched soggy cellophane. "I was holding him in my arms and looking in his face when he died," I said.

Asbery put his brandy glass, untouched, on the corner of the desk and folded his fingers into a steeple.

"Why did you come here, Haller?" he asked in a neutral voice. "Why come to me in the middle of the night about this?"

"Leo choked to death on his own blood," I said and drained the sweet-tasting brandy. "So he didn't get around to explaining who killed him or why. But I saw him yesterday. I went to his office yesterday and gave him a hard time, trying to get him to open up about Muriel Contreras and the Maranian will you drew up. It's hard to believe he was dropping by my place tonight to borrow a cup of sugar. Leo was a funny old duck, mildly neurotic, secretive. He probably thought he was restoring the Russian empire bit by bit to the disinherited. But he was also curious as hell and in his own way a world-class gossip, and he was relatively honest. I think he was coming to see me about Contreras."

"You haven't answered my question," Asbery said in his patronizing lawyer's voice. He dismantled the steeple and picked up his brandy again. "Why did you come to see me?"

"I want you to tell me why Maranian left Muriel Contreras money. I want you to help me find her."

"Because of your theory that she has something to do with your lost license?"

"Because somebody went to a hell of a lot of trouble to frame me, counsellor. And to kill Leo. Because somebody doesn't want her found."

He finally took a sip of the brandy and then jacked his voice one notch higher, as if he were dialling an emotion. "You must think I am unusually innocent and excitable, Haller," he said. "You must think you're dealing with a junior associate in a storefront law office. You come in here in the middle of the night without changing clothes, dribble blood—which may or may not come from a murder—on my furniture and talk like a hardboiled dime novel detective. Who do you think you are? F. Lee Bailey? Do you really expect your little bit of street theatre to shock me into telling you what I wouldn't tell you before, what I wouldn't tell you under normal circumstances? Do I look as easily stampeded as that?"

He looked about as easily stampeded as a boxcar. I got up and walked across the room to the bookcases and the bar and lowered another couple of ounces of brandy into my snifter. A good room to wear slippers in, I thought. A wood and leather masculine room, lined with hardback books and decorated in muted browns and greens, a room where a lawyer could settle down after a hard day handling affairs of estates and tuck into a brandy and a good book. A rich man's room. An Eastern room. California homes usually ran to *Reader's Digest* and a bound volume of bumper stickers. I dropped the stopper back in the decanter and looked down at the two books on his desk. *London Transformed,* which seemed to have something to do with London in the eighteenth century, and *Philosophical Explanations* by Robert Nozick. I flipped the Nozick book open and found there was a chapter called "Why Is There Something Rather Than Nothing?" My fingers left bloodstains on the margins of philosophy and I closed the book. Soulful Graham Greene face for the clients, contemptuous snobbery for the help. Why did I like Asbery?

He looked up at me from his leather chair, head cocked,

impassively studying my face. Why did I like him, in spite of the legal guff and the cast-iron New England formality? Maybe because he was as suspicious and unflappable as a pit boss in a casino. Maybe because he treated English with respect and used it the way an intelligent lawyer does, clipped, concise, no frills, every semi-colon in place, every simile squashed like a cockroach on a whorehouse floor.

"Moreover," he said now, "given your apparent record of violence and the fact that Leo Matz had just fired you, I don't understand why you aren't downtown right now, being questioned by the police."

"The beat cop knew me and let me go. I said I would drive down to Bryant Street in my own car." I held up my glass and watched the soft light catch the brandy and turn it a deep, rusty brown. "I must have gotten lost."

"Do you fool many people with your tough guy act, Haller?"

"I fool myself and I'm the one who mainly needs it. Tell me why an old man like Maranian left the money to a needle-shocked topless dancer, counsellor. Was it blackmail? Was it senile infatuation?"

He shook his head. Concise.

"Somebody doesn't want her found, counsellor."

"That's only your surmise."

"It's also my surmise that whoever shot the pimp south of Market was actually trying to shoot Muriel Contreras and missed."

He didn't stampede. He didn't even twitch. He shook his head again. "Sheer speculation," he growled.

"Do you fool many people with your tough guy act, Asbery? Asbery III?"

In the circle of light from the reading lamp the big lantern jaw showed a sheen of bristle, the gray hair a swirl of cowlick disarranged by sleep. Did I like him because he reminded me of my father? Two righteous New England Puritans dressing down a prodigal son? But my father's face was older, thinner, drier. Sadder. Since he had retired from practicing medicine he did little more than sit in front of the big window in Brookline and listen to the long lines of traffic swish past. He had never had Asbery's armor. And even half asleep Asbery projected a natural, boardroom dominating authority from his mesomorph's chest and beautifully tailored clothes. Maybe he was right. Maybe I was trying to shock him with cheap theatre. Maybe I was just reacting to the contrast between his intelligent, affluent house, with a wife named Dorothy sleeping upstairs, and the squalid world of the Club Eden, a couple of light years down the block.

"What do you think you would accomplish anyway, Haller?" he was saying in the hard voice. "Besides violating my professional ethics. How would knowing that information help you get your license back?"

I shrugged, suddenly uninterested in my games, suddenly remembering Leo's mottled face. "I don't know," I said wearily. "I'm just shaking bushes and throwing stones, counsellor, trying to provoke a reaction. Trying to get my job back." I balanced one hand against the desk and stood up.

He stood up too and faced me across the desk, unfriendly and sarcastic. "All things considered then," he said, "I think you had better try somewhere else, Haller. And don't call me counsellor."

I put the glass down on top of the London book. He would like the eighteenth century, I thought. A top-flight lawyer would like the age of reason. I didn't think the age of reason had ever happened, myself. "I suppose I'll have to go down the peninsula then, Mr. Asbery. To throw stones at Taghi Maranian."

He kept his face under control, slowly finishing his brandy, placing the empty glass on the desk blotter, carefully dialling urbanity on his internal computer. "I'm sorry about Leo Matz, Haller," he said in a different tone. "I'm sorry you're in shock about his death. In the morning you will probably regret this visit. After you have seen the police again."

"Yeah." I walked across the study and opened the door without looking back.

"If you find her," he said from the desk, "I'll make sure of course that you receive whatever fee Matz would have collected."

"Finders keepers, Mr. Asbery," I said and walked on down the elegant little hallway and let myself out. After a minute the door clicked shut behind me.

Up and down Pacific Avenue the expensive, delicate houses sailed on through the night. Over a clump of Italian cypresses nearby a billow of white fog turned and followed me with its eyes, like a giant friendly ghost coming in from the sea.

Across the street somebody in a dark car, a Chrysler, started the engine and drove off without turning on the lights.

CHAPTER 11

J OGGERS," FRED SAID IN DISGUST, HOLDING the big cigar clear of his mouth so that he could spit out the word. Along the sidewalk, dodging pedestrians, two men in tank tops and short shorts pattered in slow rhythm. "Why run if nobody's chasing you?" he said.

I grunted and started down the steps, dodging pedestrians myself. The street in front of the Hall of Justice on Bryant Street is never empty, not at two in the morning when I had arrived, not at ten in the morning when Yetta and his merrie men finally let me go. Leaning against a metal banister a Hispanic man in a blue suit a size too small stretched his arms around two sad-faced swaying women. Farther down the sidewalk another couple stood silently, chins planted on each other's shoulder. You see a lot of affection demonstrated at the Hall of Justice. Or what is maybe not quite the same thing, a lot of clinging to each other.

"They give you a hard time?" Fred asked, clumping down the steps behind me. Overhead the sun seemed to have dissolved into the fog, leaving no single source of light but throwing a bright, eye-watering glare in every possible direction. I blinked and the strings of colored lights on the bail bond offices across the street blinked cheerfully back. We Never Sleep, they bragged. 24-hour Service. Don't worry, Jim Bonds Can Bail You Out in a Hurry. Bee Bonds. The Bee Will Set You Free.

"Not too bad," I said, reaching the sidewalk and opening a new pack of cigarettes. One of the joggers slowed and wagged a reproachful finger at me. "The thumb-screw was being used, so all they had was the rack and the strappado."

"What the hell is a strappado?"

"It's when Frank Yetta breathes chili burger and onions in your face at six a.m. and says to tell you how it happened again because he must have already forgot." I flipped my match into the gutter between two parked squad cars and scowled up at the glare. "It's when Yetta's toy dog says no, the head is still busy and probably will be for another couple of hours. Strappado is bush league brutality."

"Yeah. Well, at least you kept your good humor."

"Where's the car?"

"I had to move it over to the pay lot. I ran out of nickels about an hour ago."

Two plainclothes detectives from the car theft division hurried up the sidewalk, talking loudly and gesturing at the street. When they saw me they broke it off and put their hands in their pockets.

"Tony," I said. "Wayne."

The nearer one coughed and mumbled a greeting. Wayne, a kid about thirty with a complexion like a waffle iron and an ambition to transfer to Homicide, looked up over my head and didn't say anything.

"You want to go home?" Fred asked.

"I thought I might just stand on the sidewalk for a few hours and run for chief of police."

"Be human, Mike. Cops are just people. You're in bad odor now. Besides, the new D. A. is slapping people down all over." He shook his copy of the *Chronicle* out of his jacket and waved it toward me. "Yesterday, look, he goes to some Gay Rights Association meeting and tells them they got to show more self-control, more restraint." I muttered something unintelligible, and we reached the parking lot and started threading our way toward the Mercedes. "At least he didn't tell them to get a grip on themselves," Fred said, folding the paper up again. I smiled for the first time in twelve hours. "There's the car," he said. "The guy moved it."

But I wasn't looking at the Mercedes. Down by the parking lot exit, half a block away, a black Chrysler with heavily tinted windows stood double-parked on the street, idling.

"You want to go home?" Fred said again, opening the door on his side. I looked at the Chrysler. The light at the corner turned green, but the Chrysler didn't move.

"Let's go to a candy store first," I said.

He jerked his head up and followed the fine of my jaw. "You sure?" he asked. "You can get into big trouble if you're wrong."

"Yeah. They can take away my license." I slammed my door and started the car.

"Go up Russian Hill," Fred said after five minutes of leisurely cruising up Market and across Van Ness.

I reached one hand to the rear-view mirror and balanced the grill of the Chrysler on my thumbnail. "The deli on the corner of Lombard?"

He nodded and pulled the porkpie hat farther down on his nose. I turned right at Vallejo and watched the Chrysler slow and signal.

The fog had burned away from the top of Russian Hill,

and in occasional flashes between Victorian gables you could see it retreating over the steel blue bay, drawing its skirts up and swirling toward the Golden Gate. At the top of the hill, just below an arrogant new high rise of condominia stacked on top of one another like safe deposit boxes, I turned right, glided one block south, and then pulled into a parking space two car lengths down from a red awning that said "Fineberg's" in long white letters. Fred and I got out and stood under the awning, looking up and down the empty street. At midmorning Russian Hill is almost always deserted except for an occasional puttering resident or an errant tourist. The Chrysler came around the corner and rolled slowly past before pulling to the curb three spaces ahead of the Mercedes.

"You want a Coke?" Fred asked.

"Why not join the Pepsi generation?" I said. He nodded and vanished into the cool, dark deli. I pulled out another cigarette, patted myself for a match, and walked out into the sunshine, toward the Chrysler.

"You want something, friend?" the driver said. He had the window rolled down and a road map of the city partially unfolded on the seat beside him. I bent down without answering and leaned in the window. A nice car, the Chrysler Imperial. Handsome gray upholstery made of crushed velour, real leather padding on the doors, an instrument panel that would fit the dashboard of a Polaris missile. Henry Kissinger is supposed to have liked the ride. Or maybe it was just the name he liked. The back seat, I decided after a careful look, was empty. Unless he had a drill team practicing in the glove compartment, it was just me and Bobby Unser.

"I said are you looking for something, friend?" he repeated in a hard, nasty voice that could break glass and cut fingers. "Otherwise, kiss off."

I got back to him. It's hard to judge when they're sitting down, but I gave him six-one or two, about two hundred pounds, a lot of that bunched up around his belt like bags of ballast on a balloon. He was maybe thirty-five and starting to go thin on top, so his barber had puffed out the hair around his temples and ears to draw the admiring eye down. His own eyes had the same watery, popped out look I had last seen on Chick Gannett's demented Doberman. Exophthalmic.

"Exophthalmic," I said. "I notice we've been taking the same route the last few minutes, and I was getting curious about that." He shifted awkwardly in the car seat to show me the ripple of his muscles, but they don't ripple so well when you're sitting behind a wheel and you feel intimidated by anybody standing up over you, moving freely. Traffic cops learn that day one of police school. He rippled anyway and let me see his fuzzy brownish sportscoat, natural shoulders, that seemed to have been made from the hide of a giant hamster. No tie. Orange shirt and dark blue slacks and loafers. Grab would have put a contract out on his tailor. I just leaned a little farther in and pressed an elbow gently where a shoulder holster might have been and wasn't.

"You notice more than I do, friend," he was saying. A pale city face, a thin, pointed nose that looked as if it had been folded out of white construction paper. A cleft chin that you could dunk in a coffee cup.

"You want your drink?" Fred asked, coming up on my right. The hard guy looked back, surprised for a moment. Then he put both hands on the steering wheel and gripped tight. Even over sixty and built like a sea-lion Fred made it two against one, and anybody halfway good could see that he carried a bulge under his left arm, the way a lot of retired cops do.

"Is this some kind of hustle?" he started to say.

I took the giant-size Pepsi bottle with one hand and kept leaning on the door. Behind the car, on the sidewalk, two elderly Chinese ladies walking past looked at us curiously. I smiled at them and took a swig of Pepsi. "No hustle," I said through my smile. "It's just that for a minute I thought this might be the same Chrysler that followed me down Pacific Avenue about two this morning and all the way to Bryant Street. The same Chrysler my friend Leo Matz told me about."

He looked at me carefully, face stiffening like dried clay, eyes unblinking, and made an ithyphallic suggestion.

"You first," I said. He reached for the inside door handle, and I leaned harder. Counting the cigarette and ash, I figured my weight at one-eight-six or so, and most people can't open a car door fast with that much weight pressing it back. The hard guy couldn't open it at all.

"Got it," Fred said from the rear of the car. The hard guy turned his face, red now, teeth gritted with the strain, and saw Fred tucking the bright silver church keys back in his jacket with one hand and holding the lid of the Chrysler's gas tank open with the other.

I flipped him the Pepsi bottle and the hard guy grunted against the door in panic. Fred twirled off the gas cap and shoved the neck of the bottle down, and the hard guy yelped as if we had stepped on his tail. I dropped my lighted cigarette in his lap and he tried to stand up in the car like a Jack in the Box.

"Jesus!" he squealed, batting his lap with both hands, twisting and hunching. "Jesus Christ!"

Then I stepped back suddenly and the door flew open and the hard guy tumbled head first toward the pavement.

"Come on," Fred said, giving the Pepsi bottle a final twist, and we started to trot toward the Mercedes.

"You ruined the engine!" he shouted after us, scrambling to get up. "You ruined the goddam engine!"

"Too bad they don't make unleaded Pepsi," Fred said between pants as we reached the car and slid into the seats. The hard guy was on his feet staring at us in disbelief. I started the engine, squealed the tires into a U-turn, and gunned uphill toward blue sky. Behind us, his hamster hide jacket shaking with fury, the hard guy was running a few steps, stopping, running again. We slammed right on Jones and sank into the wispy fog.

"That was fun," Fred said, his breath still coming in puffs. He settled back in the seat, wheezing, and tipped his hat toward the roof. "Fun and dumb. What the hell do you think you accomplished back there? I mean, I go along with you because I'm too old and too rich to worry about somebody's gunked up twenty-thousand-dollar carburetor. But what the hell do you think you're doing? You don't even know who that joker was. You didn't even try to find out." He turned his face and gave me a warning look. "And don't say it was a gas. I know you."

I steered right again and found myself behind a salmon-colored Volkswagen bug with a blue plastic turret and plastic machine gun mounted on the roof, passing the first of the stately homes of Pacific Avenue, where Edward Asbery III had his digs. Pacific to Geary. Geary to 280, and so to bed.

"You picture our pal back there as Dick Cavett?" I said. "You think he's going to pull up a chair and explain how he's been following me for two days trying to unload a subscription to *Jack and Jill?*" Fred grunted and looked out the window at the houses. I went around the Volkswagen with the gun turret. There was a foot-high miniature palm tree fastened to the dashboard, and the driver wore a Hawaiian shirt and a ten-gallon hat. L.A. plates on the bumper, of course. Los

Angeles the Damned, Mencken used to call it. "Let's just say I was grabbing hold of a bush and shaking it with both hands," I said after another minute. "What else am I going to do? I've got to make them come to me, Fred, whoever killed Leo, whoever took my license. You know that."

He pulled one of his foot-long cigars out of an inside pocket and continued to watch the pale stone buildings slide by. Cream-colored, pink, sandy yellow, polished gray, all of them soaked in fog and hauled up each morning into the sunshine as clean and sparkling as a baby coming out of a bath. The famous Mediterranean quality of San Francisco, yoking opposites like light and stone. Like Mike and Dinah, I suddenly thought.

"You're too up and down for me, Mike," Fred said, stoking the cigar. "You come out of Yetta's homeroom wearing a puss like a pickle, and ten minutes later you're jamming bottles down a guy's gas tank and flashing a grin as wide as the windshield. I thought you'd be moaning about Leo more, and your goddam license."

"Leo would have liked the candy store," I said. "He would have liked hearing about it."

Fred rolled down his window an inch and waved smoke out onto Geary. "Was that true what you said back there, that Leo told you about the Chrysler?" I shook my head and he sighed. Geary Street began to puff uphill and down toward the Japanese Trade Center and the Washington Hospital where Dinah worked. Fred smoked in silence, but when we reached the point where Geary curves south past the Cliff House restaurant he sat up straight and we both looked out to the right to see the long lines of breakers as they snarled and lunged at the shore. Down on Ocean Beach, thirty yards below the road, a few people in heavy jackets, heads bowed, were coming slowly through the dozens of slick boulders that poked like stumps from the sand. Straight ahead, across the highway, drifted a steady haze of sand, flung by the wind in gigantic handfuls. Under the Cliff House itself, as if they'd been spilled from a toybox, more boulders fanned downward to make a huge jumbled pyramid, reaching almost a hundred yards out into the surf. And beyond them the fog crouched motionless on the black water, rising to fill the whole western sky. Land's end, I thought. The Outside Lands, where the nineteenth-century mule wagons used to carry sightseers to view the sand dunes and the bleak Pacific. About as far from Puritan New England as I could get. About as colorful and Mediterranean as a block of ice.

"Welcome to sunny California," Fred said.

I shivered as I always did out there and sped up, heading toward Lake Merced and the connector to 280.

"So where is your highness going now?" Fred asked around his cigar. "After the Contreras again? Or do you just want to go over to Pacific High and flush cherry bombs down the toilets?"

"Let's go down the peninsula to Silicon Valley," I said. "Let's go looking for Mr. GreenGenes."

CHAPTER 12

HE'S OUT BACK GASSING THE SOY BEANS," the lady lab technician said, returning my card. "Or else he's still bronzing his gorgeous bod behind the parking lot."

Thirty-ish, wire braces on her teeth, an arch in her back, and a green tee-shirt that fit like a pair of pantyhose. She gave me the sweet, predatory smile of a barracuda in a goldfish bowl and turned back to the laboratory table. "I can't believe you're an insurance salesman," she said, picking up a hypodermic needle and poking it at something in a saucer. The back of the tee-shirt said "Smith College: A Hundred Years of Women on Top." I guess I hadn't expected Madame Curie. "You look like a baseball player."

"Yeah, well. Some of the guys even sell candy bars these days."

"So if you can't find Tock," she said over her shoulder, squirting a jet of clear liquid from the needle into the air, "come back and tell me about your fastball."

My fastball wasn't in the same league. I walked out of

the building and followed a gravel walkway past two more identical clapboard structures built on the model of army barracks, obviously put together in a hurry and simply planted side by side in the brown fields like shoeboxes.

The fields were brown, the buildings were beige, the hills humping up into the sunshine ahead of me were golden yellow, shiny brittle mounds of dried grass waiting for the winter rains to turn them green again. Eighty-five or ninety arid degrees, thirty miles and half a climate from the Cliff House. I stopped at the end of the gravel pathway and lit a cigarette. From behind me drifted faint grumbles of traffic on the country highway that ran through the huge expanse of fields. In front stretched a semi-circle of cultivated plots of ground, brown and black squares of varying sizes, all stitched with tiny rows of green plants and punctuated occasionally by tall wooden stakes with colored ribbons fluttering at the top. On the other side, just under the first rise of hills, stood three whitewashed greenhouses in a row, shimmering and sweating in the waves of heat.

I crunched on the yellow grass between two plots until I reached the center greenhouse and stopped again. Still nobody, nothing but the background of traffic noises. But when I circled around the greenhouse on the left, I found him bending over a workbench, wrestling a section of rubber hose back onto a compressor engine.

"Mr. Maranian?"

He wheeled with the hose in his hand.

"Jesus Christ, man, you must be part Indian—you don't make a *sound*."

"Sorry, Mr. Maranian. I didn't know you were here. The girl at the other building wasn't sure."

"Jesus, call me Tock," he said, exhaling loudly in mock relief and slipping on an automatic, empty smile. "Everybody does."

"Tock," I said, squeezing out a matching smile. He had on faded blue Levi's and a plain white tee-shirt, the first tee-shirt I had seen in years in California that had no writing on it, not the name of an Italian shoe designer or an auto parts dealer or a beer brand or a meditation conglomerate, not even a picture of Snoopy on a surfboard or I AM BABY SOFT between the nipples. He put the hose section down on the workbench, and I started to hold out the card that said Pacific Security Insurance. Then on impulse I reached in my wallet and took out the press card that Carlton Hand had given me two years ago.

He had been bronzing his gorgeous body for years, I thought as he squinted at the card, simmering it to the dry, tawny brown of an onion ring. A big, muscle-swollen body, knobby and veined with the look that only comes from lifting weights, tearing flesh down and repacking it like Spam. Styled black hair, slick and helmet tight, about six-two of adult male aspiring to the condition of hunk. But the face was at odds with the body, all wrong for it, a deeply wrinkled little monkey face too small for the head and its wide margin of cheekbone, too wizened for a man in his early thirties. The rest of him might look like a bouncer at Muscle Beach, but he had the crumpled, shrunken face of a fieldhand.

He handed back the card with an exaggerated flourish and a simian grin. "So what does the San Francisco *Constitution* want with me, Mike?" he said, tossing out the last name the way everybody does in California and turning back, not rudely, to the compressor on the bench. Dinah says the next L.A. phone book is going to be all first names. Debi, Derek, Didi, Donald, Dwayne. "Did we forget to pay the paperboy or something?"

"I told your lab assistant I was from Pacific Security

Insurance," I said to his back, keeping things clear. You can lose your p.i. license for impersonating an insurance investigator. He dipped his head and began to rock the hose back onto the engine. "I wasn't sure how you people felt about the press out here, and I thought it might get me past the receptionist. But it turns out you don't have a receptionist."

"Or a secretary or a janitor or a security guard," he said, grunting and pounding the end of the hose rapid-fire with the heel of his hand. "We got a president, that's me, and six employees, Mike. This is one of those operations held together by shoestrings and love. You want to sneak past receptionists and TV monitors and computer-flushed johns, you better drive on down to Sunnyvale or one of those other boom towns. Old GreenGenes is just a broken-down nag in the horse race of capitalism."

He took one last swipe at the hose and jammed it all the way onto the manifold pipe. "Damn," he said, and held out his palm to show me the red circle the hose had made. A restless man, like a lot of body builders, all meat and springs. "Goddam, that hurt! You saw that letter we sent out to all the media, right, Mike?"

I shrugged meaninglessly, and he rode right on, smiling at the sound of his own voice.

"Oh sure, *New West* sent a guy down here six months ago," he said, "and one of our financial backers got nervous and sent out that letter." He held up three fingers and ticked off his points. "No stories, no interviews, *absolutely* no photographs of the lab. Ever since some professor up at Davis got his patent swiped by one of his graduate students, our backers have been shitting bricks somebody's going to do the same thing to us. They think I talk too much. But what the hell—who was it said there's no such thing as bad ink?"

"Reggie Jackson," I said.

"Right." He crossed his arms with another wide open smile and leaned back against the bench. "So you think you'll just say the hell with the letter and sneak out anyway and do a story about old Farmer Tock and his down-home DNA. What's your angle, Mike? You want to focus it on me?"

I nodded and watched the chest muscles ripple like breakers at Ocean Beach.

"What makes Tock tick?" I said. He grinned the monkey-grin again. "Hey, I like that, that's good. All right, sure, to hell with the tight-ass backers. You can ask your questions while I finish setting up here. I don't know why you media people like to make things so elaborate, though. Pacific Security Insurance, my ass."

"The trenchcoat syndrome," I said. "We all want to be private eyes."

He opened the door to the greenhouse and made a sweeping mock bow to me to follow. "In that case, I hope you don't mind a little cyanide, Mr. Bernstein," he said.

The inside, bright and soupy with humidity, was as makeshift as the rest of the operation—six rows of unpainted redwood workbenches stacked high with a gardener's flotsam and jetsam, as if the greenhouse had shipwrecked in the arid valley: lines of plants in pots and plastic tubs, digging tools, coiled hoses, bags and cartons of fertilizers and chemicals, rusty coffee cans, broken white Styrofoam cups, the same sense of ungovernable litter as Leo Matz's office. Overhead a string of fluorescent lights muttered to themselves like peevish old men. To the left of the wooden door, behind a three-foot-square plywood board, a pump or motor cleared its throat and whispered back.

"We spray these plants with cyanide gas from this pump,"

Tock said. He flopped down on his back and slid the plywood board to one side. The small motor kicked over and growled and he began adjusting dials with one hand and rearranging three big plastic jugs with the other. He might wear his hair like Disco Don, I thought, but Tock wasn't afraid to get his hands dirty working.

"Not to worry, though," he said. "These plants are all legumes—peas, barley family, cereals. They have two respiratory systems like a lot of plants, one of them oxygen-sensitive, the other one cyanide-resistant. We want to study how they breathe in each system, so the best way is to shut them down one at a time. The gas smothers the oxygen in here and they only inhale through the cyanide side. People usually do it a few cells at a time, injecting the stuff with a needle like they were mainlining a carrot. You get a whole lab full of vegetable junkies, nodding their little leaves off. But I'm a man in a hurry." He looked up and grinned from flat on his back, the big pectorals bunched under the tee-shirt like a pair of footballs. I had no idea what he was talking about. New pesticides? New farming techniques?

"So I rigged up a compressor and a filter that sprays diluted cyanide gas into this baby and does it on a big scale." He attached a clear plastic tube to the top of a jug and stretched the other end out of sight. "I got it from my old man, I think," he grunted. "It's in the genes. I'm genetically wired to be a farmer, just like him. Two dumb Armenian tomato farmers from the San Joaquin Valley. Put that in your article, Mike. That's what makes me tick. I spent years bouncing around from one piece of misery to another—divorce, booze, you name it—until I figured that out. I was like a classic case of rebellion, I wasn't going to do a damn thing my old man liked. I wouldn't even *eat* tomatoes. What was it Oscar Wilde said?—'what was good enough for my father is certainly not good enough for me.'"

"Not so many Armenian tomato farmers quote Oscar Wilde," I said, revising my view of Tock a second time.

"Hey, I went to Stanford, didn't you know? Harvard of the West." He pulled his head up with a grin. "You ever been on the Stanford campus, Mike?" I nodded. "Then you know where they got the expression student body, hey? Those sororities? But I learned a hell of a lot of biochemistry anyway."

"I thought your father lived in San Francisco, Tock," I said, consulting the spiral notebook I always carry and reading a note to myself to change the Mercedes' oil at 230,000.

His head dodged back into the space beside the motor and he gave a muffled answer. "He died in San Francisco. He lived most of his life outside Fresno, a little town you never heard of, Saroyan country—just a railroad shunting, a hardware store, and a Chevron station with two Trojans machines in the can, one for the white boys, one for the wetbacks." Out popped his head, smeared across the wide brow with black grease, and he sprang easily to his feet, like a gymnast, without using his hands for braces. "He loved it, the old shitkicker. Then he had a heart attack, age fifty-five, and had to sell it all, all five thousand acres of the best farmland south of the pole. You know how deep the topsoil is in Kern County, Mike? You know how deep it is out in Iowa or Kansas, out there? Ten, fifteen inches, maybe. Kern County," he said, stacking his hands to demonstrate, "eight feet."

I thought a reporter should write something, so I wrote "eight feet" in my notebook. Tock watched me and nodded his head twice.

"That really broke his heart more than the angina," he said. "The old man sold his acres for a bundle and a half and moved to San Francisco and got so bored that he did the only other thing Armenians are supposed to know how to do."

"He owned an Oriental rug store off Market Street," I said.

Tock started walking down the aisle between two workbenches, stopping to caress the leaves of a plant, bending over, then plunging his fingers into the moist black soil and kneading the roots.

"Yeah, he owned it, but he wasn't wired to sell rugs. He was probably actually losing money the last five, six years. And he didn't really give a shit whether your Shiraz had double silk knots or a double hernia. His heart was back in the tomato fields. The last twenty years of his life, my old man was a very unhappy dude." He stopped at the end of the bench and looked back to where I stood, thirty feet away, making chicken scratches in my notebook.

"So does this look like a hundred billion dollars to you, Mike?"

I lifted my pencil in surprise. It looked like a pit stop in a truck farm to me.

He gave me the monkey-boy grin again and used his finger to trace the number on one of the cloudy glass panes next to the big Sternwood dial thermometer. I wiped sweat from my face and watched him writing zeros. The thermometer by his head registered 98.

"Yeah, yeah," he said, still tracing. "I know. Most people think I exaggerate when I say that, but it's true. *The Wall Street Journal* estimates that recombinant DNA techniques in human medicine are going to generate ten billion dollars' worth of business in the next decade, and they say that agricultural DNA techniques are going to do *ten times that.*" Even in the slippery light I must have looked puzzled because he went on with scarcely a pause. "Let me put it in layman's terms,

Mike." He picked up a potted something and delicately lifted one drooping leaf. "Most plants live on nitrogen," he said, "the way people live on oxygen. Except they don't breathe nitrogen out of the air, they take it out of the soil with their roots. But big fields of crop plants will quickly deplete all the nitrogen that's naturally in the soil. And so we have to keep fertilizing them with more and more nitrogen to keep them growing. The farmers in this country, Mike, spend more money on fertilizer than the whole state budgets of California and Texas. And they spend it not only spreading fertilizer on the ground, but cooking it up in stinking factories, and loading it in trucks and railroad cars and storing it and testing it, and you name it." He put the plant down as if it were a sleeping baby. "Half the farm budget literally goes for shit," he said.

I flipped a page in my notebook, almost forgetting Muriel Contreras and Aram Maranian. There are five kinds of plants I can identify with any certainty, and two of them are trees.

"But a few plants can actually take their nitrogen out of the air instead of the soil." Now he was reaching one long arm into the far corner of the structure and adjusting a nozzle that looked like a shower head. "Those are called nitrogen-fixated plants," he said, "and they don't need that extra fertilizer to keep growing. So what the girls do over in the lab is the recombinant DNA stuff—the glamor business, get you on the cover of *Time*—they try to alter the basic cells of crop plants by inserting genetic material called vectors from nitrogen-fixated plants. They want to change their DNA to add this ability to take nitrogen from the air. The guy from *New West* got it all wrong, of course, if you saw the article. He said it was like transplanting somebody's lungs into another person. But that's not right."

He had finished with the nozzle and turned around to face

me, arms crossed across the sweaty tee-shirt, biceps clogged in his shirt sleeves. "It's like breeding a whole new class of plants. Custom-made plants for different soils, different climates. Soybean A for Minnesota, soybean B for Argentina. We alter a cell structure based on what we know about its DNA. Then we try to grow new sprouts from it, and then new seeds. We're trying to make a soybean here that looks like the old-fashioned kind, only it breathes nitrogen out of the good, clean California smog. The man who does that for any one of three or four major crop plants, Mike—corn, soybeans, rice— is going to save about one quarter of the oil and gasoline used in this country on farms, he's going to plant crops where they never grew before, and he's going to feed the world."

"And make a hundred billion dollars."

"Oh hell," he said, coming down the narrow aisle. I stepped to one side and he squeezed past and unlatched the wooden door, but still held it closed. "I'm not really thinking about that." Big dirty fingers swept past my eyes in an extravagant gesture that took in the whole muggy greenhouse. "What I say, you know, is this could be the new garden of Eden for the twenty-first century." The hand dropped dramatically to his side in a well-rehearsed gesture, and we ducked out of Eden and into the sunshine. I took a deep oxygen-fixated breath while Tock carefully relocked the greenhouse door.

"Don't want any Cub Scouts wandering into the place while the gas is on," he said, "not even any reporters." I smiled and thought it was about as funny as most jokes about cyanide. Tock picked up a plastic jug that looked, except for the skull and crossbones, like the one I keep orange juice in.

"A lot of guys are in this to make a killing," he said, holding up the jug and examining a shadow in it. "No pun intended. That's why the venture capital people are interested.

Right now we're where the computer labs were ten, fifteen years ago—anybody with some good acres and the right kind of basic lab equipment can take a turn at bat. But I swear I'd do the work for nothing, Mike. I love it. I only come alive when I'm out here working. That's what it's all about, am I right?" He lowered the jug of poison and turned his brown, earnest ugly-man's face to me, chin riding high. "I mean, you're a reporter, you're doing what you love, that's how you define yourself. I'm a plant scientist. Nobody can stop me from being that."

He put the jug on the workbench by the compressor and wiped his hands on the same rag he had used before. "If I had time, Mike, I'd tell you about the salt that all the irrigation ditches have dumped into the San Joaquin Valley. You're going to keep your swimming pools in L.A. full, but if somebody doesn't come up with a salt-resistant tomato pretty soon, baby, America's going to be spreading mayonnaise instead of ketchup on its hot dogs. But I got to go to the lab building and do some things, and I agree with the backers about no reporters in there when we're working. Too risky. So you got any more questions for now, Mike?"

I reached in my jacket pocket and pulled out the photograph of Muriel Contreras.

"I wasn't quite straight about one thing, Tock," I said, not loving my work at the moment. "Do you know who this is?"

He took the photograph in one grimy hand, a puzzled frown beginning to peel away the smile. Then he raised his eyes slowly over the top of the picture.

"Yeah," he said slowly, in a voice like somebody gargling cyanide. "I know who this is, Mike. This is my bastard baby sister."

I reached automatically for the picture as he dropped it, serving up my head on a plate for the left fist suddenly curving in. The first punch smashed into my cheek and spun me backward and completely around. I stumbled, danced a few steps with the spade handle, and dropped sprawling to the ground like a set of car keys. He was over me before I could get up, his face black and his biceps pumping, whatever he was yelling lost in the thunder of my ear. I had gotten as far as my knees when the other fist curved in and the greenhouse fell on my jaw.

CHAPTER 13

"DID YOU HEAR ABOUT THE PROSTITUTE who hoped for a hung jury?" Fred asked.

I smiled just enough to hurt and he gave a quick look and a poke at my mouth with one stubby finger. Acrid bile tasted as if I had pennies stuck under my tongue.

"You're still bleeding around the gums a little," he said. "Is that tooth loose?" I shook my head and he sat back in the car seat. "So the kid had a punch?"

"He had a punch that would stop a two-ton double-clutching E-flat semi-trailer truck," I said. "But he suckered me anyway."

Fred held out his cigar and turned it carefully to inspect the ash. "You were probably leading with your mouth, as usual."

I looked at my swollen knuckles on the steering wheel and sucked my tooth. A construction worker in an orange vest motioned to me to speed up. Behind him, on a front-age road just off the freeway, a neon sign blinked "Dunfey's Motor Lodge" over a building a city block long that had been decorated with white plaster and artificial thatch and timber to look like a Tudor cottage. Beyond it, glistening like silicon chips in the afternoon sun, stretched the buildings of downtown San Mateo or San Bruno or Burlingame, one of the suburban sumps that catch the city's overflow at night and pump it back in the morning. More scientific and engineering talent gathered together out there than anywhere in history, they say, except maybe when Thomas Jefferson went down to his basement workshop alone. I had never seen a silicon chip. I would probably dunk it in guacamole.

"What did the backers say?" I finally asked. While I was interviewing Tock with the side of my head, Fred had been roaming Palo Alto's tiny financial district, old police badge in one hand, Irish charm in the other, opening doors, sitting on desk corners chatting up secretaries, doing what he did best. A cop with thirty years' experience on the street could interrogate an adobe wall.

"They said this Maranian could really strike it rich. They said the potential is unlimited, whatever he's doing with these plants that eat air." He swatted a foot of ash out the window and rolled it back up. "Of course that's what they got to say. Fellow named Dickstein told me they had put up about a half a million bucks so far in lab equipment and land. But they got confidence in the kid. He found some kind of nitrogen building cell he calls a hydrogen afterburner that can turn beans to gold. They think the agriculture racket is where the computers were ten or fifteen years ago, just about ready to coin money."

"How did you get all this?"

"I told them I was an insurance investigator, what else? I said we insured some of the buildings down the road, some condominiums—there's condominiums down every road in California—and did they ever use poisons and pesticides and stuff like that, that could bother our property. Routine,

routine, Mike. Nobody socked me, nobody even stuck a Pepsi up the exhaust pipe."

I rubbed my jaw with my palm and watched the city swing into view, swivelling around a hillside as if it were mounted on a revolving stage, the pyramid of the TransAmerica building slicing bright strips of blue from the sky, the smaller high-rises shimmering like glass and metal stalks on the seven hills. Long glossy cirrus clouds hovering to the west, over gray ocean. The sweet graceful curve of the city's haunch sinking into the peninsula. It still took my breath away. Even if I remembered that the shadow of the Bank of America building reaches south of Market. Even if I remembered that the best-selling local magazine is a sexual tabloid called *Perv.* Or that San Francisco has a higher violent crime rate than New York or Chicago. And more alcoholics and prostitutes per capita than any other city in the country. Gorgeous, demented old city, swaying drunkenly around the bay, cocktail glass in each hand, makeup cracked and hardening, lipstick smeared in a blood-red clot. Nova Albion, Drake had called it without irony when he waded ashore: New England, the promised land. He never imagined it would turn into Sodom by the sea, Babylon by the bay. A city of whores and lawyers. A volume of trollops. The freeway curved and the city was gone.

"What else did you get?"

"Two things. I went around to the Burger King by Palo Alto High School and tried to buy myself some information." There was a new, sad note in his voice and I turned my head in surprise. One hand was stroking his wrinkled dewlap gently. From this angle, in the harsh afternoon light, he suddenly looked less like a genial sea-lion, more like an old man growing tired. "The kids hanging around the burger joint wouldn't talk to me, not one of them. Told me to go home, pops, and oil my wheelchair." He turned his face to me with the familiar half-smile. "So I went two blocks down and found a black and white sitting there waiting for the drag races, just the way I knew it would be, and the cop bought me a cup of coffee and asked if I knew his brother-in-law Roger somebody in the Fraud section. He thinks that the kiddy corps has filled some purchase orders for your pal Tock. Not on a big scale probably, but expensive." I nodded and kept my eyes on the road. Most of the thefts from college campuses in California are done by teenagers who have taken an order from a businessman or a fence. The kids just put on an army surplus jacket, which is today's equivalent of an academic gown from Harvard to Slippery Rock, and skulk right in, looking like all the other scholars. Then they liberate a microscope, an electric typewriter, a calculator, whatever the customers ordered. They're rarely caught, and almost never sent to jail. California courts think jail would be a bad influence.

"Maranian's got a temper," Fred added in a moment. "The cop heard he banged up one of the kids pretty good when the lad tried to hold out on him. The Burger King crowd is a little scared of him."

"What was the other thing you found out?"

Fred pulled his porkpie hat farther down his forehead and slouched in the seat. Outside his window rows of pastel houses undulated up and down the hills of South San Francisco. On the driver's side, as the freeway began to funnel down from six lanes to four, the homeward-bound commuters were roaring along the center divider like Stuka bombers, diving for the first martini.

"You got to understand how venture capitalism works," Fred said in the tone of voice that meant he was going to deliver a lecture. I eased a cigarette between sore teeth and watched a cattle truck waddle down the left-hand lane. Like a lot of cops—and doctors too, people with a strong sense of fate—

Fred was fascinated by high finance. Over the years he had made himself into an armchair expert on how banks operate, on how to put and call and sell short, how to dirty cash in a slush fund and then launder it, how to dip a pension—all as unreal to a guy in a six-year-old suit from Sears as a double date with the Gabors. In his own defense he said that he had never seen a crime that didn't start with money. Or sex. Or both. But the truth was, the complete irrationality of the system intrigued him, the side that dealt lawyers like Asbery $300,000 a year, gave food stamps to pimps, and paid Dan Rather five times more than the president. Stockbrokers break out the champagne when a cop or a surgeon walks through the door, because there are no bigger believers in luck in the world. Capitalism, Fred once announced three drinks into Modesto's, is made up of random numbers.

"You got to understand how it works," he repeated. "There's maybe twenty of these venture capital outfits in the Bay Area— California has a third of the whole goddam country—and they hang around universities like General Joe's hookers, putting up money for professors with big ideas. They're like private banks that only make five or six loans a year—"

"Seed money," I grunted.

Fred scowled around his cigar. "You're going to crack wise in the mortuary," he said. "These venture people don't expect all the loans to be repaid. What they expect is that one or two of them are going to turn up aces. You got the one and a half million some company put up for Apple computers—that couldn't pay their phone bill now. You got a venture outfit that liked something called Federal Express when it was a college kid's term paper—the teacher flunked the paper. You got a guy, I'm not kidding, who starts a pizza chain with a bunch of electronic games and a talking rat named Chuck E. Cheese, the guy's a millionaire."

He paused and pulled a spot of tobacco off his tongue. "But these venture people like fast returns. They like to start an idea and retire the professor with a couple of Porsches and sell the stock to a big corporation that can run the thing. Dickstein, the guy in Palo Alto, talks too much. He put medicine in his coffee the way a lot of those guys do—it comes from getting up at five every morning to see what New York is doing—and he tried to sell me a brochure and he told me how his company had made a deal with Maranian. The company puts up half, Maranian puts up half. And it's Maranian's turn now. The money—"

He measured the new ash of the cigar with his thumbnail and puffed, an Irish ham smoking himself.

"The money," he said, having timed the pause to his satisfaction, "is supposed to come from Maranian's inheritance. That's the deal. After he pays the taxes, he'll have about half a million left, and he's signed a contract to sink it all in Green-Genes. But Asbery is the executor of the estate, and he doesn't have to dispense the shares until Contreras is found or until two years after probate. That's state law. You want to guess whether Asbery is ready to pay out half a million for Dyna-Glide soy beans?"

I didn't want to guess. I switched lanes and joined the crowd waiting on the off-ramp for Van Ness Avenue. I wanted to know about Tock's bastard baby sister. I wanted to know why Tock had unloaded on my jawbone when I brought out her picture and then had two of his six employees discard me on the roadside next to the dumpster bin.

"So Dickstein thinks his company is getting nervous," Fred said. "Asbery won't pay out the inheritance and they got other ventures to float. They got people out there who need money to breed hairless sheep and build solar-powered poker chips, they don't have to stick with corn that craps on itself."

I grunted and rubbed my jaw with one hand. Traffic on the off-ramp came unglued with a honk and I started down Ninth Street toward my office.

"Dickstein says so far Maranian's come up with the payments anyway, nobody knows how. He's suing Asbery to pay up, but that can take months."

"He could have borrowed on the inheritance," I said. "Banks will do that."

"Banks will also charge you twenty-two percent. That's a lot of seed packs."

"Loan sharks?" I said. He shrugged and looked out the window for the spot where he had parked his Buick Terrorist. "Can you find out if somebody on the street is letting him have the money?" I asked as he pointed at his car and we came to a stop.

He opened the door and got out, then leaned his head back in, cigar tilted at an angle like an anti-aircraft gun, and let go a salvo of smoke.

"You want another lecture, Mike?"

I drummed my fingers on the wheel.

"I told you before, Mike. Most cops are honest. But there's no good cop who doesn't think the same way a punk thinks. When nobody finds Contreras, the will says your new sparring partner gets half her share. That's four hundred thou. *Four hundred goddam thou.* If I needed money and I could get that much just by throwing a scare into some broken-down hooker, I'd do it. If I was too squeamish myself, I'd buy somebody to push her out of sight. And if I needed money bad enough and the push didn't work and the girl was still out there loose where anybody could find her, I'd start thinking contract, Mike, I would." He straightened and hitched his belt over his little pot belly like a geriatric gunslinger. "For four hundred thou your friend Grab could arrange a contract on Fort Meade," he said.

CHAPTER 14

THE JANITOR HAD LEFT THE MAIL OUTSIDE my office door, neatly bound with a yellow rubber band. I unlocked the door and took the package to my desk. A school for private detectives in L.A. wanted to enroll me in a fingerprint analysis course ("We Make Crime Pay"). An official-looking envelope spilled out a pinkish-gray Thermofax of Henry Sampson's ruling. A winery in Napa wanted to introduce "Resident" to an exclusive Chardonnay aged only in French oak and labelled with designs by Marc Chagall. You could charge it on your Exxon card. My landlord had left a stamped payment envelope for the October rent.

I put the yellow rubber band back and dropped them all into the wastebasket. Then I walked over to the bookshelf where I keep my coffee laboratory and ground a palmful of brown, greasy Italian roast beans into aromatic powder. San Francisco water can taste as if it had been filtered through a sweatsock, so I ran Sierra spring water from the standup cooler into an enameled blue kettle, and while it boiled on the hot plate I scooped two spoonfuls of coffee into my Melitta cone. "The man can do everything," Dinah had mocked the first time I had cooked for her in my apartment. Three weeks after we had met. Four years and five months ago.

I shifted the kettle to the center of the hot plate and remembered her amusement at my special omelette skillet with "For Your Eggs Only" embroidered on its holster. Showboating, I had taken out two brown eggs and cracked one in each hand over a bowl.

"A libber's dream," she had smiled from the kitchen doorway, where she leaned with arms crossed, hair undone, dressed only in one of my shirts. "A gentleman in the parlor, a caveman in the bedroom, an artist in the kitchen."

"This is nothing. A p.i. in Boston named Parker is so good he's writing a cookbook."

"What's it called?"

"*The Thin Man.*"

She had laughed the low, throaty chuckle that always surprises me, and I had broken an egg in my hand. Psychiatrists are supposed to have dirty minds, but not dirty laughs.

Nobody was laughing in the empty office. Even the kettle's whistle sounded mournful and off-key. I poured boiling water into the filter cone and idly picked up a crossword puzzle I had started three weeks ago and left on the bookshelf. Two words, seven letters down: camper's lifestyle. I wrote "in tents" in the space and put it back on the shelf. Paperbacks only. No hardbacks like Asbery. No Oriental rug and mahogany desk and built-in bookcases to get comfortable around. No slippers to slip into, no bond coupons to clip. Just me and Madame Matisse and a view behind my desk of the bottom of the Bay Bridge.

I poured a big cup, dropped sugar and cream into it until the coffee was a rich, healthy brown like Tock Maranian, and walked back to the desk.

Where was I supposed to go next? Back to Asbery? I hear Muriel Contreras is Maranian's illegitimate daughter, counsellor. What did that really change? It just showed me that Maranian had grown a conscience in his old age the way some people do. Most people are only human.

I took a sip of coffee, made a face to the wall, and clunked the cup down on the desk. Too rich. Like everybody else I had met in the last three days. I could leave Asbery alone and study the psychology of the goddam individual instead. Tock Maranian would pay high school kids to cadge microscopes, class. But would he drop silencers in Chick Gannett's lap and take a baseball bat to Leo Matz? Would he leave fingerprints on his little sister?

The telephone rang and I reached over the coffee cup to answer it and hear Dinah's voice asking, "Is this Philip Marlowe?"

"It's his grandson. Marlowe retired to a bee farm in Cupertino."

"I thought you had to retire too, tiger. I called your apartment first. I didn't think you'd still be in your office at six-thirty."

"Now that I'm minus a license I'm considering a new career. I think I might write an opera about modern San Francisco."

"What will you call it? *Ms. Butterfly?*"

"*Die Meisterjogger.*"

She gave the dirty laugh again and I pulled out a cigarette and lit it while she went on to tell me about her day and Shirley Mendelsohn's latest crusade against my gender. Through the window as she talked I could see a fat, ugly freighter, its decks stacked high with Japanese truck bottoms, wallowing in the choppy bay.

"And she says that for a compulsive wise guy like you, jokes represent sexual repression. They're just foreplay."

"What's foreplay?"

"I'm leaving the hospital in an hour," she said. "For dinner and a movie I could arrange a tutorial."

The freighter heaved to with all the grace of a shot pig and turned its snout toward Oakland. Over the top of a blur of dark smog the Berkeley hills gripped the edge of the continent and held on for dear life.

"I have to skip dinner and the movie," I said slowly, standing up and pulling the telephone cord tight with one hand. To hell with the psychology of the individual. I could press Christie now if I wanted to. With what I knew about Tock and modern sisterhood I could press her this time for Muriel.

"Mike?" Dinah said. "Are you there?"

"Sorry," I said. "Sorry, tigress." Twilight had begun to stretch out low across the water, and strings of red and white bridge lights were flickering on. "It needs to be a makeup exam, I think. Tonight I have to have dinner at my club."

I unplugged the hot plate, locked the office door, and took the stairs two at a time to the street. By six-thirty the night shift at the Club Eden must have already come on, fresh squadrons of topless, bottomless angels for the next skirmish in the war between men and women. Except that in San Francisco, I thought as I reached the sidewalk, the war seemed to be fought largely by mercenaries.

A powder-puff blue car glided slowly by, going the other way and sporting City Hall's latest attempt to give euphemisms a bad name: "Department of Police Services," the golden logo on the door said. The bull behind the wheel glowered at me from behind silver reflecting glasses, the car shook its fins once and was gone. I started the Mercedes and automatically wrote down the mileage in my pocket notebook while the engine cleared its throat. Then I pulled out past the precinct building, turned right three blocks later and headed up the wide, lonely spaces of the Embarcadero, here nothing more than half a mile of cobbled pavement running underneath the giant catapults of the freeway and along the deserted China Basin docks. An old-timer's shortcut to lower Market, with the best view in the city of Yerba Buena Island crouching like a yellow lion out on the gray water halfway to Oakland. There was nobody in either direction, as usual, and no sounds except the yammer of seagulls and the drone of traffic overhead. A hundred feet away from my fenders, nervous little whitecaps slapped the concrete and timber pilings and ran frothing to shore. If I hadn't been looking at the odometer I would have seen the hard guy before he rammed me.

The first collision slammed the Mercedes forward with a yelp of gears and rubber and bounced me off the steering wheel. Cursing, I whipped around to see the grill of a big sedan falling back. Behind the wheel the hard guy grinned and leaned forward. I spun the Mercedes right and accelerated across the cobblestones, and the sedan only glanced against the corner of my bumper before it shot past. Spinning the wheel hard right again, I jumped on the gas pedal. The Mercedes kept rolling straight. A fisherman far out on one of the docks got to his feet and yelled. I jerked the wheel back around and spun it helplessly through its whole circle like a man dialling a broken phone. *The Mercedes rolled straight ahead.* The sedan kicked into the bumper again just as I lifted my foot from the gas pedal to the brake, but the car leaped ahead with the jolt, twenty feet closer to the water.

I yelled and stabbed my hand under my coat where the gun used to go. The fisherman was waving a basket over his head. The sedan fell back, sped up, and slammed me again toward the bay. I yanked the emergency brake up with both hands, the sedan clipped the bumper, and the brake snapped like a finger under the impact. In the mirror the hard guy laughed and threw his head forward and knocked the Mercedes another twenty feet. The water, greasy and excited, fluttering its white lips, was lunging up the embankment for me. The Mercedes hit the curb of the sidewalk, the front tires rolled up, stopped, poised—the sedan bucked savagely into the rear like a locomotive and the tires jumped up and over. I threw open the door. The sedan locked bumpers with another thud and began grinding the Mercedes forward, rear tires over the curb now, front tires starting to drop toward slanting dirt.

I blocked the door wide with my right shoulder and fell. Blue metal whirled by, then sky, then sandy debris as I tumbled. Ten feet away the Mercedes balked a moment longer at the last rotten timber railing. Then the sedan grunted once more and it rose forward, hung its face far out over the chattering water for an interminable moment, and toppled.

I rolled up and away from the splash, scrambling along the sloping embankment while sheets of black water drummed across my head and shoulders and far out onto the cobblestone pavement. When I looked back up from my sinking car, the hard guy was holding a cannon against my ear.

"I cut your Pitman arm," he said for the third time. "I cut it half in two with a chain clip and the cobblestone did the rest. I thought you wouldn't lose the steering till you were on the fuckin' freeway or the bridge, but this was better."

I touched one hand to the cut on my chin and didn't say anything. The Pitman arm connects the steering box to the relay rods that go to the wheels. Lose it and you lose all steering whatsoever.

"So shut up about the goddam car," the guy in the back seat said. I didn't look back because I figured he still had the gun he had started with five minutes ago, a Smith & Wesson .38 that carried a fat black silencer on the end of the barrel like a garden slug on a root. "If the gonzo had totaled himself on the goddam bridge you would of been paid for how much brains you got, and you got shit for brains, Benny."

"He wrecked my engine," the hard guy muttered, but he stopped talking about my Pitman arm and concentrated on winding through Union Square traffic. Then as we turned down Powell and passed a stalled cable car stacked high with tourists, he jerked his head at me and started again: "Take a good look at the sights, Kojak. This time tomorrow night you're going to wish you'd stayed in that fat-ass German boxcar with the windows down."

"Shut up, Benny," the back seat said. Benny grumbled something to himself and turned hard right on Eddy, squealing his tires and scattering pedestrians. He had on the same fuzzy brown hamster-hide sports coat he had worn this morning, and in the rhythmic flashes of streetlights I could see the bags of fat spilling his orange shirt over his belt like fleshy lava. As he drove, his thin nose dipped and rose like a beak. A dumb thing to do, Fred had said, not to take a lawyer to Henry Sampson's hearing: Another dumb thing, he had said, to shove a Pepsi down a Chrysler. The guy in the back seat lit a cigarette and wheezed. I shifted my weight from one bruise to another. Newton's third law, I had loftily said; shove till the bad guys shove back, shove till they grab you by the throat and make you bob for apples on the bottom of the bay. One of these days I would look up Newton's first and second laws.

"Fuckin' cow," Benny said suddenly. Under a street light as we slowed for another right turn, a hooker was standing and smiling garishly at us, her long white dress slit up one side from the ankle to the ribcage. Benny grinned and sped up, jumping the curb for an instant to brush her back.

"Turn around and stop dreaming, Kojak. She's got tits like sandbags," he chuckled as I twisted my head. "She'd break your fuckin' tooth off." In the side mirror I saw the woman stagger, clap her right bicep with her left hand and give us a savage finger. Still chuckling, Benny took the next left on Turk, then half a block later swung the car into an alley three doors beyond the club.

"You can pull right up to the front," I said, my voice scratchy and hoarse. "I'm a member."

The man in the back seat swung his open hand casually and slapped my ear into my skull. "You stopped being a tough guy about five minutes ago," he said. "Get out of the car an inch at a time, wise ass, like you thought I might get mad and shoot your jewels off. Then you just walk in slow goddam motion in front of Benny and me to the door with the light. We spent too goddam much time on you already."

The door with the light opened onto narrow wooden stairs that smelled of urine and spoiled meat, not like Leo's stairway, but damper, nastier. When I stopped shivering from having half the bay in my coat and hair, I told myself as we started up, when my ear stopped ringing and my shoulder stopped throbbing and my chin stopped bleeding, I would turn around and rip Benny's head off.

"Through the door, wise ass, and open the other door over there."

We walked through a storeroom littered with cardboard boxes, light fixtures, and empty, snaggle-toothed metal shelves, and I pushed open the second door into a carpeted reception area. To my right was a glass office partition and a wider stairway, also carpeted. In front of me floated an elegant Danish teak desk shaped like a boomerang. Behind it a trio of cream white file cabinets stood at attention, flanked by two expensively framed movie posters. The first poster showed Brigitte Bardot climbing out of a pool. The second poster showed a woman being raped by a rope.

To my left a teak panelled wall contained the outline of another door and to the right of it, in gold letters the size of beer bottles, the name "Nilsson Brothers Enterprises."

The man with the gun walked around me and crossed to the door. While he rapped once with his knuckles, Benny breathed halitosis and obscenities in my ear. Then the other man jerked his head at me, turned the knob, and we went in.

CHAPTER 15

THIS IS HIM?" INCREDULOUS, CONTEMPTUOUS. "This is the guy?"

The man with the gun hitched his shoulders, rolled his jaw, and nodded.

"Take off his pants," a voice said from the other side of the room and giggled.

The office was huge, bigger than Edward Asbery's and bulging with heavy furniture. Two couches end-to-end on the right hand wall, two leather swivel chairs behind another curving teak desk, two more creamy file cabinets with chain locks run through the drawer handles, and movie posters on two walls, including one of Alice in Wonderland in a pose Disney had never dreamed of. Behind the desk, in front of drawn curtains, hung the over-sized starched collar of a home video screen. To my left, on the other wall, stood three tall video games in a row, the kind you would find in an arcade—Pac-Man, Space Invaders, and one I had never seen before, their LED faces black and shiny under the narrow plastic hoods. On a swivel stool in front of Space Invaders slouched a tall white-haired baby-faced man wearing a loose fitting yellow sport shirt, yellow slacks, and bright yellow running shoes. Six-six at least, and morbidly skinny. He looked like a french fry in a leisure suit.

In front of me another man at least as tall, almost as skinny, almost as blonde was leaning against the edge of the desk. Beside him, both hands burrowed into a dirty brown windbreaker from a Shell station, stood Benny's partner. In full light he turned out to be about the same size and age as Yetta, with a short neck and oddly flattened features that made it look as if somebody had walked across his face with a boot. Beneath the Shell emblem the name "Phil" was handstitched in looping red letters. The blonde man held up a pita bread sandwich and folded himself forward to take a bite.

"You do slow work, Phil," he said through the sandwich. "How could it take all day for a geek like this?"

"He stayed in his office too long," Phil said. "We didn't want to go in a building where there was somebody else working."

"Except if it was the old guy in there," Benny said behind me. "I wanted to go in after the old guy too. They wrecked my engine, the both of them."

Phil looked at Benny in disgust.

"Take off his pants," the man by the games giggled again. He had a high-pitched adenoidal voice, squeaky and piercing.

"Time for more medicine, Arthur," the man with the sandwich said. Arthur giggled and rolled his stool a foot to the right, where his elbow slipped off the back rest and into a game switch. Overhead, blue Pac-Man monsters were suddenly jitterbugging up and down a grid of dotted corridors, trying to vaporize a red ball with a flashing mouth. I knew how the ball felt. Arthur swivelled on his stool and lowered his head to a line of white powder about an inch long on the console counter. Next to it ran three other white lines, like military stripes, and then a gold-plated razor blade.

"My brother likes to humiliate and debase," sandwich said in a silky voice as Arthur honked the first line into his sinuses. No floppy yellow ensemble for sandwich: a tan V-neck cashmere sweater, revealing collar bone knobs and no shirt, and fat brown leather trousers that flared like Turkish pajamas. The same oblong baby face as his brother, smooth-cheeked and pink. He stretched one leg casually toward me, and the kneecap moved inside the leather like a mouse swallowed by a snake. His face over the pita sandwich was long and narrow, like a horse peering over a feed bag.

"Do you know who we are?" he said in the same arch tone. Phil watched me with his hands in his pockets. Benny edged closer to Arthur and the Pac-Man game.

"Yeah. Donny and Marie Osmond." I raised my right hand slowly and reached toward my breast pocket for a cigarette. Before I had it halfway out of the pack, the Smith & Wesson had jumped back into Phil's paw and Benny was pointing his cannon at my ear again.

I asked: "Can I use my lighter instead?"

The sandwich man smiled, one tooth at a time, and cocked his head at Phil. "The geek is full of wisecracks."

"They're a form of sexual repression," I said, lighting the cigarette. "You wouldn't have heard of it." I tasted warm cottony smoke and exhaled. They were also a defensive reaction to being scared witless. Phil was built like a cinderblock, and he had probably used the big pistol on something besides tin cans. On the other hand, if they were going to do more than flood my car, they wouldn't have bothered to bring me to the executive suite first. "You're Piers and Arthur Nilsson," I said, still leading with my mouth as usual. "Slam and Dunk to your many friends. You run about half the hookers in the Tenderloin, you make movies a gynecologist couldn't follow, and you picked the wrong way to ask me up for a sandwich."

"So tough, so tough," Piers said. Or maybe he was Slam. They both had the faintest possible Scandinavian accents, reminders that they were supposed to have come over as school children. And that they still used their Swedish connections for lend-lease pornography. Hands across the sea, among other things. Bring me your tired, your poor, your huddled masses. "You don't think much of us, do you, geek?"

I shrugged and blew smoke uphill toward his face. He had a tiny mouth, almost lipless, that puckered into an O the size of a coughdrop. "I think you're nasty, brutish, and short," I said.

Arthur honked another line of cocaine, tossed his red nose high, and started the high-pitched giggling again. Behind his right ear the Pac-Man monsters were scattering in panic, like chubby blue atoms.

Piers said "short" and held the smile.

"Your flunkies also tried to open a carwash with me inside," I added stupidly. Never complain, never explain. Getting even is the best revenge.

"Flunkies." Piers rolled the word around his tiny mouth. His tongue popped out and in like a sparrow in a birdhouse. "Phil and Benny are independent businessmen," he said. "They're subcontractors. We hire people like them by the job. This particular job was to ask you around for a little chat. We don't particularly give a shit how they got you here, do we, Arthur?"

Arthur squeaked something and began to look at me with bright, interested eyes, as if I had just materialized in the room.

"What's Arthur's job?" I asked. "Dreaming up pornographic video games?"

Piers finished the sandwich and stretched his torso around to the top of the desk. "Haller," he said over his shoulder. "Michael Haller. We heard you were a motor mouth." He turned back around with one of my business cards in his hand. "Private Investigator," he read. "California License 19-1964." He held the card delicately by one corner, as if he might sail it across the room, then let it drop to the carpet. "We understand that last part is out of date." I inhaled more smoke and didn't say anything. My card flopped over once in a floor draft, then lay still, playing dead. "You wonder how I got your card, Haller? A girl named Christie gave it to me," Piers said. "She works downstairs, Christie. She's what you might call a middle-level whore, wouldn't you say, Arthur?"

"Christie can suck the batteries out of a flashlight," Arthur giggled in the same slight Scandinavian accent. He had dragged a set of black nylon handcuffs from one of his pockets, the kind of handcuffs they sell along with the rubber suit and the rawhide whip in the front room of the Club Eden, and was twisting them around his long bony fingers. Piers had pulled a small tin-colored globe from somewhere on the desk, and was slowly rotating it between fingers and thumbs. The globe had half a dozen black indentations and a rusty keyhole on top. The Nilsson brothers had restless hands.

"Arthur threatened to put Christie in one of his movies, I think," Piers said quietly.

"Christie would go down on a fire hydrant," Arthur said.

I clenched and unclenched the fingers of my left hand, and Phil straightened his shoulders and rose on the balls of his feet. Arthur was widely rumored to have made several snuff movies a few years ago, real movies with real prostitutes turning into real corpses. He was known for sure to have turned up as an actor in one of his own S-M films, but not acting.

"We also understand you got a little rough with her, Haller."

"I paid my five bucks and recited the first amendment backwards," I said, keeping my voice steady, not thinking of Christie, not thinking of Christie's comfortable, intelligent face and elegant dancer's body. "Eden is open to anybody with a pulse and a dirty raincoat. Why the subcontractors?" Arthur got up from his stool, shook out his arms in the loose yellow shirt, and walked over to stand with his nylon handcuffs by Phil. Six-six maybe when he stretched to full height, and no longer giggling.

"One," Piers said. "Nobody comes in and pushes our girls around." He popped a smile like a bubble. "Nobody but us. Two, all of our girls work out of the clubs. We don't let any geek with a hardon follow them home or make a date somewhere else. That's money out of our pocket. Three, we let one private snoop in to bring some hooker home to mama, all of a sudden we got a dozen private snoops on the doorstep wanting somebody else."

I raised what was left of my cigarette to my lips. Grab would have said the same thing.

"You finished with that weed, Haller?" Piers said. "I don't want your goddam ashes on the rug." I glanced down automatically at the lavender carpet. Piers reached behind him and pulled out a silver ashtray shaped like an oak leaf. As I rubbed the cigarette butt into it, Phil gripped my wrist with one hard hand and batted the ashtray away. Arthur slipped the nylon handcuff over my wrist while Phil grabbed the other arm and held it up and Benny loudly cocked his pistol.

"Arthur will want to watch," Piers said.

CHAPTER 16

IT WAS A PROFESSIONAL BEATING. Knowledgeable, quick, indifferent.

They took me back to the storeroom next to the outer office, and there Benny ran a double cord between the cuffs and hoisted my arms up to a hook screwed in the wall. Then he split my legs three feet apart and tied one ankle to the back leg of a wooden desk, the other to a clamp in the floorboard molding, leaving me as exposed and defenseless as a baby's belly.

Phil never bothered to unzip his windbreaker. He bent down and tested the knots, straightened up, and hit me five times fast in the stomach. Paused to check the knots again and started more slowly from navel to heart.

At first I kicked back, uselessly, and tried to roll my hips to one side or the other, dodging his fists. Each time he simply steadied me with one hand like a laundry bag and hit harder with the other. After fifteen punches I lost count and stopped struggling. The sides of the dank little room swam toward my face, swam away again, oscillating like walls of water. Sweat filled my eyes and plastered my hair to my skull. Arthur's lower lip flapped like a gill. Benny's long gun separated into gray and red streaks of light. With a deadpan face and fists like flagstones, Phil stooped, swung, straightened. Stooped, swung— blunt arcs of knuckles and forearm, the grunt-slap rhythm of a man beating a rug. Of a man beating Leo Matz with a club. The last thing I saw through a film of pain was Leo's face floating toward me. The last thing I heard was Arthur beginning to yip with pleasure.

When I opened my eyes again I smelled wine.

Strong red wine aged in plywood and giving off the bouquet of a courthouse spittoon.

I coughed, scraping my cheek back and forth against gritty pavement, and raised my head a fraction. Inches away stood a pair of muddy shoes propped on their heels, one sole peeling away from an instep and drooping like a leather leaf. I blinked and refocused and let my eyes travel up shapeless gray trousers to a pair of knobby hands and a transparent plastic raincoat. Head tilted back against a brick wall, red eyes set in a complexion like a dirty mattress, a wino with a jug in his lap stared at me silently.

I raised my head and pushed up on my hands and knees and the pain came rolling down my gullet, spilling bile through my teeth, wringing my belly like a wet towel. When I unsqueezed my eyelids, the wino was lifting the jug and swallowing in loud gulps that made his Adam's apple jump. I lowered my head again and stared at the pavement, a wobbly old dog waiting for the shakes to pass. Cigarette wrappings, old pieces of screwed-up cellophane. Somewhere many feet to my left, lights worried back and forth on a street, a horn sounded. The wino lowered the jug to his lap and belched, and a smell like swamp gas drifted over. I tried to stand all the way up, slipped in a puddle, staggered backwards and began to slide helplessly down another wall, ending in a long-legged sprawl exactly like the wino's. A knowledgeable profession-al beating. No blood drawn, no bones broken. I felt humili-ated, debased, unmanned, and there wasn't a mark on me. For a weird, chaotic moment I closed my eyes and it seemed as if Phil's fists had released a hot tide of Puritanical guilt into my belly along with everything else, as if I had somehow actually deserved such a beating. As if the beating confirmed that I had lost something else, something essential and inward, when I had lost the license. I shook my eyes open and frowned at the wino, and we sat facing each other for a long minute on the floor of the alley. Then he raised the jug again to a waxy tongue covered with ulcers the size of fishscales, and I dropped my head between my knees and vomited.

The doctors say that maybe in times of great pain the body releases hormones that anesthetize it. Peptide hormones. Inner opium. Nature's own Mickey Finn. They find the stuff in dying mice, caught by traps or snatched away from cat's teeth. They aren't sure yet about people. I stood in the doorway and put one hand against the wall to steady myself. A man or a mouse? My insides were collapsing in slow motion, floor by floor, staircase by staircase, brick by brick.

Dinah had let herself into the apartment as usual and was sitting curled on the couch in her favorite position, shoes off, feet tucked under, reading a magazine and drinking a cup of coffee. From the radio on the other side of the living room floated the polite, sedately mournful conversation of two vio-lins and a cello.

I swayed, watching her, not watching her, listening to my

pulse kick down the doors to my cerebellum, and my shadow tugged at the corner of her magazine.

"You're late," she said, looking up, then sucked her cheeks hollow. I followed her eye and saw my left jacket arm ripped along the elbow and the caked mud and slime on my trousers. Across the room the violins whinnied in alarm. She uncurled her legs and stood up very slowly.

"It was an accident," I said. I swallowed with difficulty and tasted filmy saliva on my teeth. I tried to think of a joke to finish. Indestructible Haller. The manliest man's man since . . . "He hit before I could run," I mumbled.

Her hands were already pulling the jacket off, popping buttons open, and her face had taken on the stiff seriousness I had seen once or twice before when something had gone badly wrong with a patient. At the first touch of finger against bruise I winced and flopped back, and she pushed harder, kneading my torso like bread dough.

"Have you spit up any blood?" she said, still touching, loosening my belt and pressing hard with her thumbs.

"No." I cleared my throat, started to say something else, couldn't. She had left the drapes open to the bay, the way we usually do on clear nights, and over the balcony, skimming on black water toward the Golden Gate, the filigree of bluish white lights traced the silhouette of a ship.

"You've obviously vomited."

I started to say yes, then simply nodded.

Her fingers had my shirt tail out and were probing the small of my back, kidneys, hipbone.

"Did they hit you back here?"

I nodded.

Her fingers came back and pulled the trousers open.

"Here?"

I shook my head. She was asking more questions. I heard my voice, scratchy and soft, answering. My eyes wandered to the delicate lights of the ship, jerked to the shelves on the far wall I had built two years ago to hold the books and records. The music had stopped. Dinah was asking if a bone or a muscle hurt when she pushed, but the ship and the shelves and the furniture were dissolving, her voice was dissolving, and I brushed past her, stumbling toward the couch and not making it, on my hands and knees on the floor beginning to cry.

She prescribed a long, hot shower and a palmful of Zomax pain-killers from her tote bag.

When I came out of the bathroom, there were clean clothes on the bed and a cold bottle of Beck's beer on the bureau next to the photograph I had taken last summer of her riding the merry-go-round in Tilden Park. I put on the clothes and drank half the beer in one swallow. Then I padded gingerly back to the living room.

"Now I know why Holmes kept Doctor Watson around," I said from the doorway. She had returned to her place on the couch, legs curled, magazine open on her lap. But she had been staring through the French doors toward the bay. It was a stupid, unpleasant remark. Somebody had yanked my license away and somebody else had taken my manly muscles, hung them up like an empty sack, and mugged me in the ego. Naturally I was kicking out at the nearest normal person, the person who had pulled me bawling off my hands and knees. If you lose your license to work, do you lose everything? What to make of a diminished thing?

"Watson was an ophthalmologist," she said without look-ing around. "He couldn't have known much about internal hemorrhages."

"Whereas a psychiatrist . . ."

She turned to face me and even from twenty feet away I could see that her eyes were moist and bright. "Have you given any thought to becoming a CPA?" she said. "Or a florist?"

I walked across the room and snapped off the radio, which had switched to a quartet of contemporary twelve-tone mu-sic. The shower had loosened my belly and thigh muscles and I walked almost normally, wincing only when I had to bend forward and my lower back trembled like the springs of a tram-poline. Tomorrow, if I didn't spend the day in the shower, my muscles would stiffen and turn the color of burst plums. For the next few hours I would hardly feel it.

"That sounded like dolphins talking in outer space," I said, gesturing with the beer bottle toward the radio. She nodded and bit her lower lip. Tears had run down each flushed cheek from the corners of her eyes, leaving wet streaks that caught the lamplight. A chubby redheaded wren, her brother had once called her. We had met in the basement of the San Francisco city morgue, of all the places in the world, in front of the baroque, polished metal elevator doors that the architect must have thought would take your mind off the brackish smell of formaldehyde in the corridors and the chilly, air-conditioned silence crawling out from under the doors. She had come to identify the body of a patient, an anorexic girl who had rented a room in a Tenderloin hotel, piled the furniture against the door, taken off her clothes, and stepped out the window. I had come to check a John Doe against my missing persons list, the way I used to do every month or so, like a ghoulish schoolmaster taking attendance. I hadn't gone back in years. A ship somewhere out of sight nudged its foghorn, and I walked to the couch and sat down beside her. She pulled a Kleenex out of the purse on the coffee table and started to rub her nose. I bent my head forward and kissed the inside of her wrist. Dinah-joy, her father calls her. On our third date she had told me that her idea of the perfect man was someone who made passionate love to her every night until one-thirty in the morning. And then at two o'clock turned into a pizza.

"What's the magazine?"

She flipped the cover to show me. *Scientific American.*

"Shirley Mendelsohn wanted me to read the article on the adactylidium mite," she said and held up a page with a photograph of a goggle-eyed, bandy-legged silky green insect chewing on a laurel leaf. It looked like Truman Capote in combat fatigues. Dinah took a swallow of my beer and handed the bottle back.

"I don't want to ask," I said.

She sniffed. "It seems the adactylidium mite is a natural radical feminist," she said. "The female hatches her eggs within her own body and always gives birth to just one male and five or six females."

"Just one male." I finished the beer and arched my back to ease a newly discovered muscle.

Dinah nodded. "Poor old thing. He copulates with all of his sisters inside the mother's body, fertilizes them, and then promptly dies without ever seeing daylight. Mendelsohn said he serves the only significant male function. She said to show you the article."

We were skating along the surface, making familiar patter to cover other issues, the way we sometimes did when one of her friends asked if we were ever going to get married or did we ever want to have children. Foreplay. She took my empty beer bottle and went into the kitchen. When I was nine or ten my father had talked long and seriously one night over the dinner table about the Depression, about how he had washed dishes in a Hayes-Bickford Cafeteria in Scollay Square in order to pay for medical school, about how he had constantly wondered if he would make it through the week, let alone ever graduate and become a doctor. He told me that every day he had pictured himself in five years as a bum, a derelict standing in a soup line, dressed in burlap and staring at the sidewalk, and he had never gotten over that picture of himself. When Dinah came back with two more beers, I was standing in front of the French doors, looking over the tiny balcony and wondering where the hell all the ships had disappeared to. Among other things.

"Are they the same people who killed Leo Matz?" she asked, standing beside me.

"I think so."

"Do they have anything to do with Muriel Contreras and your license?"

"I don't know."

"But you're going to keep looking for her? This was a kind of warning, but you're going to keep looking?"

"I have to have my license, Dinah."

She was suddenly brusque and busy, pouring her beer into a tall glass and straightening some books on the shelves. "Mendelsohn gave another in-service talk today about sexism and language," she said briskly. "Did you know there's no male equivalent word in English for 'nymphomania'?"

"Satyriasis," I said and started the second beer.

She stared at me. Then marched down to the other end of the bookshelves and took out my old Webster's Second, bought for my freshman year at college and nearly as battered by now as its owner.

"You are an infuriating man," she said after a moment, snapping the dictionary closed.

It's foolish to say we don't love people for the way they look. Dinah stood in front of me, arms akimbo, red hair catching the bright glow spilling from the track lights overhead, the high breasts swelling the white blouse, the legs, not quite stocky, slightly apart and rigid in the brown tweed skirt. I put down the beer and gathered both her hands in mine and kissed her gently on the mouth.

She blinked twice and said nothing. I kissed her again.

"People get mad when people they care about get hurt," she said. I kissed her again, less gently.

"You don't feel like that," she said, putting her hands on my shoulders. "You can't feel like that."

I had started to say I would do my mite when somebody knocked loudly on the apartment door.

"My God—you look terrible!" squawked the widow Margot.

I propped one shoulder against the doorframe and watched Edward Asbery shush her with a flathanded wave while he tried to inspect my face.

"You look white as a sheet," she said. Far down the hall behind me Dinah made an inquiring, worried noise.

"What happened, did you miss the turn to Pacific Heights, Asbery?" I said rudely. Margot stopped fidgeting and stood up straight on her dignity. "Or is this business?"

He rolled his shoulders and twisted his jaw in a way that reminded me of Phil. Any man would have reminded me of Phil. Except that Asbery was wearing a black pin-striped suit with creases that could slice steak and carrying a fur-collared overcoat on one elegant arm. All I could see of Margot was a bowl of shiny blonde hair, a fur wrap, and several pounds of precious metals clinging to a stiff neck.

"Taghi Maranian came up to the city tonight," he said, laying the New England frost thick across the name. "He came to the restaurant where Margot and I were dining and made a remarkable scene. Margot and I have just left."

"I dined at my club," I said, and watched the brainy, patrician brow wrinkle in puzzlement. "What the hell," I sighed. "Come on in, counsellor, and have a beer."

Dinah already had her coat on and her paisley tote bag in one hand when we reached the living room.

"You won't need me," she said in a tone I didn't quite understand, and nodded, not politely, to Asbery and Margot.

"I'll call you in the morning."

She touched my elbow for a moment and walked around me to the hallway entrance.

"I've changed my mind, Edward," Margot said suddenly, sloshing her words together like ice cubes in a Bloody Mary and making it clear that Tock hadn't interrupted them before the cocktail course. "This is all wrong," she said more distinctly. "I don't want to stay."

"Margot—"

"All wrong," she said and pulled the fur wrap tighter. "I'll take a cab home. You stay if you think you have to. But this man lost his license to work, you know. I don't care if Tock . . . what Tock did to him." And she turned bright little animal eyes in my direction.

"I'm taking a cab," Dinah said from the door. "You can share if you like."

Margot swivelled inside the wrap to look at her—presentable, affluent, obviously annoyed at me. I made introductions while she nodded her approval, glowered in my direction, and nodded again.

When Asbery came back from seeing them to a cab, I was sprawled in my big chair opposite the couch and tenderly massaging my gut where Phil had worked on his short game. The aspirin, the shower, and the beer were all wearing off at once, and the last face I wanted to see, then or later, was Asbery's impassive Bostonian mask.

"Did Taghi do that to you?" he asked, standing quietly in front of me, both hands at his sides in a pose from the Brooks Brothers fall brochure. He wore an orange silk foulard that had cost thirty dollars and that looked like a malaria culture.

"He started a trend," I said, "but no. Tock lost interest after the first couple of punches. Later on was by a couple of guys on Turk Street—call them Bambi and Thumper—who wanted to please their bosses. The first boss likes to watch people hurting, women people if he can find them, men people if they're handy. The other brother has a face like a choirboy and keeps a pineapple choker on his desk to fidget with."

Asbery made his expression change to impatient puzzlement again. I bent forward in the chair and let a muscle spasm go off across my belly like a guitar string breaking. From my navel to my throat I felt as if I had been stripmined.

"A pineapple choker," I repeated and reached for my beer. "Make yourself a drink if you want it, counsellor. They're in the next room on a shelf." He didn't say anything and I sipped flat beer and grimaced. "A pineapple choker is a gadget extortionists liked to use in the eighteenth century. A metal globe about the size of a golfball that has ten, twelve double-edged six-inch spikes packed into the center on springs and held in place by a lock. Your renegado would grab a wealthy victim on a dark night on Hampstead Heath, yank his mouth open and stuff in the ball. Then he would turn the key." Asbery shifted his weight and put a hand in each pocket in the naval officer's classic watch pose. "When your renegado turned the key," I said, wrenching myself out of the chair and starting toward the bar myself, "the spikes all jumped out at once like an exploding pineapple and lacerated the victim's mouth and throat and tonsils. And the hell of the thing was, you couldn't remove the pineapple without the key to the lock, because that was the only way the spikes retracted. Or you could, but it'd be like pulling out a Swiss Army knife."

I found the scotch bottle on the tray in the dining nook office that stands to the right of the French doors. Asbery had turned to watch me but hadn't taken the hands out of his pockets. I shook Laphroaig scotch out of the bottle and reached in the aluminum bucket for ice cubes. The only things plastic in my house, I had told Dinah in some phase of immature rebellion now forgotten, should be my records.

"To get the key," I told Asbery, "most victims paid through the teeth. Cheers."

He stood in the half light of the open door and watched me drink half an inch of whiskey before he spoke.

"You are a remarkable fund of information," he said dryly. "I've misjudged you."

"You want to know Woody Allen's real name?" I said, walking back into the room and brushing past him on my way to the big chair. "Allen Konigsberg. You want to know when the Declaration of Independence was actually signed? July second." I lowered another half-inch of Laphroaig, which was settling between my bruised ribs like tar. "You want to know where Muriel Contreras is or who killed Leo Matz? Find a detective."

He stood in his vice-admiral's pose for a long time watching me as I sipped scotch and squinted out the window at a lattice of ghostly lights sailing on top of a cushion of gray fog. Then he took the hands out of the pockets.

"Maybe I will have that drink," he said, and walked into the next room.

I was still staring at the fog when he came back with a tall glass of mostly scotch. Hot and cold flashes were playing tag in their hobnailed boots up and down my abdomen, and my mind was as sharp as a secondhand stick of Wrigley's, but the liquor was staying down. Cracked ribs, Dinah had diagnosed. Massive insult to the abdominal muscles and inner organs, she had added in medical jargon, but apparently nothing worse. You will know if they've ruptured your spleen or if you have internal bleeding, she said, because your skin will begin to feel clammy and cold and you will become suddenly, desperately thirsty, which is the first sign of shock. By then, she had said grimly, you will be leaking enough blood into a subdural hematoma to fill a jeroboam.

"Are these all your books?" Asbery said, lifting his glass a fraction in the direction of the wall behind me. I ignored him and concentrated on my hot flashes of abdominal pain. Never let lawyers get away with saying the obvious. Do you know how to save ten drowning lawyers? my father used to ask my uncle in some secret joke ritual between brothers. My uncle always said no, my father always said good! and they both burst into laughter.

When I didn't reply, he turned away from the books and faced me.

"I suppose that was a condescending remark," he said, not quite apologizing. In the glare of the track lights I could see that his cheeks had an angry flush, and I remembered that about twenty-four hours and two beatings ago I had decided that he held the key to my ever getting back my license. I had also decided in some perverse way that I liked the son of a bitch.

"Let's start over, Asbery," I said wearily. "You didn't come up here to buy a paperback. And Tock Maranian didn't send you into shock by using the wrong fork. What do you want?"

He stared down at me for a moment, then walked across the room to the spot where Dinah had been sitting. He didn't curl up his feet under him, but he sat back with his left arm stretched across the top of the couch and looked almost human. Unbending with inferiors would never come easy to Asbery—there is no such thing as laid-back Yankee—but take away the half-acre office, the deferential secretaries, the view of the city at his feet, and maybe, just maybe, you had jazz.

"I suppose I had better be candid with you," he said, then stopped. His eyes roamed to the bookshelves behind me, to the French doors on my left and the balcony and the long view of the cottony bay. Later I could ask Dinah if they were soulful eyes. Right now they looked like frozen brass, and uncharacteristically restless. "I asked several people about you yesterday," he said, "after you came to my office." He stopped again and leaned toward the coffee table where I had left a pack of cigarettes. He took one without asking and lit it with a paper match from a book beside the ashtray. Then he blew smoke from his nose into his lap and waved the match out with a snap.

"Margot and I are having an affair," he said.

I swallowed another ounce or so of scotch and used my tongue to keep the ice from falling out of the glass.

"Gee," I said.

He held the cold eyes on me for a long moment, then tapped a millimeter of cigarette ash into the ashtray.

"She's not his mother, of course," he said finally, "but that accounts for a certain amount of the general ill-will he has for me."

"How about the specific ill-will, counsellor? Does that have anything to do with stepmom?"

"No." Asbery unbuttoned the middle button on his pinstriped jacket and revealed an opulent tie made of black and gold silk. The cuff link that flashed against the jacket consisted of a yellow topaz and a black ceramic foil. His tie clip was a gold stick holding a pearl the size of an olive. A lawyer in Asbery's bracket charges $120 an hour to draw up your will. We have twenty-two times more lawyers than Japan, and one-third as many engineers.

"No," he repeated. "There are two specific reasons for his ill-will. The first is that he thinks I'm delaying the disbursement of the money he inherited from his father and thereby preventing him from spending it as he likes."

I watched the second hand jog around the clock on the end table by Asbery, as tireless as a dog chasing its tail, and wondered if I had ever heard anybody say "thereby" out loud before.

"I am, of course," Asbery said, and I looked up from the clock to see a wintry smile evaporating. "The will has been probated, but not executed. We haven't found one of the principal legatees, as you know, and until we do that or until two years are up, the trustee—and I am the trustee—doesn't have to disburse the money. Taghi has filed what's called a petition for reasonable allowance with the court, but so far I've limited him to what I already give Margot, which is fifty-five hundred dollars a month."

"You can't run a soy bean ranch on fifty-five hundred," I said slowly. "Not with employees and electricity and laboratory equipment. That's less than seventy thousand a year." My belly rumbled and I pried myself out of the low chair and stumbled around the coffee table on my way to the bar to plug the leak. When I came back I had a full glass and another bottle, which I slammed down hospitably on the table, between the plaid beanbag ashtray Asbery was using and the copy of *Scientific American* that Dinah had left. Smoke spiralled up from the ashtray and broke into thin gray branches like a fishbone, and I batted them with my hand on the way back to the chair.

"It's his money, Asbery," I said when I had settled into the chair and gripped one arm of it hard. *My chest was heaving like the sea. "It's going to be his money. Why won't you let him have it?"

He laughed a short, high-pitched bark that showed his teeth, and leaned forward for the bottle. "You've met Taghi," he said. "He's a crude, bumptious man with no sense of money or responsibility. This GreenGenes lab—I've seen it twice on surprise visits—he'll never discover anything there except bills and more bills. He'd run through his bloody inheritance in six months if I let him. Soy beans," he said contemptuously.

I made a mild sound of protest. "I thought he went to Stanford and had respectable backing."

Asbery barked the peculiar laugh again and refilled his glass. "Did he tell you Stanford, Haller? Our friend Taghi Maranian went to Hayward State College, dropped out twice, took seven years to get his degree, majored in something called communications sciences, and learned what little biochemistry he knows from a night class at a community college on the peninsula. You're an investigator, Haller, look it up. Call Stanford, ask for the alumni office. They keep a special secretary there just to handle inquiries from people like you and from employers with job applications in front of them who wonder if the nice young man who can't write two grammatical sentences in his native language really studied at a fine private college."

There are people who think about their college years every day of their lives: bright, golden, irrecoverable years. He punched the cigarette hard into the ashtray and tilted his chin up at me with the assurance of a man who kept his Harvard diplomas on the wall. A lot of anger ran underneath Asbery's pinstripes, I found myself deciding fuzzily, a lot of undirected passion leaking into his own subdural hematoma. My mind wrenched itself abruptly from one track to another and I found myself picturing him making love to the pneumatic Margot on the Persian rug in his office, showering her with candied torts and whispering dirty codicils in her ear. I shook my head, and Asbery went on talking about the high standards at Stanford. All wrong, I thought. As a lover he would be about as playful as Chick Gannett's Doberman. He would be like one of those geysers in Yosemite that suddenly erupt steam through ice.

"A smallish firm in fact," he, was saying as I blinked him back into focus. "They won't take a loss if they can help it. These are heartless people, Haller, these venture capitalists. They prey on academic suburbs and count on academic naivete. And academic greed. If I gave Taghi eight hundred thousand dollars they'd suck it up into a court order within hours. I was a friend of Aram Maranian for fifteen years," he said. "I introduced Margot to him. I drew up his will. I have a certain responsibility to his estate, I think, and to his children."

"Including Muriel Contreras?"

He flushed. "Including Muriel Contreras," he said. "You wanted to know: all right. Her mother worked on Aram's farm in the San Joaquin Valley, a domestic worker in the house. After his first wife died . . . " He shrugged urbanely and pointed his big jaw toward the window and the view of the empty bay, where the fog was settling down on the water like a quilted blanket and a few stars were poking their heads through the eastern sky. To the west, over Mount Tamalpais, the new moon looked like a dirty dime.

"Aram was a religious man," Asbery said. "He was an elder in the Armenian church here, gave thousands of dollars to it." He dropped another two inches of my scotch into the glass and rolled it back and forth between his palms. "The liaison," he said, and it flickered through my mind that the word was unusually impersonal, even for a lawyer. "The liaison lasted only a few months, until Aram sold the farm and moved to the city. The codicil was his idea, when he knew he was dying of stomach cancer. One of the woman's sisters had written him about the girl—he never saw her, never knew about her. I see a lot of guilty conscience codicils—every attorney does—and I always advise against them. I told Aram he had no proof the girl was really even his daughter." Asbery put down the scotch without tasting it and pulled out another of my cigarettes. "He always blamed the cancer on the dyes in the Oriental rugs," he said irrelevantly.

I sipped my scotch too and stared at Asbery's sleek, fleshy face. What he said about codicils was true enough—guilty consciences were how Leo Matz had made his living. In the cramped light of my apartment he had a jaw like a cowcatcher.

"If I were Tock," I said, sounding drunkenly belligerent, "I'd take you to court and force you to pay." Ice clung to the rim of my glass for a moment, then lost its grip and began to slip down the side. "I'd make you disclose the accounts of the estate too."

He glanced at me with something like interest in his eyes. "The people I asked said you would have made a good lawyer, Haller. You have the brains for it."

"But not the heart."

He almost smiled.

"No. He can sue, of course, but he wouldn't win. And he wouldn't come to court for years."

"You would see to that."

"I would see to that."

"My partner and I once arrested a lawyer at San Francisco airport," I said. "He was an estate specialist from a small town in Indiana, and he'd cleaned out his firm's trustee checking accounts and stuffed his suitcase with half a million buckaroos. When we caught him he had seven different passports and a Pan Am ticket for Hong Kong in his pocket. He also had on a skirt and blouse and a blonde wig on his head. His wife just thought he'd run off with a waitress again."

Asbery stood up without looking at me and carried his glass and his cigarette stiffly to the French doors, looking in the shadows less like an elderly roué than like a crowbar in a J. Press suit.

"Let me educate you to the fact, Haller, that in California an estate attorney has to post a bond to cover each estate bank account he handles, and a judge moreover can examine the account's bank records at the end of any fiscal quarter. It does not, however, do the attorney any good in the legal community to have his integrity questioned, even pointlessly. Since Aram's illness began four years ago I've handled his affairs without a whiff of scandal or complaint, except for Taghi Maranian's little petition." He raised his glass but didn't drink. "An estate attorney has to have a subservient streak," he said enigmatically, and drank. Then he gestured with the glass toward the bay, rapidly clearing overhead, and the great dim shadow of Mount Tamalpais and the necklace of lights around Sausalito. "Most people think California is lush, gorgeous scenery, you know," he said in another tone of voice altogether. "But it's really an austere landscape, brown and angular and harsh and cruel, like New England. That s why I stay here, Haller."

I sank back like an astronaut accelerating in an easy chair and let my body hurt and my mind drift. Asbery was feeling the drink. Or Asbery was loosening up. Or Asbery was passing along the guff by the shovelful. I tipped the scotch bottle in the direction of my glass and measured the dose by the sound.

"You said there were two reasons for old Tock's ill-will, Asbery. What's number two?"

He turned from the window with an approving smile, like a ramrod professor hearing the right answer for once, and said, "You *would* have made a good lawyer, Haller," and for some reason it made me mad.

"Shut up about what I would have made, goddammit!" Some compartment of myself watched Asbery's well-bred face blanch at the outburst; the rest of me went right on shouting. "It's *too late* to be telling a man he could have been something else." I was out of the chair somehow, stalking across the carpet, circling Asbery. "The goddam world is littered with the ghosts of what I could have been. I pick up a newspaper and read a byline and see the ghost of the kid reporter I started out to be. I go past a bookstore and I see the ghost of the writer I never turned out to be either, lounging up against one of the tables, turning over somebody else's book. I end up being the one thing I never expected to be—a goddam missing persons dick chasing other people's ghosts—and now some maggot-brained kid and a Sacramento bureaucrat pull that away from me, too, and you show up in your three-piece suit to tell me what a wonderful lawyer I would have been."

I stopped as abruptly as I had started and walked away from the French doors, blowing air like a whale into the silence.

Asbery coughed and said, "I didn't realize," hesitated, cleared his throat, started over. "Obviously losing your license would be a terrible thing," he said. "You project a rather powerful physical confidence, Haller. One doesn't think of you as losing the thing you value most." He swallowed another inch of scotch and put the glass on the coffee table. "I couldn't stand not to practice law," he said slowly and distinctly, as if he were talking to someone in another room. "I had better go see about Margot."

"The second reason," I said as he reached the hallway, "would be that Taghi doesn't want you to find his sister."

He picked up the fur-collared overcoat he had draped over a chairback when he had come in. "Taghi," he said, pulling out each concise word with tweezers, "vigorously does not want her found."

CHAPTER 18

HE'S CONNING YOU," DINAH SAID.

"Raspberry-pineapple-almond," I said, reading the ice-cream package on the kitchen table. "Whatever happened to vanilla?"

"At three in the morning a person should step out a little," she said. "*Time* did a whole feature last month on the new ice-cream flavors," she said, licking the spoon deliberately, like a redheaded cat. "The cover story, in fact."

"Was it a scoop?"

She finished licking the spoon and grinned. "You're already recovering, I think."

"I'm glad you came back." She didn't say anything. Through my kitchen window I could see the front edge of the next door building, and one light, behind a shade, on the fifth floor. Beyond the edge of the building a smug, fat star was perched on nothing at all, burning up its calories, staring in. "What did you think of Margot?" I asked finally.

Dinah sniffed and got up to see to the coffee pot. "All

legs and breasts," she said from the stove. "Like one of those packages of chicken parts."

"He's not conning me," I said. "Tock unloaded on my jaw because I was looking for Muriel Contreras. Tock has eight hundred thousand reasons for me not to find her. Tock is the con man. Tock didn't go to Stanford, Tock didn't study biochemistry, Tock can't last another month without his cash."

"I don't like Asbery," she said, coming back with two of the flower-covered clay mugs that she had given me one Christmas. "He leaves a trail of smarm across the floor."

"You're not used to formal New Englanders," I said. Dinah had grown up in the foothills of the Sierra Nevada, in a small town called Placerville whose original name in the gold rush was Hangtown. "He said he couldn't stand to lose his license and not to practice law," I added for no reason at all.

She looked at me quizzically. "I said it was all right for you to drink beer," she said. "I never dreamed that you and your New England lawyer would sit down and polish off half a bottle of raw scotch."

"I experienced a sudden desperate thirst," I said from the table. "Probably shock."

She walked over and poured more coffee into the mug, then stood looking down, one hand cocked on her hip. "You have the constitution of a Mexican mule," she said in a pleasant voice. "You should be in bed drunk or unconscious. How do you feel?"

I felt as if my torso had been set in cement. I felt as if Phil had dropkicked a blasting cap into my gut.

"I feel fine," I said.

"Do you remember what you said the other day about Freud?" she asked. "When we were talking about my interns?"

"I say so much crap," I said and stubbed out my cigarette

hard, flushing at the thought of my outburst to Asbery, flushing at the thought of every half-assed drunken remark I had made in the last two days. In the last thirty-eight years.

"You said he never took the obvious explanation. He never took the most recent symptom at face value. You said that in his theory there was always an earlier crime that triggered the one that came to the surface."

"Yeah." I creaked to my feet, grunted once with pain, and stood staring out the kitchen window. The light two stories up had gone out, the fat star had ducked behind a cornice. "I know. Tock's motive doesn't explain the Nilsson brothers."

"They wouldn't do . . . what they did to you just for seeing that girl," she said.

"They're sadists," I said. "They would."

She shook her head.

"Sometimes I think maybe Henry Sampson did me a favor," I sighed after a long silence. "Maybe I should just let the license go and call somebody up about a real job. A job I can actually do." She put her hand through my arm and didn't say anything. "You know what I did the other day, after I couldn't find any lead whatsoever in the files at either the *Chronicle* or the *Constitution?*" She looked up and shook her head. "I went over to the games arcade at Pier 39 and spent five dollars playing a new Japanese game called 'Whack-aMolie'—don't laugh—it's true. A board the size of a pool table covered with lots of little stucco prairie dog mounds and holes, and you pay a quarter and get a Styrofoam bat and every time a little kamikaze mechanical mole pops up grinning in one of the holes you cream him with your bat for a point. It's going to put you people out of business."

But she was laughing too hard to listen, and standing

on her toes and reaching for my neck with both arms and pulling my head down into a busy, slurpy kiss that didn't end until long after we had stumbled down the hallway and kicked shut the bedroom door.

When the telephone rang, Dinah stirred and wiggled one arm farther under the pillows. I sat up slowly and swung my legs over the side of the bed. The telephone kept ringing. Like a man wrapped in rubber bands, I hobbled across the cold floor to the table by the window and picked it up.

"Mike?"

I looked at the clock on the bureau. "It's four-thirty in the goddam morning, Fred."

My mouth was full of dead leaves and sticks, from navel to throat my body burned with a dull underground heat.

"Mike, a guy I know at Bryant Street just called me."

"Yeah." I lifted one arm, stiff like a plank, and pulled the curtain aside. Black overhead, black up and down the empty street.

"San Mateo Sheriffs office called Bryant Street, Mike. They found a body and they want a pickup in the city." I let the curtain swing back, whispering against wood. "They found Tock Maranian in his greenhouse, Mike."

My voice fell off the roof of my mouth in dry flakes. "Who do they want picked up?"

"Your notebook was in the greenhouse, Mike. The one you keep your mileage in." I turned my head and looked at the top of my bureau three feet away. Wallet, keys, pencil, watch, checkbook. While I had showered, Dinah had emptied my pockets and arranged them in a little mound. I always kept the notebook in the jacket next to the checkbook.

"It had your name and address, Mike. Half the cops in

San Francisco seen you write mileage in that notebook." His voice faded, came back louder, urgent. "Homicide called Yetta maybe fifteen minutes ago. They got to wake up a judge and get a warrant first. Don't do nothing but get dressed, Mike. Get your clothes on and get the hell out of there."

He hung up before I did and the click at his end sounded like a plop of water from the end of a faucet. The electronic buzz made Dinah turn and work her other arm under the blankets, a triangle of shadows up and down.

When I had dressed, I walked silently down the hallway, keeping my shoes on the center of the narrow runner, and went to my desk. From the bottom drawer I took out a green metal toolbox, opened it, and lifted a screwdriver and a roll of electrician's tape. The packet of fifties under the tape was held together by two pale rubber bands. I turned on the desk lamp, pushed back my battered Olympia portable—my tripewriter, Dinah's niece had once called it—and counted. Six hundred and fifty dollars, mad money. I picked up the memo pad that said "Mike Haller" in block letters across the top and started to write Dinah a note. Far away, past the close-up silence, down one of the slanting streets, I heard car motors grinding. I wrote her name, stopped. Thought of Yetta. Crumpled the paper into a ball.

As I came down the hallway again, she turned restlessly and moved her head into one of the shafts of chilly gray light coming from the sides of the curtain. A blossom floating on black water. I patted my jacket where the gun wasn't and opened the door onto Friday morning.

The headline in the *Chronicle* was about a guy accused of smuggling valuable poisonous snakes from the San Francisco Zoo to private collectors around the country. Not a word from San Mateo, not a syllable about a body.

I folded the paper on the counter and the man on the next stool let one dirty hand scratch along the corner of the green sports sheets while the first finger of the other hand continued to stir his muddy coffee. I nodded and he licked his lips at me as if he might speak, then simply took the paper.

There were eight men and two women spread out along the Formica counter. All of the men wore windbreakers and stubbles of beard, and all of them sat propped motionless over cups and plates, only occasionally rattling silverware or speaking softly to the cook behind the counter. One of the women wore an olive drab Army overcoat and sat with two paper shopping bags between her calves. The other wore a rabbit skin jacket, a red satin dress with a scooping neckline, and sat chewing gum and watching Van Ness Street struggle into the light. I was the only man in a sportscoat and button down shirt, but I hadn't shaved either and in the polished chrome strip above the stove my eyes looked as red-rimmed and wounded as everybody's else's.

I could turn myself in and call my lawyer. Depending on the judge and the precise charge I could be out by noon. Or in the basement of Bryant Street with half a million dollars of bail sitting on my shoulders. The Bee Will Make You Free.

Not me.

I touched one hand to my jacket again and the guy on my right slid his eyes toward my armpit and hunched down a little deeper into the paper. I looked at the congealing yellow eye of the egg on my plate. Looked out at the tungsten street lamp dropping a pale blue arc of light halfway over the humpbacked street. By the newspaper racks a cab was idling its motor while the driver stood in front of the hood, arms crossed, and stared at a black building. Yetta could haul her in as a material witness, I thought, but manhandling a female doctor like a drunk and disorderly was one fast way to kiss his captain's bars goodbye. He would storm up and down the apartment, he would rip every drawer from its socket and every book from its shelf, but he would let her go.

I put three dollars on the counter and stood up. The cabbie raised a face like a sheet of paper and watched me move toward the door. A cabbie would remember a fare this time of morning. I would walk to the East Bay Terminal, despite the cables of pain across my chest and back. I would either follow O'Farrell Street, straight through the Tenderloin, or go across Market, dodging the shadows and lowering my head at every black-and-white.

I crossed the street and headed for Market.

You stroll down San Pablo Avenue in the flatlands of Berkeley with your legs crossed and your jacket buttoned. You go past bank fronts better fortified than the Alamo, past rows of windows boarded up with plywood—Chinese laundries, secondhand clothes stores, dark, sticky-smelling bars with handpainted cardboard signs—everything and everybody open for business at seven in the morning. You walk around old men sitting on the sidewalk and shouting at the commuter traffic, around young men urinating against brick walls, around hookers in hot pants leaning against bead-curtained doorways, yawning and scratching an invitation, and pimps in leather and stainless steel spreading the fingers of one hand wide to study their rings, spreading the other hand, letting mud yellow eyes drift toward the pocket where your wallet would be. Once in a while, if you look up over a clutter of McDonald's arches, flat tenement roofs, and bony antennas, you will see the tall campanile of the University of California two miles away and rising out of a tranquil green and beige hillside. Up there young people in turtlenecks and Levi's skirts are about to start another day of worrying about Renaissance allegory and macroeconomics. Down on higher education's dirty hemline I was about to buy a car.

A '62 Ford car, wider than the *QE2*, with bigger fins than Moby Dick. I paid a fat man in a white shirt soaked gray with perspiration three hundred dollars for it. He wrote out temporary papers in the name of Edward Asbery, and I launched it south onto San Pablo, remembering my sunken Mercedes and Benny's demented face in the mirror. At Ashby I turned left and climbed a few struggling blocks until I reached the BART station's crowded, anonymous lot and parked. Diagonally across the street, next to the Paradise Parlor of Massage—"California Coeds," the sign in the window said—stood the open door and the three linked balls of Western Jewelry and Loan. I walked past a forty-year-old California coed sitting in a window seat with a flyswatter in one hand and entered the Western.

There was already a customer ahead of me, a lanky boy of about fifteen in an Army fatigue jacket and bell-bottom pants, his two fists working in the jacket pockets, his blonde hair frizzy except for a strip down the center dyed purple. Behind the glass-top counter an old man in a tee-shirt and a vest was staring down one end of a silver flute, holding it just above a polished wooden case lined with felt.

"Ten dollars," he told the boy.

"Mothafuck," the boy said.

The old man behind the counter sighed and looked at me and then tipped the flute around to stare down at the other end. Under the flute case the glass shelves were lined with watches, rings, knives of all shapes, tiny manicure sets zipped open, ceramic cases for cuff links, trinket jewelry. Behind the old man's head hung a row of electric guitars, flat and thick as nail files, varnished a slick apricot color and ornamented with sharp-pointed curlicues. Taped to one of the guitars was a large printed sign that said "Proof of Legal Ownership Required on All Loans. Calif. Code 1961-D-614." The old man looked at me again and I leaned heavily against a stretch of counter displaying brass cocktail shakers and electric clocks. My chest was a sea of pain.

"Fourteen dollars," the old man said and put the flute back in the case.

"Mothafuck," the kid said, but stood there still working his fists. The old man waited, and after a minute reached in his vest pocket and began to lick his fingers and count out dollar bills from a roll. When he had finished, the kid snatched the money off the counter, pushed me hard with one shoulder as he squeezed by, and disappeared onto the street.

"Conservatory student?" I asked.

The old man looked me over and brought up a cigar stub from somewhere beneath the counter. His face was lined with a few deep, criss-crossing wrinkles, like the palm of a hand.

"Yeah, he's a student at the goddam Juilliard," he said. "What the hell do you want?"

The gun cost me almost as much as the car, but it was fifteen years younger and as far as I could judge had been fired no more than a dozen times. "Retired schoolteacher's weapon," the old man had kept saying as he stroked its barrel and worked the safety. A hell of a way to correct papers, I thought; back to basics. It was probably stolen, of course. Most guns used in crimes in this country are stolen, usually from law-abiding homeowners who buy the things legally and stick them in the nightstand drawer as if their bedroom were the OK Corral. What they don't realize is that their NRA decal on the window is catnip to burglars, who fence to pawnshops and dealers, who sell in their turn to the criminal element at large. And *that*, according to Frank Yetta, Henry Sampson, and the state of California was what I had joined the moment I had slipped the pistol into my armpit holster.

I drove back across the Bay Bridge in my new Ford and worked the back streets from Geary past Golden Gate Park and into the dreariest, flattest section of the Sunset district, where I parked in front of a discouraged-looking Chinese restaurant and went in to meet Fred.

"I don't know why the hell you gotta pick this place," Fred said, staring over his shoulder at the empty tables and the one waiter folding paper napkins behind the cash register. "I'm not about to eat chow mein at ten o'clock in the morning." He put down the plastic coated menu and scowled at the plate of noodles and the cup of tea in front of him. "I don't like Chinese food," he said. "Three days later you're hungry again."

"And they serve a martini like an oil slick," I said. "But nobody else is going to come in at ten o'clock either." I took a sip of martini and a sip of tea. The pain had crept up my neck like a vine and into my eyes. My brain was a wad of gum under a chair. "It wasn't in the papers," I said.

"They're not sitting on it," Fred said. "It'll be in this afternoon or tomorrow. They found him in his greenhouse with a couple of spoonfuls of cyanide in his belly, which probably came from a jug of plant poison. The people all said he worked late most nights after they left. One of the lab girls came back around midnight to look at something in a test tube and saw the lights off in the middle greenhouse, where they're supposed to be on all the time. The one thing they probably won't put in the paper is that before somebody spooned in the poison his face had gotten a close shave."

I looked up in surprise. "He was a hell of a strong guy."

Fred poked a fork tentatively at the noodles. "When you're not expecting it, Mike, one of those things would rattle King Kong."

He meant what the street boys call Gillette knuckles, three razor blades taped to a wooden bridge and held between the fingers of a fist. Even a glancing blow will slice facial skin into fillets, not hurting so much as terrifying the victim. I saw Tock's wrinkled monkey-face dodging back, a fist looping out of the shadows again, bloody strips of flesh, Tock crashing among the heavy benches of the greenhouse, the tumbling pots of dirt and plants.

"He was your best suspect, Mike."

I lit a cigarette and looked out the restaurant window at the Ford. In the hazy morning sunlight it looked like an albino tuna.

"He had motive," Fred said, shaking his porkpie hat. "I really thought if you were going to hook up your license and the Contreras thing, he had to be the boy. I thought he smelled like the kind of guy would go into a bar on Eddy Street one day and find somebody who would contract on the girl for lunch money. I was taught motive first, last, and always."

"And now?"

He held the palm of one hand out flat, as if he were playing a card. "Chick Gannett?" he said. "You never followed up whether he moved or not. A punk kid like that would use razors."

I mumbled something I didn't quite hear myself and rolled the cigarette along the rim of the ashtray. My mind made a funny leap, dodging the headache. Asbery had no children, according to my lawyer, who had three teenaged daughters of his own. "Daughters are a consolation," my lawyer had said in his mock literary way, sucking loudly on his pipe. "Daughters are a consolation for marriage," he had added after a moment.

"You can't do it, Mike," Fred said, leaning forward and speaking more quickly and intensely than I ever remembered him doing. "You got too many cops in this town know your mug. That piece of scrap metal you're driving now has got papers on it that go to the DMV today; three days later you're on the stop list. This is a small town, Mike. You can't investigate a murder when you're running away from Yetta and every black-and-white comes down the block." He slowed down and leaned back. "Your lawyer gets the thing reduced from murder one to material witness with his hands behind his back."

"Maybe," I said. "Or maybe Yetta fights bail and I move into Bryant Street."

Fred lifted a forkful of noodles halfway to his mouth, stared and replaced it carefully on the plate like a divot.

"You're a damn good investigator, Mike," he said in his lecture voice. "You get inside people sometimes and lose your skin, and you can talk to people I want to spit at. You can talk to some queen down on Castro Street with a Cheerio in his ear, and you can go talk books with a three-piece lawyer like Asbery. I can't do that," he said, wagging his face and making the old man's loose flesh wobble. "But I know the streets like you never will, and you don't want me to say it, but I'm a cop and you're not and never were, and I'm a much more logical guy than you are. You do missing persons so good because you're not logical. You're . . . intuitive," he said, rubbing his thick fingers together for the word. "You snag people the damnedest ways. I've seen you pick up something casual in a case—like a guy's hobby or the way somebody tells you he orders a drink—and you turn it into a hook. You don't track people down as much as you kind of cast your hook out where you think they'll be, and that's fine for figuring out people that get sick of life one morning and bugger off to Reno. That won't solve a goddam murder." He picked up his white egg-shaped teacup and blew on it. "Besides, you're so up and down over the goddam license you can't keep your mind on your fanny."

"How long before Yetta's people pick me up?"

He shrugged and slurped brown tea. "They're looking. If you go home to change shirts or go to your office, they'll take you. You hang around dumps like this and stay away from downtown, maybe two or three days." He finished the tea and read the bill. "I talked to Dinah like you wanted," he said. "Yetta took her in and questioned her, but they let her go after a couple of hours. Yetta can't treat a class woman like he can treat you. They'll be watching her, of course."

Still reading the bill, he pulled out a cigar long enough to be a walking stick and said without looking up at me, "I see you got a new piece for the shoulder holster." I went back to the martini and shoved him a book of matches. "I hope to hell you went over to the East Bay or somewhere to get it," he said "because Yetta is going to be standing on top of the goddam pawnshops around here." He licked the end of the cigar and struck one of the matches. "Guy in a bar told me the only way to get gun control in this country would be to shoot a congressman a day until they passed a law. He figured it'd still take about six weeks."

I reached in my jacket pocket on the other side of the holster and pulled out the four yellow pages I had clipped from the telephone booth outside.

"Ballet classes," I said. "You take A-K."

CHAPTER 19

I T WASN'T THE MAGAÑA BELLY DANCE CENTRE.
And it wasn't the San Francisco Conservatory of Ballet.

I called six more dance schools from the restaurant's pay phone before customers drifting in began to look curiously at my stack of change and spread-out yellow pages. Nobody notices a man who isn't there. I pocketed the money and tried the booth at the corner of the block.

The Smith Studio of Classical Dance had no student named Christie, didn't give classes at night, and informed me testily that they ran a dance school, not an escort bureau. I ran a pencil line through the name and looked up from the next entry to see a black-and-white lazily riding the current toward me. Fold the yellow pages and crease them. Put them in your inside jacket pocket. Wiggle a finger in the coin slot. Walk. Walk at a normal pace back to the Ford. The black-and-white slowed and turned at the corner. Exhale like a harpooned whale.

I slouched into the Ford, still trembling, and lit a cigarette off its coil lighter. In a store window across the street, beneath a whitewash sign that said "The Best and the Brightest—50% Off," a bald man was arranging a display of floor lamps. Farther down the block two girls wearing dark blue parochial school uniforms were sitting on a concrete bench by a bus stop. One girl was holding a stopwatch over a lapful of books. The other girl, using all her fingers at once, was twirling a Rubik's cube in a blur of colors.

I started the Ford with three pumps of the gas and three turns of the key and sat staring at nothing. Sleepy, dirty, unshaven. Fifty percent off. An uprooted flower child. The next black-and-white might have an observant cop at the wheel. The next edition of the paper might have my photo and a caption in ninety-point type that said "Have You Seen This Man?" I could wait until evening, I thought, just driving from phone booth to phone booth, going through the motions, and then send Fred to the Club Eden to find her. But one of Slam and Dunk's erotic stormtroopers might still be keeping an eye on Christie's visitors. And Christie might not talk to Fred. And Christie might have the night off.

The two schoolgirls on the bench had exchanged stopwatch and Rubik's cube. For my best time with the cube you would have needed a calendar. I wrestled the Ford into first gear and joined the bump and grind west on Santiago, sniffing toward Ocean Beach and the giant range of fog mountains building on the horizon. At one o'clock I had a hamburger and a root beer at a drive-in between Lake Merced and a bleak low-income housing development that looked out on two private golf courses. "The golf links lie so near the mill," I quoted to myself, a jingle from a New England childhood, "That almost every day/The laboring children can look out/ And see the men at play." At three o'clock I had called all of my schools, L-Z, and gotten nothing, not even a song and dance.

I copied the numbers of the public school extension classes as a last resort and squeezed the Ford into a space on Sloat Boulevard outside the main gate to the zoo. At four-thirty, in front of the brown bears, I met Dinah.

"I should feed your carcass to the grizzlies," she said, planting herself in front of me, face bright. She wore a tailored brown suit and a quilted red Chinese jacket, and she hunched her shoulders high against the cold foggy air so that the collar of the jacket framed the angry flush on her cheeks. "Lieutenant Frank Yetta practically tore the door down at five o'clock this morning and hauled me off to a terrible smelly little room in the Hall of Justice Building. If your lawyer Raggio hadn't poured some of his oil on Yetta, I could still be there."

I sat down on the bench in front of the bear pit and waved a hand weakly. "Fred was supposed to explain," I said, then stopped. The pain had started again in my belly, smouldering in my lungs, making me swallow with every other breath.

She sat down abruptly beside me, lips thin, voice softening. "He did. I know. I missed a staff meeting and two patients and I left another meeting early to come here. No," she said as I raised my head, "I wasn't followed."

I looked down the asphalt path toward the new monkey cages and the pre-cast concrete bulge of the reptile house where the man had been caught yesterday smuggling poisonous snakes to collectors. What kind of person collected snakes? I would ask Arthur when I saw him. "I started to write you a note in the apartment," I said, "then I figured it wouldn't help to have Yetta find it first."

She continued to hold herself rigidly on the bench, looking to her right, where a few people had gathered to watch the polar bear rock back and forth in his pool of fishy water. "I suppose I should make a citizen's arrest or something," she said.

"Your picture's in the afternoon paper. Mendelsohn brought it into the cafeteria and showed me. They found your car too, halfway under Pier 30, completely ruined—that was in the same story, and Raggio made Yetta admit that the notebook could have fallen out earlier in the day and you could be a victim instead of a suspect. He said the law distinguishes between suspicion of homicide and homicide itself and Yetta said the law was an ass and Raggio said what did that make somebody who was sworn to uphold the law and Fred said a toilet seat and got thrown out of the office." She took a deep breath. "Fred was just fiercely loyal to you," she said. "He would have been thrown out right away if he hadn't been an ex-cop."

"I put him in a spot," I said to the back of her head. "He covered for me once. He can't do it again." I stopped to swallow more lava.

"Are you going to call Yetta?" she asked, turning her face to me and peering over the collar. I shook my head. "Are you going to call your lawyer?"

I smiled through my chin stubble and the polar bear splashed the squealing crowd with a pawful of water. My lawyer ran a quiet, low-key office just off Montgomery Street, drawing up papers for people who wanted to incorporate a business, drawing up papers for some of the same people who wanted to declare bankruptcy. His most exciting legal case had been in 1969, when a fat man without the right change had gotten stuck under a pay toilet door in a downtown hotel and sued the city. He did my business so he would have something to talk about back home in Moraga every evening. When I had called at nine o'clock that morning he had practically jumped down the telephone.

"He's an officer of the court," I said. "He can't counsel me unless I'm willing to turn myself in."

She sighed and put one finger against my cheek, drilling gently just above the corner of my mouth, a gesture of delicate exasperation.

"Which you're not going to do," she said.

I didn't answer. Above the bear cages rose the spindly necks of the dredging cranes on Ocean Beach Highway, hauling sand back to the beach in an effort to make the world safe for condominiums. I shivered and Dinah looked me over with a professional opaqueness in her eyes.

"You're probably stiff as a board today," she said. I pulled a tiny bag of roasted peanuts from my jacket pocket and offered it to her. She smiled wanly. "My brother has a fellow accountant in El Cerrito he wants me to meet," she said. "A nice bachelor with his own business and a tract house on a hill and no warrant out for his arrest."

I looked at her round face and red jacket. I closed my eyes and I could still see the elegant white neck and the lines of dark red hair on the nape. Does the loss of one thing lead to the loss of others? When one fear gets a toehold, do all our other fears come swarming to join it like predatory insects?

She took the bag of peanuts and pulled on my elbow. "Let's go see the other monkeys," she said.

She wanted me to go to Asbery.

"I tried that, too," I said. A siamang gibbon with flat yellow teeth held up one of the peanuts between leathery fingers and screeched something complex and rude. A group of Japanese tourists laughed uproariously and swivelled their heads to see if I'd answer. "I drove up to his house in Pacific Heights at one-forty-five—the office said he hadn't come in today—and at one-forty-eight I was backing down the steps and Asbery was telling me that he could be disbarred just for talking to me."

"I don't like him," Dinah said stubbornly. "He's cheating on his wife, and he has a sexist manner. I thought from the minute I saw him that you ought to check out everything he told you."

"He was with me last night," I said. "And before that he was in a public restaurant with Margot. Tock left them and went back to Palo Alto and got killed there while Asbery was soaking up malt scotch in my living room. You saw him yourself."

"Did you check the restaurant he said they were at?" I looked at the gibbon, who scratched his head and puckered his lips. "He could be making off with the Maranian estate," she said; "he could have been robbing Tock."

I shook my head impatiently. "Come on with the wild guesses, Dinah. Half the lawyers in San Francisco know him. The guy is bonded up to his Harvard tie in order to be executor of the estate. He can't be skimming."

"Did you check his bond?" she asked. I flipped a peanut into the air and worked a muscle in the side of my jaw. They will routinely waive the bond for lawyers with ten years' practice, I had found out. "You like him," she said. "You don't want to think about him because you like him so much."

"I don't like him. He's arrogant and aloof and has a cruel streak right down the center."

"He's also extremely intelligent, you said. And resourceful. And he makes word games the way you do—you told me. He talks like the Dean of Harvard Law School and something in you still likes that type of man. He's some version of yourself. What you might have been if you hadn't dropped out of college and run off to be a Bohemian."

"Everybody is some version of yourself," I said irritably. My stomach was curling over like a leaf in a fireplace, and I didn't see why I was standing in the goddam San Francisco zoo and arguing about my subconscious.

"Not everybody specializes in tracking down missing persons," she said.

I pulled out a cigarette and over cupped hands followed the clouds of fog pumping out of the Pacific two blocks away. My eyes burned. The wind vaulted over the sea wall and the highway and began to tug Dinah's red hair into wisps of flame.

"Shrinks certainly cut a man down to size," I said. She drew in her breath sharply, and I turned to her in more pain than ever.

"I didn't mean that," I said. "I'm acting like a two-year-old when his toy's been taken away. I'm sorry."

She shoved her hands in the pockets of the red jacket and the gibbon muttered something about selfish clods. "Losing your license to work is not just losing a toy," she said finally. "Come on and walk me to my car."

We passed a security guard at the entrance who had unfolded the afternoon *Constitution* on a glass-topped counter. I glimpsed the name Maranian, but no picture of me before we hurried out onto Sloat Boulevard and into the full force of the wind. The guard never looked up.

"I left the Velveeta-mobile right there," Dinah said, pointing toward her bright yellow VW bug. I opened the door for her and squinted over the roof to make out the whitecaps at the end of the block, sliding under the curtain of fog and scattering toward land. The zoo lies at the southern base of the old Outside Lands, reclaimed from the sand dunes along with Golden Gate Park. From its western border the cold, gray ledge of Ocean Beach leads up through the sea-rocks to the Cliff House, the old Sutro Baths, and the northwest rim of the peninsula. And just opposite the gate, like the state totem of California, stands the twenty-foot-high maroon plastic head of a dachshund wearing a white chef's hat, and underneath it a sign: "Doggie Diner."

"'Roll on, thou goddam Ocean, roll,'" I said, quoting Byron.

Dinah stood between the open door and the car and held her face up to the wind. "You're still going to try to find this Muriel woman, even though everybody including the police is telling you to stop?"

"I have one more possibility," I said. "After that, if I have to I'll go to see Yetta."

"You don't know about Dr. Stanley Milgram's famous experiment," Dinah said.

"No, but I saw the movie."

"He was a Yale psychologist. He devised an experiment where volunteers were taken into a laboratory room and ordered to administer electric shocks to other volunteers behind a big glass panel. The ones getting the shocks were really actors Milgram had hired from New York, and there was no electricity. But the actors yelled and jumped and pleaded with them not to do it."

"And?"

"And about seventy percent of the volunteers went ahead and pulled the electricity lever anyway."

"Because people are naturally cruel?"

"No, because Dr. Milgram looked like a man with authority. He ordered them to do it and they did. Scientists all over the country repeated the experiment dozens of times. They couldn't believe that people—Americans—would cave in to authority so easily. But the results were always the same: seventy percent obeyed the man in charge."

I leaned my forearms across the top of the car door and

watched a seagull glide into the fog and disappear. "What about the other thirty percent?" I said. I didn't want to hear Fred's lectures or Dinah's psychology stories. I wanted to find Muriel Contreras and see if the Nilsson brothers came scuttling out of their horny shells. I wanted to take whoever had killed Leo Matz and snap him across my knee like a stick of kindling.

"Nobody knows why they defied authority," she said. She caught my ears with both hands and pulled me forward, kissed me hard and sat down in the car. "You tell me, sugar-cake," she said.

CHAPTER 20

FRED HAD THREE POSSIBILITIES ON HIS LIST. The first turned out to be an extra-credit high school class in the Twin Peaks section of the city, run by a fat woman in a gray sweat suit who blocked the doorway and stood on her toes to prevent our peeping at the girls. Behind her the girls had also stood on their toes and giggled. Her Christie was fifteen, wore braces on her teeth, and had a smile like a hubcap.

The second one was on the other side of the city again, out the avenues toward the ocean, deep in a neighborhood of oriental restaurants and overcrowded apartments.

"It's eight o'clock," Fred said, folding up the map, "and the carburetor on this goddam boat you bought is gonna take a pistol to its head if you try any more hills."

I got into line on Divisadero and started north toward Geary.

"You look like hell, too," he said. I rubbed one hand over my chin, more or less smoothed two hours earlier by Fred's electric razor, and grunted. I was neat, clean, shaved and sober, and I didn't care who knew it. "Yetta called me up before I left," he said after a few more blocks. "He told me he'd reduce the charge to material witness if you came in by noon tomorrow."

"With what Yetta told you and fifty cents you can get a ride on the bus," I said.

He stared down the barrel of a new cigar and shrugged. We had had the same conversation over and over since six o'clock, when he had shaken Yetta's clumsy tail to his satisfaction and picked me up at a Lombard Street motel. I turned left above Golden Gate Park and started to look for street numbers. When we reached it, two blocks south of Geary, the signs said "Song of Thailand Restaurant" on the ground floor and on the second, under a crude black and white drawing of a man hitting a brick, "San Francisco Studio of Marital Arts."

"My wife always said 'marital arts,' too," Fred muttered as we climbed long narrow stairs. "I told her marital arts was hitting below the belt." We walked into a room with gym pads littered across a raised hardwood floor and kids in crisp white karate outfits ripping warmup blows at the air. A Korean man about my age, but wider, taller, stronger, detached himself from the students like the cab of a Mack truck and rolled toward us with a half smile on his face and a black belt on his waist. Beyond the karate students, in a far corner of the big room lined with mirrors and handrails, half a dozen women in pastel-colored leotards were stuffing clothes into canvas bags and repacking a portable record player.

"You want karate lessons, please?" the Korean asked.

Over his shoulder I saw a mane of metallic blonde hair bobbing up and down in a mirror. He followed my eyes and said in the same polite singsong, "Dance class over now. Men only. Tae kwan do class next. You want karate lessons, please?"

Fred started to explain and I walked half a mile around his massive left shoulder, not quite breaking into a run, and headed up to the group of women.

Most of them were in their late twenties or early thirties and had the air of serious exercisers, students or nurses or young mothers whose bodies were beginning to feel the pull of time and gravity and who didn't mind the inartistic atmosphere of a cut-rate gym. At the other end of the room a gray-haired woman wearing thick white ankle socks around her tights looked up from the record player, and beside her a moon-faced chubby woman in purple crossed her arms and frowned. The others continued to pack their canvas bags and the blonde head with the long, straight back to me went right on bobbing.

"Help you?" the gray-haired woman said. The chubby woman pulled her arms tighter. Behind me an adolescent voice yelling a karate cry suddenly skidded up the register into a Henry Aldrich squawk, and several of the women smiled, looking at me, looking away. In the mirrors Christie's face bobbed up, looked straight ahead at my reflection and bobbed down again.

I gestured and said something with her name in it, and except for moon-face the women lost interest and stepped aside.

Christie kept bobbing. I hadn't really expected to find her, I realized; and I didn't know what the hell to say—half of my mind was still driving compulsively back and forth across the city, grinding out fantasies of persecution and revenge; the other half was automatically wedging me into the corner of the mirrors, facing her and the whole expanse of the makeshift gym, and cranking a smile up from somewhere.

"Hello, Christie."

"Michael Haller," she said at the top of her deep knee bend, keeping her eyes on herself in the mirror, keeping her smile small but amused. "I'm supposed to be surprised, right?" I remembered the heart-shaped face, the peroxide hair now clinging in damp patches to her temples and brow, but I had forgotten the expression of poised intelligence at odds with the brass voice and the muscular, high-breasted body. I had not forgotten the muscular, high-breasted body.

"You told me you took dance lessons," I said, trying to match her casualness. You do not stampede your last reason to stay out of jail. You do not push just because the next guy through the door could be wearing blue serge and announcing police services. "I went through the phone book calling studios and asking if they had students named Christie. You should have let me follow you home."

She moved the smile up a fraction. "Piers Nilsson the boss himself came down to see me at the club about you," she said in the same calm voice. "And then you don't show up the next night like I kind of figured you would, and Tony the bouncer tells me you got warned off." She took a breath and went down, parting her knees a little and twisting the thin lips in concentration. "Ten minutes later, detective man, and you would of missed me for sure. This class only meets twice a week, and we don't ever stay this late unless Bruce Lee over there's in a good mood."

I raised my eyes for a moment to see the ballet dancers shrugging themselves into jackets and sweatshirts as they moved in a group toward the exit, and halfway across the room Fred standing with his hands in his pockets, porkpie hat tilted toward the talkative Korean. Moon-face walked past them, staring back at me and whispering something to the gray-haired woman.

"I need to see Muriel Contreras, Christie. Things have changed, there's more money in the inheritance now, I came this soon to ask you to help—"

I stopped abruptly because I was talking too fast and because Christie was beginning to close her eyes and bite her smile. Somebody who dances five nights a week at the Club Eden would not want strange men to rush her, to push demands.

"Let me finish these first," she said, blinking back to me when I grew quiet. "I always do fifty of them after the lessons. If you're long-waisted like I am, you've got to keep the old thighs from turning into watermelons." She went down again, not unconscious of me, and I glimpsed dark strands of pubic hair curling under the seams of her leotard, nipples half-flattened by the pressure of cloth. Love is blind: lust is bug-eyed.

"Two more," she said, tossing her hair.

There is a standard procedure in looking for people like Muriel Contreras, I reminded myself. You go to the places they are known to go, and you tear a fifty dollar bill in two and give one half to somebody who hangs around that place, a clerk, a ticket-taker, a regular; the other half of the bill is theirs when they call in with a number or address. Christie flicked her eyes at me and pumped down again. I thought if I tried to offer her money she would turn her face back to arctic and walk away. I gripped the dancer's balance bar and thought that if I made a pass at her my queasy belly would turn to floor wax.

"I told Piers Nilsson you wanted a date," she said, finishing the deep knee bend with a gymnast's little spring and positioning herself a foot away from me. "The bouncer made me give him the card with your name on it, but I didn't say anything about Muriel."

"What did Piers say?"

She looked down her chest and used both hands to knead the pink roll just above her pelvis. Not deliberately provocative, I thought, not on the make for the irresistible clean-shaven Haller, but one of those women whose hands are always full of flesh.

"He was nice, for him. He said he didn't want any kind of cops in his places and for me to tell him if you ever came back." She turned and stooped to pick up the last canvas bag and pull out a wraparound skirt and a denim jacket, her spine stretched out like a knotted cord under the pink cloth. "I told Muriel," she said. "I told her you hadn't pushed and you had nice eyes." She turned around to face me again, face somber, hands working the skirt around her hips and buttoning. Back of her, Fred was inspecting two teenage boys as they advanced on each other with a flurry of kicks and snapping sleeves. "Muriel is in real bad shape, Mike Haller," she said. Canvas sandals replaced the dancing shoes. "She's been sitting in her place all alone for two weeks now, with her dope in one hand and her *TV Guide* in the other. She won't eat, she won't go out."

"Can I see her, Christie?"

"You look terrible," she said, making a last hitch of the skirt and gathering up the bag.

"Can you get her to see me tomorrow?"

"She won't talk to you. She won't talk to any man. She's scared to death of men. You work in a scumbag place like the Club goddam Eden, Mike Haller, and you either get so scared of men that you turn into a vegetable with tits or you get to hate them so much you can literally feel it, every time you prance your ass out on that two-by-four stage and spread your legs. Look at them," she said with a jerk of the head. Two lines of white-clad boys were growling and stamping the floor in rhythmic hieroglyphic patterns, thrusting stiff fingers and feet at each other with rapid, angular blows. "If they're not born with it, they learn it as soon as the daddies get hold of them. We got eight women come here twice a week to dance in front of mirrors. The rest of the week you got every goddam adolescent boy in San Francisco in here learning spiritual perfection and how to put a foot through somebody's crotch. I gotta leave for an appointment."

She swung the canvas bag over her shoulder and started for the exit. Fred read my face and disappeared down the stairs.

"She would talk to a woman," Christie said, stopping suddenly. Ten feet away boys kicked and counter-kicked, slapped and grunted in spiritual perfection. "You got a woman partner, Mike Haller? Muriel needs help. I don't want her to lose any money she's got coming, but she's not going to talk to a man, not a man alone."

I took a deep breath. A warm spot at the back of my neck spread over my ears and cheeks and made my eyes water. I saw a bright, angry face superimposed on my empty office.

"There's a woman she can talk to first," I said. "A doctor I know."

Christie stood tapping her sandal for a moment, head cocked to one side. Then she reached into the canvas bag, fumbled with one hand, and came up with a tiny blue dime store notebook.

"Write her address down. I go to work at one tomorrow. Say I'll bring Muriel at eleven. You better be straight, Mike Haller, or she'll bolt and you'll never see her again, not ever in this world."

I wrote Dinah's home address on the first sheet of the notebook and gave it back. She dropped it into the bag without looking and turned for the stairs. As I started to follow the door swung open and Fred clambered up toward me, flapping one hand hard to shoo me back and mumbling excuses to Christie hurrying past.

"Look for a back way out," he hissed. "Some goddam broad is talking to a black-and-white outside." I spun and sprinted for the EXIT sign at the other end of the gym. Behind me Fred was calling out how to reach him later, but I was already elbowing a yellow belt to one side and plunging down the darkened stairs, dropping like a stone through a lake to the black alley below.

CHAPTER 21

"COME ON, MAN, WILL SHE OR WON'T SHE?" I put the telephone receiver back on the wall, picked up my cigarette from the ashtray, and turned around slowly to six menacing black faces lined up along the counter. The seventh black face in the room belonged to Grab, and he was slouched in his usual boneless way into the corner of a wooden booth and grinning. The Down Home Deli had three more telephones in the storage room—specially altered to flash lights instead of ring, and permanently connected to a phone booth by Golden Gate Fields—but not even Grab trusted me enough to be alone in there. At best one of the regulars would stand near the windows watching for patrolmen.

"That man got himself a redheaded fox," he told the others. They stared at me as if I were a scorpion that had crawled out of the wall. "She kinda short and kinda flat, but she the main one for—how long, man? Four years?" He lifted a paper bag from the table top to his lips and took a long, luxurious swallow. Inside the bag would be a bottle of Chivas Regal, the only whiskey Grab will drink. "The slicker likker," he had once told me.

They could use it for their next ad campaign in *The New Yorker.* He thumped the paper bag back on the table and uncoiled from the booth a vertebra at a time, pausing at various stages to inspect his silver calf-length leather raincoat and to pat the red feathers into place on the ostrich skin boots. Over the raincoat lapels, drooping shyly like stowaway daffodils, peeked two flared yellow collar points.

"You look like the goddam daughter of the rainbow, Grab," I said.

He shook himself straight and held out the front of the coat as if to air it, collecting everyone's attention.

"When you first come to the city, Haller, you moving with all *kinds* of action, man. I seen you around some *talent.* Then you just kinda poop out, man. Now you might as well be married, the way she got you hopping." He cocked his head toward the ceiling and threw his voice into a falsetto. "Gotta call my fox, Grab, gotta ask her permission can I stay out late." He snapped out his left hand without looking at it, and one of the men at the delicatessen counter handed him a black felt five-gallon hat decorated with a madras hatband and another red feather. Stetson hats were originally manufactured in Philadelphia, I could tell him, and were about as wild west as English muffins. Another piece of useless Haller information. In jail I would write books and articles on trivia.

"So is she cool?" he asked again.

I nodded. Dinah had protested, insisted that I call my lawyer too and see Yetta if she didn't show, but finally had agreed to cancel her appointments and wait for Christie. I would stay outside her building for at least half an hour, she said, or until she appeared at the window as a signal. Then I could come up and for the first time actually speak to Muriel Contreras.

"Time to split, Haller baby."

I shrugged my shoulders once defensively and walked along the row of stools, past the faces set in cement and their physical air of intimidation, and joined Grab at the door to Eddy Street. While I stood back from the light, he stepped outside, fingered the brim of his hat and glanced up and down. Across the street, in the plasterboard lobby of a welfare hotel, an old woman leaned around an aluminum walker and stared bleakly at us. Nearby, assorted shapes and shadows were blowing softly like scraps of paper, in and out of narrow doorways, down the mouths of alleys. In daylight, an English friend had once said, big city American streets look like deep, fortified canyons; at night like illuminated sewers.

"No bacon," Grab said. "Not even on the hoof. Nobody here but broken-down whores and junkies. The pigs been laying off the whole Tenderloin the last two weeks, so we must be in between elections, am I right? Eddy Street just one big sore waiting to be scratched, you know? Come on and walk down the street, Haller baby, you OK."

He led me two blocks west and turned up Hyde, stopping once or twice to look hard at a car or a distant figure silhouetted in the streetlights. A vivid, dangerous figure himself, enjoying his power over me on the street, holding himself casually, with a slight stoop in the metallic raincoat, as sharp-edged and amoral as a razor. Then he turned again, walked thirty feet down a fetid alley the width of a clothes hanger and pushed open the service door in a brick building.

"This gonna cost you, Haller, you know that?" he puffed as we started up the stairs, one bulb at the top of each landing, ankle deep in litter. "You come poppin' up eleven o'clock at night looking like some kind of Geritol commercial and talkin' about how the Man comin' down on you, it's gotta cost you." He stopped at a landing and looked down at me while his shadow swooped and swam across the gray walls behind him. He adjusted the brim of the gigantic hat again and showed a mouth of brilliant white predatory teeth. "I give you credit for now, Haller, but when I bring the bill around it gonna *hurt,* man, it damn near gonna kill you."

"Just get me off the street, Grab. I don't need the Holiday Inn."

"Shit, man, I'm gonna put you up in style. Old Grab run an underground railroad for the brothers, man, but I'm gonna put you in the Pullman."

He dug out a ring of keys from the raincoat and began searching through them. I stood silently and waited. It had taken me almost two hours to stumble out of the labyrinth of streets and hillside pathways back of the karate gym and then to thread my way down O'Farrell and Eddy to the delicatessen, the nearest thing Grab had to an office. Another hour for one of the countermen to reach him and bring him around. My chest and belly no longer burned with old layers of pain, but in the chilly night air my legs had turned to rubbery stalks and my eyes blurred with exhaustion. Grab twisted a key with a flourish and pushed open a door that had no name and no number.

"That one is Charlie Sleeve," he said, kicking the door shut behind us and pointing through a murky room to a black man behind a bar and aluminum sink. Incense, or perfume, or disky clouds of tobacco and marijuana smoke hung against bamboo patterned wallpaper. "And that one over there you already know. Make my man a Chivas, Charlie," he said, snapping fingers, "*after* you make mine."

The one I knew was the nun, the soul sister, now costumed in a pop-top Hawaiian gown, sitting on one of three oversized couches in the room and speaking into a red telephone. Nearby stood two stereo speakers the size of ice cream wagons and scattered around them half a dozen enormous cushions covered in radioactive fabrics. The rug was big enough to have fit in Edward Asbery's office, but the design just missed being Harvard Yard: long swirls of chocolate, yellow, and white spiraling into irregular, glittering borders; a junkie's eye view of the Milky Way.

Grab strutted over to the nearest couch, turned, and sprawled lazily onto it, like a brown egg dropping into a skillet.

"I knocked down two apartment walls in this rathole," Grab said. "Made one big ranch. I got nine rooms up here, I got half the top floor of this whole building, and nobody knows I got it, 'cept the brothers I stash while the Man downstairs. I tried living out in Hayward one time, in the mothafucking, lawn-mowing suburbs, but, hey man, I gotta be downtown, you know?"

Charlie Sleeve brought him the Chivas and straightened to look me over before going back to the bar. A black man about my height, balding, broad across the shoulders but running to pudgy, the lower half of his shirt ballooning with fat and giving a gentle, effeminate waddle to his walk. When he reached the overhead light at the small bar I could see that his right sleeve was buttoned and sewn around a stump where his hand should be.

Grab followed my eyes. "Charlie kind of retired since he had his accident," he said. "Sit down, man, you ain't going nowhere, sit down." I took a chair next to Grab's couch and Charlie carried me a highball glass filled with six inches of oak-colored liquid and two oblong pieces of ice. The woman on the telephone twisted so that her back was to us and Charlie waddled back to the bar.

"He kinda like you," Grab said. "He got kicked out of his chosen profession too, except they was more to it than kicking. Old Charlie he used to be a showtime burglar—name Charlie Warren then—you dig?" I nodded and siphoned off an inch of scotch. A showtime burglar operated by sending potential victims phony promotion letters from public relations firms and free pairs of tickets—to movies, to car shows, to ball games—to anything at all that would get them out of the house or apartment at a specified time.

"Old Charlie made the mistake of sending his tickets to some *bad* Italian dude just moved in a condominium in Ocean View. But the dude come back early—he give the tickets to somebody else—and he kinda lose his temper and hold Charlie's fist down the new garbage disposal in the kitchen sink while another Italian dude turn it on. He say that the *last* time Charlie put his hand on *his* shit."

"I need a car tomorrow morning, Grab. Can you do that too?"

The woman at the telephone cradled it loudly and stood up, arching her back so that the folds of the Hawaiian gown swept the rug at her heels.

"She wants to know when you gonna send around that stuff you promised, Grab." For some reason Grab seemed to like having me there and playing his version of the attentive host. He pushed a dismissing hand in her direction and swallowed scotch. The woman glowered for a moment, then turned and stamped through a bead-curtained doorway behind the couch. A second or two later the big speakers in each corner popped to life and began to churn out the clotted sounds of electric guitar chords and a background chorus of shrill female voices.

"You like that shit?" Grab asked over the din.

I shook my head. "It sounds like a duck gargling ball bearings," I said, and he chuckled and cakewalked over to the curtain, where he disappeared for a moment. The music faded to a grumble.

"You do say what you mean, Haller baby," he said, returning and flopping back on the couch. "Lot of white boys be sitting there with they legs crossed twice and watching every which way for the bad black boogie man. But you the same uptight asshole to everybody. Charlie don't like soul music either," he said, wagging his head once in that direction. "Charlie even took a fox to the Fairmont one time to hear Frank Sinatra—back when he had his hair and his figure and those sweet-snapping fingers. Italians put him out of another job, too, you know. Sure, Charlie, you used to be a free-lance cocksman, star in X-rated movies right here in San Francisco. Charlie used to do some rough shows, Haller baby, whip the white girls with a stick, but nobody want a fat one-handed nigger in the movies now."

"The car, Grab."

"Get me another drink, Charlie." Grab unbuttoned the raincoat with an expansive, lordly gesture. I listened to angry voices rattling behind the curtain.

"You gonna need to make some money to pay for all this good service, Sherlock," Grab said over the rim of his refill. "Maybe you better do what Charlie used to do, go down to Kaiser Hospital tomorrow morning and donate to the sperm bank, man. Twenty-five dollars cash." He leaned forward, grinning broadly. "But for that job, baby, you know you gotta have *pull*." And he roared back against the couch, splashing Chivas Regal down the arm and shaking his head from side to side with laughter.

Charlie Sleeve walked between us and exited down the hallway.

Grab's face recovered its usual hard expression in an instant as he watched the beads swing to and fro along the edge of the rug.

"You know what the saddest words in the world are, man?"

I was tired of Grab's boisterous aggression. I was tired and frightened and out of my world, and I wanted to cut him short.

"Yeah. Prices slightly higher in California." I sank my glass into the shaggy rug. "Cut out this garbage, Grab. I want to go to bed. I want to get set up for tomorrow."

"'I wish I was white,'" Grab said. "Those the saddest words in the world."

I sat hesitating on the edge of the chair, hearing the little waves of free-floating middle-class white guilt hiss and gather in my ears.

"I'm not talking no black is beautiful shit," he said. "I'm talking about realistic, man. I'm talking about knowing black is *bad* in this country and you ain't gonna change that if you march for the next century, man. Charlie don't see that. That's why I'm always on his ass. Moaning about his white women in those stud flicks and white jazz music, man, and conking out that good frizzy hair when he had it." He tipped the glass up and let the scotch drain into his mouth. "I get you a car tomorrow," he said when I finally stood up. "Go on down the hall, take any room you want."

I had reached the beads before he said in his familiar jive voice, "Money is *green,* man. Ain't black or white."

I took the last room I could find along the darkened hallway, far from the occasional whoops and shouts of Grab and the woman and Charlie Sleeve. It had a bed, a bureau and a mirror, an easy chair, and a closet stacked high with Zenith television sets still in their boxes. Too weary to lie down, I lit one more cigarette and leaned against the window pane and thought how impenetrable and how unpredictable human character was. I had long ago guessed at the subtle intelligence Grab manipulated under the pimpster's gaudy act. But I would not have guessed how eagerly he would put me under friendly obligations, or how near the surface and still internalized his wounds were. For that matter, I thought wryly, grinding out the half-smoked cigarette, I wouldn't have guessed how violently the loss of the license would derail my ego, or how impatient Dinah would become when stability started to turn over into dependence. A personality is only a front door to a city. These violent delights have violent ends. Hamlet, King Lear, somebody. I closed the curtain on the city and climbed fully clothed into bed. Down the hall the black woman's voice suddenly rose in anger: "You know what having a baby feels like, man? It feels like shitting a pumpkin!" Then sirens coursing through the Tenderloin drowned out his reply.

CHAPTER 22

KNOW THAT MAN," CHARLIE SLEEVE SAID.

"Say what?" Grab said.

"That man driving that car." He pointed the coffee cup in his left hand toward the back of a late model sedan turning left on Hayes. "He was in one of the movies."

"With you?" Grab asked contemptuously.

"Never mind," Charlie said and relapsed into sullenness.

"Somebody done shot the spots off your dice, Charlie baby," Grab said. He dipped one hand into my shirt pocket and came up with a cigarette, which he lit with a monogrammed gold lighter. "Charlie had the movie fever bad before the accident, man," he told me. "*Loved* that S-M."

"Stage struck," I said, and he wrapped a smile around the cigarette.

"You might be all right yet, Sherlock, you just get over the idea there's only one kind of work you like to do."

"I should find a hobby, cultivate outside interests."

"Yeah, man, find a hobby."

"Shut up and watch the door, Grab."

"They only been up there ten minutes, man. You got plenty of time."

He made a motion with his thumb to Charlie, who rose ponderously from the wire-backed chair and waddled back to the cafeteria line. I stopped tapping my fingers long enough to pull out one of my own cigarettes, light it, then resume squinting through the bright window. Dinah had moved to the new apartment on Russian Hill six months ago, into a co-op building on Hastings Terrace, just below the crest of the hill itself, a convoluted neighborhood of narrow streets and stone stairways landscaped like Machu Picchu that led up and down the hillside between buildings and through occasional patches of semi-public gardens. To the right of our coffee shop, across the street, stood another apartment building with a quilt and yarn shop and a bakery on the ground floor. To my left an alley, wide enough for one car at best, running uphill into sunshine and green shade, and then the canopied door of Dinah's building.

Charlie sat down, making the vinyl cushion wheeze under his weight, and pushed a tray with three yellow coffee cups onto the center of the table. I waved away his silent offer of cream and sugar and chewed my cigarette. Eleven-fourteen.

"You ever get hold of your partner, man?"

I shook my head and watched the entranceway across the street. A middle-aged woman was bending to help a very old woman fit a key into the front door. Fred had not answered at his apartment when I had called at eight, or at the office half an hour later, or at ten-thirty when I had tried both numbers again.

"Cops got him downtown," Grab said through a mouthful of Danish. "Want to know how you pull you disappearing act."

I checked the watch again: eleven-fifteen.

"You sure you don't want me and Charlie to sashay up with you to meet the chicks, Hallerbaby?" He tore another piece of Danish with long, spidery fingers and began to lick the icing.

I ignored him and watched the front door swinging shut behind the two women. Four flights up, on the corner, Dinah's front window reflected a gray sheet of empty sky. They had waited just long enough by the buzzers for me to see Christie's blonde hair over the turned-up fur collar of her coat and the taller, more angular figure of a stooping dark-haired woman who had to be, after three weeks, and two deaths, and one license, Muriel Contreras.

"Three chicks, Haller, three dudes," Grab said, still smiling wickedly, riding me with that mixture of hostility and friendly interest I could never quite get used to. If you grew up black, he had once told me, you grew up knowing how to play the dozens, which the encyclopedia later confirmed happened to be an old slave game of insult trading. And the dirty dozens, Grab's favorite, was the version of the game where the insults got ugly. "You ask the horse-face one all those questions you wrote down in your pocket this morning, man, and then we party—how about it? Charlie be in hog heaven with that blonde white girl. Come on, Haller baby, relax. You supposed to be so cool, you sitting there like you ready to jump through the window. Let Charlie—"

I threw my chair back so hard it fell over and skidded while Grab toppled to one side and yelled and Charlie hoisted his coffee cup chin-high off the table. Before either of them had reached his feet I was pounding across the sidewalk and squirming between two parked cars, shading my eyes with one hand and staring up at Dinah's window.

Halfway to the canopy, as a van driver stood on his horn and waved his fist, Grab caught up with me, one hand clutching his sportscoat shut, the other hand dragging me backward. In the corner of my eye I saw Charlie Sleeve lumbering into traffic. "Jesus, man, you—"

"You know the Nilsson brothers, Grab?"

"Shit, man—"

"I just saw the crazy one circling the block in a white Lincoln. You go around to the back of the building and watch the door. Tell Charlie to get the car—I'm going up."

He said something else in protest, but I had already shaken his fist loose and chopped the edge of my hand savagely across a row of buzzer buttons next to the big glass door. My key had gone down to the bottom of the bay in the Mercedes, but I couldn't have taken the time to find it anyway. One part of my mind was screaming that I should never have used Dinah, never, never for a second put her in touch with the kind of world I lived in; another part was turning to ice, numbing itself and making the arms and legs go through the motions that would get me in, get her out.

Somebody buzzed the door, and it had barely started to click when I threw it open with one shoulder and bulled toward the stairs.

At the first landing the middle-aged woman was helping the old woman fit another key to another lock. Both of them straightened to stare, slack-jawed, at the gun in my hand. One flight up somebody angrily demanded who had rung the bell, then screamed. A door popped open as I scrambled around a corner, swaying and cursing, and a thick Spanish accent joined the clatter.

At the fourth floor I snapped the safety on the pistol free and stalked down the hallway, my breath caught on brambles in my throat, my right shoulder just brushing the surface of the wall. Six apartments per floor. Dinah in 4-F, facing front, overlooking the street, green wooden door that opened inward. How long had they been there? Why would Christie have told them? I pushed questions down with an effort and tried to think which way to go in, where the windows and the shadows were.

Twenty feet of blue-patterned runner carpet, a large marble vase of dusty ivy, then Dinah's door. If I were mistaken, if I went through the door with a gun in my hand and was wrong, Muriel was gone, lost maybe forever. If I hesitated, made the other mistake . . . if Piers Nilsson and Phil were in there with Dinah . . .

Louder shouts from the stairwell. Footsteps one flight below. I dropped to a crouch and stopped at the marble vase.

A sliver of sunlight on the carpet outside her door.

Another step, and the door was swinging lightly an inch each way in a draft. I slammed the heel of my hand hard against the wood and spun through on my knees like a homicidal dervish.

Empty—two windows glinted, silver teeth in a mouth of sunlight. Chairs overturned, end table smashed into brown spikes, Dinah's tote bag on a shelf. I dove toward the tiny kitchen—blank. The bedroom, the study facing north— blank, all blank. From somewhere far below a siren gulped and fell.

On the stairwell landing a man, white-faced, wedged into his doorway, waved a fist and shouted at me as I sprinted past, reaching for the door to the fire stairs at the other end of the corridor.

Grab was covering the exit, I told myself, clambering down metal stairs, slapping my palm against the banister pole at every corner. But Grab didn't carry a gun in his over-sewn, eyepopping getup, and Grab wouldn't get in the way of real trouble—trouble with bullets and white women—not for me or anybody. I hit the last concrete square with both feet working, my elbow already twisting and pushing the steel safety bar, and the door fell back in panic and I was running down a narrow sunken rampway, then up and downhill over the Machu Picchu steps.

Two sirens now, closer, hounding. And Grab was suddenly in front, at the edge of one of the Russian Hill parklets, emerging from lilac bushes and pointing wildly downhill. I flew past him at full speed, left arm lashed across my ribs to hold the pain in, and kept on moving, jolting down the endless stairs as if I had been running for days, thighs pumping in jitterbug, slick city shoes catching on damp stone. More bushes stretched over the path, a bed of orange poppies along a wall, low fir branch—I swung wide and ducked. Just past a renovated carriage house the overgrown stairs twisted again and I saw a flash of lemon-colored hair, green coat. Grab shouted my name yards behind me—I tripped, careened, exploded into the clear daylight of an alleyway leading over a driveway, and down again toward Broadway, through a maze of concrete walls and parked cars. Blonde hair, the weedy figure of Piers Nilsson turning, red hair vanishing around a corner. Still moving, I raised my pistol, braced it for an instant with the other hand, somebody shot a cannon and high behind my head glass began to rain down on pavement.

When I regained my feet they were gone again, and Grab was coming at a lope. I pushed up and off and ran through a white blur toward the corner of the building where they had disappeared, throwing my head back just long enough to see Charlie spinning the special knob on his steering wheel and backing Grab's Cadillac up the alley. Grab stood straight, hands on hips, cursing.

At the next corner I slid to a stop and poked my head low around. A wide passageway between two brick buildings, ending in a set of wooden steps. At the bottom, I thought, my chest scalding with pain, would be the steep slope of houses built over the Broadway Tunnel—open, busy, the logical place to have a car waiting. Nilsson and Phil were shoving two women toward the steps. Another head bobbed at shoulder level, already descending. My skull was coming apart in fragments, like pieces of tile. Phil wheeled at my voice and I raised the pistol. Piers flung one woman toward the steps, the other broke free and staggered a yard toward me, falling in terror as he fired twice more, cataclysmic booms that shook the walls. Half of our soldiers never fired their rifles in Korea, the Army learned in horror—too afraid of the sound, of the sight of another human being in the path of a bullet. I swayed and leaned against jutting brick, lifted the barrel up and let it drop slowly, crossing his black hair, until the sight divided the base of his throat and the whole world sat on the end of the barrel. My breath stopped of its own accord the way they tell you a thousand times on the firing range and my finger began its microscopic contraction—the woman stood up again, and I stopped, and then they were gone.

By the time I reached the top of the steps, Piers was pulling the back door closed and the big dark sedan was gathering speed, pulling into traffic and heading for the maw of the tunnel. I spun in every direction. No red hair, no blonde hair. Behind me, at the end of the passage, Grab was yelling and pointing to his open car. Closer, six feet away, sobbing and hunched over in a coat too heavy and too bloody, wobbled Muriel Contreras.

CHAPTER 23

YOU CAN COME GET HER ANYTIME," Piers Nilsson said. "Just stroll right up Turk Street and knock on the door."

I watched the ash on my cigarette make one final stretch toward the center of the ashtray and begin to crumble into soft, ghostly particles. On the other side of the ashtray, crossed on the coffee table and caked with dust, rose Grab's white suede boots, and above their sharp points his brown face, half-smiling, eyes closed while the soul sister massaged his shoulders. Her name was Silvia, he had told me, and she had hands that could zonk a buffalo.

"On the other side," Piers said in his faint accent, and I pushed the telephone closer to my ear, "I can see where you might not like the idea of walking up a public street too much. I hear the local pigaroos have your photo in every squad car these days."

"Let me talk to her."

"You've been watching too much television, geek. You don't talk to anybody but me."

"Let me hear her say she's all right."

"She's busy chatting with Arthur. You remember Arthur? He's got both girls off somewhere talking movies, talking show biz. Arthur's so excited he's pissing down both legs. You understand what I mean, geek? You understand what I'm saying?"

Behind the couch Charlie Sleeve pulled back one edge of the window shade and peered down at the street. Whatever he saw made him frown and draw the shade to a slit of light. Next to him, bending over the bar sink, was the huge black man with the shaved head who had driven Grab's car to my office. On the other side of the sink another black man in an African shirt stood with his arms crossed and his pursed lips working slowly back and forth across his face. Calling in the troops, Grab had explained; making a circle around the leader. The leader was now cranking his head to one side so Silvia could tie a striped barber's apron around his neck.

"Why don't you call in the police, geek?" Piers taunted.

"How much money do you want, Piers?" Plenty of people had seen me caroming across Russian Hill with my pistol in my hand. But according to the radio, nobody had reported seeing Dinah and Christie and Muriel taken out of her apartment at gunpoint. She had cancelled her whole day's appointments. Nobody would begin to worry until tomorrow morning, when she didn't show up at the hospital. A night with Arthur. A day and a night.

"I don't want money, little man," Piers said. "What do I want money for? We lead a rich, full life, my brother and I. A lot of booze, a lot of dope. All the ass we can grab." He chuckled. He liked that. "All the snatch we can snatch," he said, aiming for the elegant variation, keeping his voice silky and obscene. I leaned forward and pinched the glowing end of the cigarette between my thumb and forefinger and didn't feel a thing.

He would be sitting in his over-furnished office, I thought, behind the curved teak desk, fingering his eighteenth-century torture toy as he talked. She would be—where? upstairs? or locked in the cavernous labyrinth of the Club Eden? in one of those dark moldy rooms I had passed on the way to Christie's show: private rooms for members only, plasterboard erotic coffins. Or somewhere else completely, with Arthur? I braked my mind to a halt and skidded away from the picture of Dinah in the same room with Arthur. Tall, stringy, demented Arthur, whose face had glistened as he watched Phil roll one fist after another into my belly.

"So you got something else to tell me, geek? Otherwise I might want to hang up and go join little brother in the game room. You ever hear of a game called 'hot nips,' geek? You start with a girl and a cigarette lighter."

He was piling it on, I decided, watching my knuckles whiten. He would be quick to pile it on, but he would be wondering all the same. He would understand that Dinah wasn't Christie, that there was a limit to what he could get away with. Arthur wouldn't know about limits. But Piers would be running his bony fingers over the spiked blades of the pineapple choker and wondering what kind of deal I wanted to offer.

"We've been having a chat here too, Piers," I said, thinking I would throw up any second, thinking my belly was like a torn sack. Silvia began to clip the edges of Grab's mini-Afro with tiny silver-plated scissors, slow, careful snicks, her pink tongue curled up in concentration.

"That's wonderful," Piers said. "Who gives a shit?"

"You left Muriel behind, Piers."

"Yeah."

"We just had a long talk with Muriel, Piers." I moved my head two inches and looked at the far corner of the dim room, where Muriel was huddled in one of Grab's beanbag chairs, still wearing the blood-stained overcoat, her face buried in the crook of her arm, her shoulders rising and falling to some tearful inner rhythm. Junkie rhythm, Grab had called it scornfully. The blood came from a deep cut in her mouth, somebody's watch or ring in the struggle out of Dinah's apartment; but the quaking came from a deep, unquenchable terror. From the moment we had shepherded her into Grab's back seat, she hadn't said a word.

"She talked a lot about Tock Maranian," I said into the telephone. Piers said nothing. I thought of Dinah, took a long, desperate stab. "She talked a lot about Edward Asbery, too," I said. "And how to skim a will."

Piers laughed out loud. "Who the hell is Edward Asbery?" he said. I jerked a cigarette from my pocket and raised my eyes in surprise to see Charlie Sleeve extending a lighter in his good hand.

"You still want her, Piers?"

"Yeah." The voice had softened, not quite to a whisper, and Grab had held up a palm to stop the scissors. There would be a book about it somewhere, a book about the psychology of negotiations, telling how both parties limber up through ritual fencing, with thrusts and parries and lies and counter-lies, before they come down to the nub, to the place where they had known all along they would end up. I took a deep breath and heard it rattle into my lungs like coal coming down a chute. I had known where we would end up from the moment I had turned and seen Muriel Contreras staggering away from the wooden steps at the foot of Russian Hill.

"Yeah, I still want her, geek," Piers said.

I said nothing.

"You don't know why," he said. "But you don't have to

know why, do you? What you need to know is that I got your redheaded girlfriend, Haller. Arthur and I got her right here."

"And Christie."

"Forget Christie, Haller. Christie is as good as dead." I said nothing. "You got yourself to thank for that," he said after a moment. I said nothing, watched Muriel's shoulders rock. Grab was still leaning forward with his palm up, staring hard at me while Silvia held the scissors suspended over the black curve of his hair.

"Call it a Mexican standoff," he said, coming to the point at last. I said nothing. "We trade cunts," he said.

When I put down the telephone Grab had closed his eyes again and Silvia's hands were fluttering like pale brown sparrows over the inverted nest of hair. I glanced at the cigarette Charlie had lit and saw that it had gone out some time ago between my fingers. I dropped it into the ashtray with the others and stood up, feeling a great black hollowness. You have yourself to thank for that, he had said. For Christie, for Dinah. For Leo. I looked at Muriel. When I handed her over to Arthur and Piers, she too was as good as dead. The fingers of my right hand crawled like a long-legged, desiccated insect into my shirt pocket and closed around another cigarette. I had hung up with a threat. I could be proud of that. I had told Piers that if Arthur or anyone else touched Dinah, if he played games or got out his cameras and his toys . . . I looked down and saw veins like pencil leads across my hands and wrists.

Grab opened his eyes lazily. "Actually, man," he said. "You one hundred percent ice."

CHAPTER 24

"THEY'RE GOING TO KILL HER," FRED TOLD ME. "You're going to hand over Miss Chula Vista over there and they're going to sandbag everybody and toss what's left over the rocks into the goddam ocean, and she's going to be just as dead as if you took out your goddam gun and shot her yourself."

He stood in front of me with his hands jammed in his jacket pockets and the cigar stump in his mouth and glowered.

"Shit!" he said suddenly, flinging the cigar into the sand. "Shit, shit, shit!"

I turned away and leaned my elbows against the seawall and squinted into the glare, watching the breakers thirty yards away tumbling over each other like puppies.

"Call the cops," he said.

Two girls wearing tank tops and shorts jogged by in the sand—joggle, Dinah calls it—studying the seawall and the sidewalk for likely men. They took in Fred's porkpie hat and old man's quivering dewlap, my grim, unshaven face and slept-in clothes, and joggled on past.

"Call the goddam cops," he said. "Let me call them. They can cover that parking lot like a goddam bird net. I know somebody—I know Riggs in the specials—he can have a SWAT team on the roof of the Cliff House and another one coming out of the park entrance. Riggs can put on the helicopters—"

"No cops," I said, and he lunged a step forward and grabbed me by the front of the jacket to yank me around.

"*Mike, you're going to kill that girl!*"

I shook his hands loose and he stepped back and slapped me across the cheek and nose as hard as he could, and my own hands went up into fists before I turned away again and hunched my shoulders against the wind.

"It's your goddam license, isn't it?" he said. "You think you call in the cops and they find out your hotdogging has turned into a kidnap and there goes the goddam license forever." He grabbed my right shoulder and dug his fingers in, shaking me as if he wanted to snap the bone in half, and I lowered my head so that all I could see was the edge of the pavement and my dirty shoe tips, gritty and white with blowing sand.

"By Jesus, you're something," he said.

I clenched my teeth and raised my head, not trusting myself to look at him. Thirty yards of beach, then half a mile of boiler gray surf, then a wall of fog that climbed straight up to the top of the world. When gulls sailed into it they disappeared, emerging somewhere else moments later, like clowns coming out of trick doors. North, toward the point where the beach narrowed and the giant offshore rocks began, I could see the stern of a navy cruiser slipping sideways into the wall and vanishing. Fred released his grip from my shoulder and I swallowed once and finally straightened to face him. His anger rolled over me like a wave.

"You call in a SWAT team," I said, "and they're going to

shoot somebody. You line up cops at the park entrance, at the Cliff House, in the Sutro goddam Baths, and the Nilssons are going to spot them, and they're going to turn around and take Dinah where we don't know how to follow, and then she really is gone."

He worked the muscles in his jaw for a moment, staring at me with fierce black eyes. "In thirty-five years of police work," he started belligerently. Then he rubbed his face with his palm and the eyes went dead. The hand sank to his side. "I don't know," he said in a wearier voice. "I don't know. I'm a cop. I came up learning you have to go by the rules. But there aren't any goddam rules." He shoved his chin toward the breaking surf, not looking at me. "I used to make neighborhood speeches when I was in the sex crimes section, and I'd advise the women if they get assaulted not to fight back, not to do anything to make the rapist mad, so they wouldn't get hurt. Hurt worse. Ten years ago I changed and I told them to fight back and scream like hell for help. When I retired I didn't know what the hell they should do. I had one woman yelling like a banshee outside a Safeway on Divisadero and the punk runs off like he was dismembered. The next one yells and the guy puts an ice-pick through her throat."

In front of us the waves chased each other's tails and came up frothing.

"Where's that goddam one-arm fat boy you sent up there?" Fred said.

"I told him to take his time. He saw them outside Dinah's building, he knows them."

"He knows them from being in the same goddam sado movies with them," he said in disgust. "This city." He held up his watch so that I could see the hands at five-thirty. Then still not looking at me, he began stripping the cellophane from another cigar. "Why the goddam Sutro Baths?" he muttered. "Did he say why the Sutro Baths?"

We would talk in normal voices, I thought. We would stand talking and leaning against the sea wall at Ocean Beach half a mile from the spot where, an hour from now, Arthur and Piers Nilsson might or might not return Dinah. Where I would hand over Muriel Contreras and they would drive her someplace else for whatever preliminaries Arthur had mapped out. And after that, while fear clawed up and down the sides of her skull like a wild animal, Phil or somebody like him would press a small caliber pistol indifferently against her temple.

I gathered liquid in the bowl of my mouth and spat. We would do it that way because the alternative was to let it be Dinah. My stomach squeezed up my throat like a rising balloon.

"He insisted," I was saying. "I wanted someplace downtown, and he insisted. He said downtown was too public. The parking lot over the baths ought to be empty at six-thirty, but there's still going to be a busload of tourists on the lookout point or in the restaurant. Enough people," I said. "A simple exchange."

He grunted. "That parking lot's a city street with a city name. Merrie Way," he said. "You understand that the north end of it runs right into the service road for Lincoln Park?"

I nodded. I understood that. The Sutro Baths themselves stretch fifty yards across the hollow of a cliff—an elaborate complex of roofed swimming pools that burned down twenty years ago, leaving an outline of broken walls and troughs like a Roman ruin. Beyond the Baths, Lincoln Park teeters around the tip of the whole city peninsula, just above a shelf of dangerous rock-lined beaches, until it runs into the base of the Golden Gate Bridge.

"That's where they'll dump her," Fred said with a jerk of his head toward the car sitting at the curb. I didn't look. Muriel would still be there, huddled in her coat in the back seat, too terrified or weary or spaced out to get up and move. She was afraid of men, Christie had said, and why not? But she had also turned her brain to salad oil with who knew what combination of heroin and cocaine and red, white, and blue striped pills. Recreational drugs, the slick magazines lightheartedly call them, the young moderns with politics by Leary and values by Gucci. I had tried for three hours to talk with her, to ask if she had ever seen Chick Gannett or Leo Matz before, or if she had known about her half brother, or had any idea that she had inherited money. She had only dug her face deeper into the coat and whimpered *"madre con los ángeles"* over and over. What she needed, of course, was an addiction clinic, psychiatric treatment, a refuge from Eden. And with eight hundred thousand dollars she could have bought it. But what I was giving her was the Nilsson brothers.

"He's coming now," Fred said.

In the distance Charlie Sleeve's purple shirt advanced down the middle of the sidewalk, his head bowed slightly against the stiffening wind.

"She knows something," Fred said, looking back at Muriel. "For them to do this. She saw something or heard something, even stoned like that."

I didn't answer. I didn't answer because I didn't believe it.

"They won't hurt Dinah," he said. "Not now." I nodded and watched Charlie Sleeve approaching. Piers Nilsson was willing to exchange Dinah now because I couldn't call in the cops. And afterward, he had made it clear, if I tried to press charges, Dinah would never live to go to court. The last fleck of Navy cruiser plunged into the fog. He had too much at stake, he had said, and too many subcontractors to let me go to the police, now or ever.

"But they'll come after you both," Fred said. "After they hand her over. *If* they hand her over."

"Dinah first," I said. "You take Dinah away first."

"I got you your pictures," Charlie Sleeve announced.

He had a Polaroid camera that he wore around his neck and balanced on the stump of his hand to operate, allowing him to blend easily enough with the dozens of tourists always milling around the Observation Point and the telescopes for Seal Rock. Mingle, I had told him; cover the parking lot and the restaurant slowly and photograph everything. Sullen, not quite openly hostile, he had shifted his gaze to Grab. Haller likes to look a place over first, Grab had said sarcastically. He likes to see who's going to burn his ass to butter.

"You wanted all the cars," Charlie said in a wooden voice. "I stood by the hamburger place and took the whole parking lot."

"Louie's Restaurant," Fred said, and Charlie nodded but kept his eyes on me. I spread the first slick photograph on the wall. Nine cars scattered across an unpaved rectangle that ended abruptly in a rank of eucalyptus trees. I recognized none of the cars.

"The swimming pool," he said. The light was better over the shallow green water, and explosive patches of spray, cotton balls of ocean, could be seen just beneath the last ruined wall. A beautiful spot for a swimming spa when old Adolph Sutro had levelled the trees and gouged the cliff open. Nobody in his right mind would go a hundred feet farther down and step in the cannonading surf. Just at the edge of the picture stood the service road entrance to the park, one vehicle wide, crossed by a single white guard plank.

"I went on up in the park," Charlie said. "Up to the other parking lot by the steps."

Fred took the picture. "By the steps to the beach overlook platforms," he said.

"These the cars," Charlie said stolidly, and handed me a picture of a bigger, emptier lot. I glanced, snapped it impatiently on top of the others.

"And I was in the movies with this guy," he said and held out the last one.

I gripped the thin cardboard with both hands and lifted it into the fading gray light. Overhead a gull wheeled to look, Fred bumped me, crowding. I stared at a profile in the top right corner of the photograph, streaky and underexposed, and felt my mouth turn to starch.

"I was in the movies with him," Charlie said, "only he didn't know they was taking movies." His voice had changed for a moment, as if he were smiling, but I didn't turn to see. Fred's hand was pulling the photo lower. "Two niggers and two white girls," Charlie said. "Bad S-M, man."

"Who the hell is it?" Fred said, grabbing a corner. I let my hand drop and he snatched the whole picture away.

"Edward Asbery III," I said.

"Bad S-M, man. He didn't know they had a camera in the mirror."

Fred's face had grown squarer. He tipped the photo in front of his belt buckle and said something drowned out by waves and traffic.

"Who were the white girls?" I heard myself asking.

Charlie tilted his head toward the parked car and smiled an ugly, triumphant smile. "It was four or five years ago, man. I can't swear to it. I'm pretty sure she one of them."

Fred started to speak and I cut him off.

"It doesn't change a thing," I told him. "It doesn't change a goddam thing."

Charlie held up his good hand so that we could see his watch stiffen at six o'clock.

CHAPTER 25

THEY CAME IN A VAN. A YELLOW DODGE VAN the shade of Arthur's leisure suit, with opaque tinted windows and the graceful aerodynamic lines of a loaf of Wonder Bread.

I climbed out of the front seat and watched the van sniff its way to the end of Merrie Way, circle, and park near the north end facing the ocean.

"You want me to keep the motor running?" Charlie asked from the car. I shook my head, and he did something with his foot that made the engine shudder, then gently cough itself quiet. In the back seat Muriel stirred and moved her head. In the front seat Charlie stared straight ahead, without expression, at the curtain of fog blowing back and forth across the horizon. I took one more useless glance around the parking lot—deserted now except for us, the van, two or three cars near the entrance—and started to walk along the sidewalk to the center of the wall.

They let me wait.

When I reached the broken gate in the wall that we had agreed on, the doors of the van were still closed, the tinted windows impenetrable. I stopped and pulled out a cigarette. Nobody moved from the van. Seals honked on the big rocks far out in the surf and fog, a tourist bus grunted out of its space by the Cliff House, but the van sat, holding its brown windshield up to the last rays of the sun and the cold wind. I turned my back on it and looked down at the ruins of the Baths, rectangles of shallow green and black water framed by crumbling lines of concrete, and at the lean, muscular waves hooking and crossing into the rocks below. Did I know any Greek? she had wanted to know. Thalatta, thalatta. The snotgreen sea. The sea like a blue-gray bruise. The sea like a scab. Wishful thinking it had been to call it the Pacific. On a chilly September evening, blistered with whitecaps, teeth bared, it looked as peaceful as an exploding bomb.

"Right on time, geek," Piers Nilsson said to my back.

I tapped cigarette ash over the edge of the wall and forced myself to turn around slowly.

"Or am I late?" he said.

"You're on time," I said, just to say something while I squinted and tried to guess where the gun was. He wore silver reflecting sunglasses, aviator style, a blue nylon windbreaker and tan trousers, and he loomed over me with six-feet-six of sneer and bland contempt. If he wore a gun, I thought, it was inside the windbreaker. If he wore a gun, he had no immediate plans to use it.

He pulled out his own cigarettes and lit one, taking longer to look around the parking lot than I had, stopping once to turn and show me the lipless smile on the oblong, horsey face.

"So you didn't bring any cops, little man," he said, coming back to me finally.

"Where is she, Piers?"

"Arthur said we put you on the spot. A moral fucking dilemma. He didn't like it. He said you'd double cross us. He said he didn't trust anybody who was too crooked to be a cop." He inhaled smoke and began another slow, frowning survey. "A former private cop who got busted. You like it here, geek?" he said. "Down there is like a fucking ruin. We shot background down there for a Roman orgy scene one time." A hundred yards away, on the other side of the Baths, oblivious, a handful of tourists clustered around the pay telescopes pointed toward the ocean. Behind Piers one of the three remaining cars in the lot crunched gravel and fired a salvo of rock music as it headed out. Then the sea wind kicked harder and the thin sunlight rippled through the fog and Piers sucked some more around the edges of his cigarette. As nervous as I am, I thought. As careful. As untrustworthy.

"Arthur thought you might get ideas," he said, fingering the rim of the glasses and studying the short ramp up to the lot from Point Lobos Road. "Like trying to block the exit over there with your car once we were through dealing, or like bringing a gun and trying to run off with both girls at once. I told Arthur not to worry. I told him I read you as too sentimental about little red to do something risky like that. I told him you'd shit nails first, but you'd end up doing business like an Eagle Scout."

"Arthur never talked that long in his life. Cut the stall."

He pulled out a short length of smile. "I also told him a guy that had his picture in the want ads yesterday wouldn't call any goddam cops."

"Bring her out, Piers." Over his shoulder I could see the van. Twenty, twenty-five yards away, under shaggy eucalyptus branches and pulled parallel to the beginning of the woods. Dinah would be that close. If I bulled him aside and ran I would be there in ten seconds. I leaned my hips carefully against the wall and listened to Piers taunt.

"But now I look you over, geek," he said, "and that's not a pocket comb I see under your armpit. So maybe Arthur was right after all, you want to be fancy."

"It's a .357 Magnum," I said. "It can fire a bullet through the engine block of a car. Bring her to me and you'll never know I had it."

He coaxed the rat-tailed smile out again. "So tough," he murmured. "I had forgotten so tough." He twisted his long head toward Charlie's car at the other end of the wall. "Is that her in the car with the nigger?" I didn't answer. He jerked his head as if he were biting off a knot. "Bring her to the van."

I straightened from the wall and flexed the fingers of my right hand in the damp air. The fog was drifting on shore now, in long feathery wisps and sugary puffs. In twenty minutes or half an hour it would be too dark in the lot to see well, the last tourist bus would have gone.

"Dinah first," I said. "You bring Dinah here, then you can go to the car."

He leaned forward, tilting his silver glasses toward me, and took the lapel of my sportscoat between thumb and forefinger, speaking softly, as if he were discussing the fabric. "We don't want the whore that much, Haller baby. Arthur and me, we don't have any moral dilemma at all. You want the girlfriend, you bring me the Chicana."

I exhaled smoke I couldn't taste and waited. Piers laughed.

"I'm going to do something to help you make up your mind, Haller baby," he said. "You just keep your popgun in your pocket and remember two things. One, if you want little red all safe and sound, you gotta play ball. And two, you're the guy who came carrying the cannon, not me."

He walked to my right, along the uneven concrete sidewalk under the wall, until he reached the car. Charlie looked at him, at me, and shifted his bulk behind the wheel. Piers stooped and ran one hand into the radiator grill, grunted and stood back as the hood swung up, yawning, toothless. Then he gave me a flash of silver glasses and stretched a long arm beneath the air filter.

"Distributor cap," he said when he returned, holding it for me to see. "Now Arthur won't worry that you might back the car into the middle of the road all of a sudden, or dump the girl and try to follow us home. Or whatever else a bright guy like you might think was fun." He put the distributor cap in his windbreaker pocket and grinned, small pointed teeth under two tiny reflections of my face. "Phil told me you like to monkey with cars, geek. You got two minutes to bring us the whore."

He had swaggered across the lot and already disappeared around the other side of the van before I stepped on my cigarette and looked one more time around the lot. A dark Buick still sat parked near the exit. A diesel bus labelled "Golden West Parlor Tours" was just pulling into the space by the telescopes, tourists arriving for sunset and seals. The other bus, the other cars had gone.

I walked around the open hood and unlocked Muriel's door. She raised her eyes to me and said something in Spanish, and I put one hand under her coat sleeve and tugged.

"Lamb to the slaughter," Charlie said, watching in the mirror. "I didn't think you'd do it, man."

She stumbled out of the car, an awkward bulk of coat and elbows and black hair, and clutched drunkenly at my shoulder.

"Silvia give her some nighty-night pills," he said.

Muriel wrinkled her brow at the sound of his voice and lowered her face to find him. Taller than I had guessed from her photograph, I thought again, holding my mind up, at a distance, circling. With cinder gray skin and a heavy, bovine figure that suggested sensuality and an old age coming of easy, comfortable fat. There was nothing in the face she raised to me that suggested she knew what was happening now, before she had her chance to grow old. Afraid of men, Christie had said, but she had made what living she could performing for men, linked to men pimp-by-pimp, trick-by-trick. Man-forged manacles I hear. From her mother, Christie had said, she had gotten the idea that men would always use her.

"It's six-forty," Charlie said, sarcasm out in the open. "If you don't come back in five minutes, you want me to stroll down to the auto parts store and charge a cap?"

Muriel peered from one to the other.

"You sit where you are, the way we arranged," I said.

"Yes, massa," he said with a mock salute.

In front of the van we paused, Muriel's weight dragging my arm as she looked vaguely at the surf and the ruined pools and asked me a question in Spanish. I didn't know Spanish. I didn't answer. You wouldn't do it if she was white, Grab had observed casually just before we left, and Charlie had turned his head with a hiss. I pulled her off the sidewalk and we took three steps along the rough, uneven ground. This close to me her hair smelled of cheap shampoo, her body was warm under the coat. I dragged her another step. My car disappeared from view, the big empty lot contracted to a strip of gravel between the van on the right and the thick undergrowth and trees of Lincoln Park on the left. I pulled the gun from the shoulder holster and shoved it out of sight in my right jacket pocket, gripping tightly but holding my finger off the trigger. It wasn't a .357 Magnum, I thought, it didn't fire shells the size of brickbats. It was a snub-nosed .38, unlicensed and unsilenced, a gun I had never fired and never meant to. Not with Dinah in range.

"I'm cold," Muriel said in English. I looked over her shoulder to the back of the lot, a short chalky cliff bounded by shrubbery. Where was Asbery? Charlie had only seen him at the other parking lot, half a mile away beside the vista point stairs. Too far away to reach the Baths. Too far away to make any sense. We took another step and halted by the sliding door.

"Frío," Muriel said, *"tengo frío,"* and the handle rotated and the door slipped open a foot to reveal Arthur's long narrow face, his eyes bright under girlish eyelashes, his lower lip rubbery and drooping like a worm. In the black rectangle behind him shadows floated, as if in an aquarium. From beneath the grinning face a hand suddenly poked a small pistol into daylight and aimed at Muriel's breasts.

"We could cancel the deal right here, Haller," Piers said, sliding the door another foot and appearing beside his brother.

Muriel whimpered and tried to shake off my arm. The gun barrel wavered, moved in the direction of my feet, drifted up again in disjointed circles.

I exhaled slowly, a whistle of breath, watching the barrel wander, and my finger crawled back from the trigger in my pocket. Just little brother's treat at Halloween. Just junkie jamboree.

"You wouldn't let Arthur load a pencil," I said and Arthur smiled at me, uncomprehending, delighted. "Where's Dinah?"

Piers wrapped his fingers around the yellow edge of the door and held it like a curtain to block the interior while Arthur looked down at the pistol and scratched his wrist with his left hand.

"She's right behind me," Piers said, still bent double like a giant straw to fit his head through the open door. "Belted in and being good. We stuffed a gag in her because she's got a big mouth, like you. She kicked Arthur so hard we had to give him extra medicine."

"Let me see her."

"You're really going to hand over the whore, Haller baby?" he said, teasing his pleasure out. In the black interior, straining my eyes, I could see shapes like a blanket, a back, red hair.

I watched Arthur's gun and made a conscious effort not to swallow, not to lick my lips. In the distance, over the march of my pulse, waves dove fearlessly against the cliff and rocks. Hours passed. "Yeah," I said. So tough. So scared. "I am."

Piers widened his smile. "And we're going to hand over little red?"

I didn't answer.

He made the jerking motion with his head again and Arthur looked around, interested.

"The Buick by the driveway, right?" he said.

I nodded.

"One wrong move and the U.S. Cavalry comes charging out of the Buick?" he said. "More niggers?"

"Bring her to the door," I said and let my hand fall away from Muriel's elbow.

Piers shrugged and a flicker of motion crossed his silver glasses and I pushed Muriel hard with both hands, a soft pillow falling, and turned. Phil emerged from the trees behind us raising a double-barreled shotgun to his hip.

"Outflanked, Haller baby," Piers said. "Give Arthur the gun."

I shot twice through the jacket and missed and Arthur jumped on my back screaming. As I flung him off my shoulder, staggering, Phil maneuvered to the left, through the trees. I ripped the gun free of the jacket.

"Get *her!*" Piers shouted.

At the rear of the van Muriel was crawling on her hands and knees.

Phil swung his face, then the gun toward Muriel. Swung his face back to me.

Behind us the door rolled shut, and Arthur lunged up again, flailing in panic, long arms buffeting me like sticks. At thirty feet a shotgun would turn us both to pulp. Phil hesitated, his face caught for a moment in a shaft of eerie light between two trunks. I drove the gun barrel into Arthur's face and slapped him backwards with it, two steps, three, and he tumbled, arms and legs revolving like a windmill, dragging me down to one knee and somehow batting the pistol away. Headlights swept over us and tires began to move. In the open lot Muriel was running, coat gathered to her chest, already halfway across a space the size of a football field.

I swayed to my feet. The pistol was gone. Piers or whoever was driving would reach her long before I took another step. The van gathered speed. A dozen yards to my left Phil lowered the gun and watched. By the exit Fred's Buick began to turn. In slow motion, far away, beyond anyone's reach the van shifted gears, dipped once and hit her back with a sound like the thump of a door.

Phil raised the gun. The van skidded, circled back to us, lights bobbing for me. Into the yellow beam, his face wild, his white hair flying, lurched Arthur, coked to the last, mouth still stretched wide in surprise an instant after Phil's shot blew his midsection into crimson splinters.

CHAPTER 26

ARTHUR COLLAPSED LIKE A BREAKING WAVE.
When I looked away, Phil had vanished into the trees.
Behind me a woman screamed in a thin, steady voice, a wire in
the wind. The van veered sharply to the right, hesitated, turned
toward the exit again and found it blocked by Fred's Buick.
From the tourist bus stepped Grab, then a tall black man with
a rifle.

The van darted left and accelerated back down the middle of the lot. Three feet beyond what had been Arthur I
saw my pistol, propped with its handle in the air like an
upended bug. I started to run and the van roared past, still
accelerating as it shattered the white guard plank and curved
out of sight, two red lights swallowed by the trees of the park.

By the time Fred caught up I was sprinting along the center
of the service road, stretching the pistol forward like a runner's
baton.

"Is she in the goddam car?"

I nodded, out of breath, sinking into the seat. He spun

the wheels and jammed the Buick through low-hanging branches woolly with moss that danced and scraped across the windshield.

"Grab's driving to the other lot," he grunted. "It's the only place he can come up." The car bucked and he swung the wheel hard one way, hauled it back. Ahead of us no red lights, no van, only muddy ruts following a slope. "Where's the guy with the shotgun?" he said.

"Gone." In a quarter of a mile or less the road would stop. I squeezed my eyes closed and tried to picture. We had come there a year ago, less, picnicking with her brother. Wooden stairs up the hillside to the second lot and the lookout point. Walking paths down the cliffside, treacherous paths laid out with metal stakes and ropes, skirting the cliffside and the ninety-foot drop into the Golden Gate channel. If he went up the stairs . . . If he panicked and left Dinah in the van . . .

"He's turning around!" Fred shouted.

Lights high-beamed, blinding, the van ground across a fallen limb toward us, rocked to a halt. Fred wrenched the steering wheel with both hands and slung the Buick sideways.

"Don't use your goddam gun!" he shouted, but I was already out of the car and running again, and the van was whining into reverse, lumbering backward toward the base of the lookout stairs.

I scrambled crabwise up the slope, rocking and sliding over the slick dirt, a cannon loose on deck, clawing the underbrush with both hands to reach the stairs first. Somewhere overhead, in the crash of surf and hoarse rush of the wind, sirens rose and choked.

Whatever Fred shouted next the wind and motors chewed apart. A gunshot cracked, impossible to know where. When I broke through to the walking path, the van had stopped catty-cornered to the stairs and the back doors lay flung open like windows. Far down the path the tall, spiky figure of Piers was ducking away into shadows, carrying or pulling someone smaller. In the parking lot above me sirens were converging like wasps. I glanced toward them for a moment, hesitating, and then bowled downhill into the shadows.

And suddenly everything stopped.

No noise but the clapping of waves far below, on my left. No light but the pale, shimmering reflection of twilight off fog. I stood at the head of the path. Nothing moved. I took a step.

Where could he go? The path led to no more stairs, only to steeper cliffside trails, dead end beaches. I kept to what I thought was the main path and moved ahead softly, testing the ground with each step, balancing. In the Army, a decade before, we had held night maneuvers, rifle squads sent into the Texas hills to set up lines of defense and send out patrols, and my lieutenant had gotten us lost. We had marched for half the night, twelve men stumbling after each other's shadows. Overhead the branches criss-crossed the California sky like the veins of an eye. I angled to the other side of the path and stopped again. Ahead of me lay a clear space where hikers had worn away the underbrush, and at the end of it a makeshift stone wall overlooking the cliff and the gray, swollen Pacific tumbling in harness.

From where I stood I could see the path branching in two directions downward. The nearer path, coiling through rocks and wind-whipped shrubs, came to a halt at an unpainted redwood deck with a bench and guard ropes. Beside the bench stood a faded white sign warning visitors not to go farther. The other branch, unofficial, no wider than a pair of shoes, plunged over the cliff and vanished.

I looked back. Nothing moved. No Fred, no Grab, no

squadrons of police or joggers. Ahead of me the great orange bridge arched seven hundred feet over the water toward the north coast and the sprinkled lights of Marin County, a postcard for tourists. Below, jutting into mist, brown patches of beach and darker, jagged outlines of boulders and seal rocks on the edge of the sand, teeth in wet gums. In the channel itself the huge wall of sky and fog billowed on, obliterating light moment by moment as it advanced toward the bridge. We had marched for three and a half hours in darkness and silence and come out at dawn by an all night gas station on the outskirts of Austin. I put one foot into the clearing. We had been driven back to camp, humiliated, in a school bus.

Nobody shot me, nobody called my name.

I ran crouching infantry style to the point where the illegal path went down to the sea, sprawled headlong on my belly and looked over, and then understood.

The path wound in three loops down a hillside of shrubbery and sand to the beach, no more than a narrow shelf of brown sand littered with man-sized rocks. At the far end the rocks jutted out into the breakers, bigger rocks, truck-sized, extending a hundred yards into the channel and forming a narrow, broken promontory. Once around the far point of it, and he would have another short range of open beach, and then the maze of trails that led uphill again to Presidio Park and the avenues. Once around that promontory and Piers and Dinah would disappear into the city like birds into the fog.

"Mike!"

Blue windbreaker in pale green shrubbery, a crown of red hair—gone. I knelt on the rise of ground and leaned forward, weaving over ocean, taking my breath in shallow, painful gulps. They were on the third loop, almost to the beach, below me and to the right. I aimed and cocked. Legs, hair—gone.

Then a moment later reappearing. If he crossed the beach, I thought, he would have to clamber over the promontory of rocks at the other end. There was no more path. And it was a two-handed climb in the best of circumstances. He would have to drop her. I took a deeper breath. He would have to leave her.

Or else he could wade around the promontory with her.

I stood up slowly and leaned farther out, clutching the top of the wall. For whatever reason he wanted her by now—hostage, victim, simple revenge—he hadn't carried her this far to suddenly quit. If he went rock by rock, holding on with his free hand, he could do it. Anybody could do it. They had reached the last turn before the beach, on my left now and seventy feet below. I shoved the pistol into the holster. A ten degree slope, no worse than a sliding board, no bumpier than a set of stairs. I vaulted the wall like a mad gymnast and skidded feet first toward the ocean.

Three-quarters of the way downhill, working my legs like brakes, I misjudged and a rock caught me by the shoulder, lifted me up, and thumped me sideways along the slope. I ricocheted off a loop of path and mowed down shrubbery like corn. Somehow my legs turned and my head flipped and the sky abruptly rolled underfoot like a sheet of gray, then green and brown rolled up again, a bone-cracking collision with hard sand and buried rock, breathless silence. Silence for ten seconds, thirty. An ocean of foam exploded over the rock and whirled me completely around like a cork in a drain.

I wobbled to my feet and stared. I had ended up yards too far to the left. On the beach ahead of me Piers slung Dinah to the sand and raised his arm.

I took a step and felt my left knee buckle. Piers fired twice harmlessly, stopped, fired again before another wave shrouded me in foam and sent me skidding forward into shallow water. As I stumbled up, soaked and burning with pain, he fired once more. In that wind and light he would do more damage throwing the gun itself. Overhead on the observation deck somebody shouted and shot back, a faint cracking noise like bone against rock.

Piers turned and lifted Dinah effortlessly to his shoulder in a fireman's carry, and they began to move along the beach toward the silver outline of the promontory.

I stood up unsteadily and began to run as if I were made of glue. It hurt simply to breathe; it was unendurable to move. I put my head down and ran doggedly, erratically. Boulders sprang out of the mist in front of me like pop-up targets, sand crumbled into water underfoot. To my left the giant waves crashed closer and closer, pressing in. Between the rocks gray flags of fog. When I reached the end of the beach, Piers and Dinah were already twenty yards out into the water. With one hand Piers guided himself along the rocks, with the other circled Dinah's waist and hauled her forward. I pulled the gun and stepped in after them.

No one spoke. In the heaving, freezing water we worked grimly, foot-by-foot, outward to the narrow head of promontory. Once Dinah squirmed around and I saw her face, her wrists bound with cord, her mouth opening to shout, and then Piers wrenched her forward again, face down through the water. All around us the fog was descending in billows from the sky, ghostly wings flapping, and the gray water was bursting and withdrawing in a slow, demented rhythm. I would never catch up, I realized. Each breaking wave folded my left knee and tripped me head first toward the rocks. One step forward, two steps backward. My waterlogged coat and trousers pulled like weights. Ahead of me Piers, with his height, his two good legs, was receding into the fog. The endless waves swelled and dropped, and the pressure of water meeting rocks bounced me leftward again, like a raft in white water. I would never catch him by wading alongside the rocks. I stopped for an instant and stared ahead into the seamless gray of fog and water. If I swam, away from the promontory, through the first line of breakers, and calculated the distance correctly, I would come out beyond Piers and Dinah in the calm of the channel; I could circle back. If I swam and miscalculated, the Pacific would smash me against its teeth like a piece of shell.

I looked at the pistol in my hand, dripping salt water and useless, and shoved it for the second time into the holster. Then I kicked off my shoes and launched hard to my left, pushing off against slippery rock when the waves paused and drew back. People had swum this far, I had seen them. In their wet suits. With goggles and flippers. I rose on the high curl of white, twisting and gasping for air, and kicked. In an instant the promontory was gone, the sky was gone, my eyes were plastered with hair and foam. I swam clumsy strokes against the pull of the waves, riding the surface. A huge rock appeared, vanished. I gritted my teeth and kicked. The water retreated ominously, sucking my clothes forward like flaps of skin, and the honks of seals suddenly carried clear and close by. The fog moved its lips along the surface of the water. Too late, microseconds too late, I dove forward and the edge of the continent came down across my shoulders with a roar— an explosion of sound and weight and pain that went on and on and on. The world turned black, then white again, then eternally black, and the ocean poured itself down my throat.

When I bobbed to the surface, my coat and shirt were strips of rag, my socks had vanished, and I was floating on my back just beyond the line of breakers, rising and falling with the unhurried rhythm of the water. Many yards in front of me, rounding the point of the promontory, Piers moved methodically through waist-deep water, still clutching Dinah, pushing inland toward the brown crescent of the next beach. Then the fog rolled between us again, obliterating. I floated, gently rocking while the water around me tucked and crashed toward shore. In two minutes, three, he would reach the easy water, wade ashore and start for the up-hill paths to the city. With Dinah. With Dinah. I wouldn't move. My arms and legs floated in rubbery chill, spread-eagled, body warmth seeping out pleasantly into the water. Something smooth brushed my leg. I drifted quietly and tried to remember what sharks attacked. Not blood, not scent. Dark outlines, I thought, they attack silhouettes of things on the surface. My legs rubbed whatever it was again. A store of useless information, Asbery had said. Sharks. Hypothermia. Death by freezing. Jeroboams of blood. *Tengo frío.* The fog hissed aside again, coiling, and I saw them walking, Piers upright, six-feet-six, halfway back down the promontory toward the shore. The Outside Lands. I would float peacefully in the cold Pacific until my blood ran out or turned to glass or I sank smoothly downward, dragged under by fins or rocks or seaweed. I watched Dinah kick. A wave curled and broke. They went down, stumbled up. I would float downward forever. I would never fail. I would never fail again.

Slowly, slowly, as if reaching one hand out of a dream I turned over and looked into the channel stretching behind me. The great bulk of the ocean was bearing down out of the fog, a giant wave, a haymaker hurrying to lift me up and carry me under. I brought my head back around for hours, stretched the other arm forward and with an inarticulate sound of pain began to kick.

He never saw me coming. He had timed the big wave

and turned away, one long arm wrapped around a thin, up-right stone that stood at the edge of the promontory like a spar. One more outsized breaker, he must have guessed, thir-ty feet or so of rock ledge, and he would be coming ashore. I rode the crest in like a torpedo, and when it boomed and started to collapse I flung myself sideways hard to the right, aiming for any part of his arm wrapped around the stone, colliding high with it and wrenching Dinah loose and van-ishing into the everlasting foam again. Then the suction of the wave boiled pebbles and sand back over us, and when I stood up, Piers was ten feet away, his left arm held straight at his side, his brow torn and bleeding. The fog smothered us and I lost him. In another moment it drew back like a cur-tain and we were knee-deep, side by side. I hit him with my right fist, swinging in and down and smashing the bad arm. He wrestled my head, slipped, staggered backwards and sat down in the water. He stood up again with a double-edged knife in his hand. I grabbed the left arm with both hands, jerk-ing it straight up as the knife entered somewhere out of sight in the water below, taking the full twenty seconds you have before the severed nerves begin to scream and breaking his arm over my knee. As he pulled the knife free in a rush of blood I swat-ted it away. The pain sprang up my side, climbing like a fire. I hit him once in the windpipe with my forearm. Twice. His face darkened. His eyes went white. I hit him again, back and forth with my forearm in rhythm with the waves, crushing the wind-pipe, watching him gasp for air where no air could go, sink and rise, and swinging again until his throat and mouth were red paste and he flopped backwards into the surf and rolled over on his face.

When I turned to the shore Dinah was on her hands and knees. When I fell down beside her she said my name. When

Fred appeared over us, his voice faint and metallic, he told someone else I was still conscious.

True then. Not true a moment later.

CHAPTER 27

THEY PAINT THE GOLDEN GATE BRIDGE constantly, all year long, starting at one end and working up or down, then crossing to the other side and repeating. By the time they finish one complete circuit, the wind and salt air have eroded the new paint, and they have to start all over again. If I hold my telescope steady between the French doors of my apartment, I can see the painters on the scaffolds loading their electric sprayers, almost see the brilliant orange drops falling two hundred feet to the whitecaps below.

"What did Doctor Susens say this morning?" Dinah asked from the other room.

I flexed my left shoulder tenderly and swung the telescope an inch to the left, where with the help of a little spray and imagination I could make out the first of the seal rocks in the channel. He had come to the parking lot that afternoon to watch the sunset, Asbery had told the police. He was a New Englander, he loved the California landscape, he had said. He had come because the Nilssons had forced him, Christie told them. They had wanted him tied in so tight to the kidnap that he could never run.

"He said the pneumothorax was completely healed now, there was no damage to the myocardium, and the intercostal muscles would take another month to heal because I insist on using them to breathe. He said in six weeks I would be completely back to normal."

"You have the jargon down already," she said, coming into the living room behind me. "Just my luck to fall for the strong, verbal type." I fiddled the telescope back to the right and watched the waves lick at the northern base of the bridge with five foot tongues. "I ran into Doctor Kaplan at a meeting today," she said. "The neurosurgeon at the V.A. Hospital. You'll never guess what his new hobby is."

"Sculling."

She made a clucking sound, full of disgust. "You're already back to normal. He makes wine. He gave us two bottles of his own handmade wine. Chardonnay."

I turned around from the telescope and looked at the bottle she held up, full of butter-colored wine and carrying a blue label that had a bright drawing of a bunch of grapes, the handprinted words "Chateau Kaplan," and underneath them a French motto which I mentally translated as "Take Two and Call Me in the Morning."

"There are still some things about California," I said, "that are different from New England."

She kissed me and put the bottle down on the coffee table. "I stuck the other one in the refrigerator to chill," she said, bending and starting to sort through envelopes. "You haven't opened your mail." I shrugged and she glanced at me with a frown before going back to the envelopes. Three weeks had entirely healed the long cut on her scalp, and the Ace bandages on both her ankles had come off five days ago, although stairs sometimes gave her trouble when she was tired.

The nightmares, once or twice a night in the beginning, had tapered off to nothing. A fine, healthy body, her doctor had told me, an even healthier, normal mind. She will heal faster than you will, he had said, looking stern and Viennese; far faster than your feelings of guilt.

"You're brooding again," she said without looking up.

"I did open one letter," I said. "I put it on my desk. Asbery's lawyer is taking a deposition on Friday and said I have a right to have counsel present."

She was reading a brochure from a company that sold waterbeds and called them "sleeping systems." "Will he be there?" she asked, still reading.

"He remains under doctor's care, just the way he was from the minute the judge granted bail. He'll be under a doctor's care for the next three years, until the fiduciary misconduct charge comes to court. By then the records and the witnesses will be so scrambled that they'll put him on probation and he'll enjoy a miraculous recovery."

"But he'll have been disbarred," she said, looking up finally. "Surely by then he'll have been disbarred?"

I picked up my gin and tonic glass and nodded without much enthusiasm.

She got up and walked around the table and started to swing the eyepiece of the telescope lightly back and forth with one finger. October is the clearest month in San Francisco. The fog has rolled away with the summer, and the brief rainy season hasn't yet begun. At the end of the telescope the enormous bay stretched out on its back, sunning. Two or three cumulus clouds kept their distance and paddled slowly eastward, toward Sacramento and the mountains.

"Whatever else," she said, "he's lost his job. He'll never work as a lawyer again, and that's the worst punishment he could have, worse than the pictures of him having sex with those women in leather and chains, worse than the divorce. It's the one thing he can't stand." She put her head lightly on my good shoulder and touched my collarbone with one finger. "You should know," she said. I chewed ice from my gin and tonic and didn't answer.

"I've worked with people like that," she said after a moment. "Mendelsohn and I were talking about it today. They have a tremendous capacity for anger, and almost none for sadness. I could give you a lot of psychoanalytic jargon about the Marquis de Sade and his mother, but what it boils down to is that sometimes a person like that places all his value on his public identity, on his job or social status."

"The Harvard All-American," I said.

"They're terrified to let the public face slip. It's their way of denying their guilt. The Nilssons were good psychologists—pimps and pornographers usually are—they knew when they threatened Asbery with their pictures he'd do anything to keep from losing his position, his work. You can't imagine the guilt and shame those people feel. It's a sickness."

"Post coitum omne animal triste est," I said, making Boston Latin proud of me. But I wasn't thinking of Asbery anymore. I was thinking of two days earlier.

"Did you see this?" Dinah asked, holding up a brown envelope.

"He's in the last booth," the bartender had said and had put down the glass he was polishing in order to lean over the bar and point. "He's talking on the telephone."

I had thanked him and pushed past the stools and into the gloom. Small's Club, two doors up from the Down Home

Deli, a class bar by Eddy Street standards, with the hookers well-disciplined and herded into one corner of the room so that serious dealing could go on without distractions. They watched me going down the rows of booths, but none of them spoke.

He had a red pushbutton telephone on the table in front of him, and he was reading a morning newspaper folded over twice commuter-style and drinking what by then would be his second or third Chivas of the day. "Sip, don't swallow," he'd once told me. "Sip like a butterfly, sting like a bee."

When I slid into the booth he kept the newspaper propped on the telephone and looked me over for a moment, smiling. Then he reached one brown hand across the table and pulled back the lapel of my sportscoat, scraping the rough cloth of the bandage I was still wearing across my whole left side.

"Worse than I thought, man," he said. "You got a dead alligator on your shirt."

I didn't laugh and he let the smile fade away slowly.

"Give the man a Chivas," he told a passing waiter.

"Martini," I said. "Up, with an olive."

Grab shook his head as the waiter drifted away. "They going to carve a martini on your tombstone, Haller. That stuff pure rat poison, man. Gin kills rats."

When I didn't say anything, he snapped the newspaper with a knuckle and pointed to a headline I couldn't see. "Your lawyer friend gone cop a plea, Sherlock. He gone tie 'em in knots. Shit, man, all he do is skim four hundred K's out of this dude Maranian's will and use it to pay off ol' Slam and Dunk. That's honest blackmail, man. That's white-collar crime, that's honkie crime. He be back home in Pacific Heights in time for Christmas."

I picked up the martini and held it while he pushed the newspaper to one side and ran his fingers up and down the long points of his shirt collar.

"So what's doing, Haller? The doctor give you the all clear yet, man?"

"I spent part of yesterday afternoon with Lieutenant Yetta on Bryant Street," I said, putting the martini down again and looking over his shoulder. I was the only white man in the room. From the bar three or four black faces stared at me as if I were wearing a sheet over my head.

"Is that right? I know Yetta. He a candy cop. He can't give you any more shit now, man. After that hearing with the judge, you so clean you shine."

"They picked up Phil and Benny down in San Diego, Grab. Working in a garage by the Navy Yard, and Yetta flew down for the questioning."

Grab reached under the newspaper and came up with a pack of cigarettes. He extended the pack toward me and I shook my head. He took out the goldplated lighter that would have cost me half a year's income and flicked it under his cigarette.

"Phil confessed to killing Tock Maranian," I said. "The Nilsson brothers hired him to do it. The Nilssons were ready to stop anybody who was going to get in the way of Asbery's steady flow of payoffs. Tock was in the way because he was pushing to get his share of the inheritance. Muriel Contreras was in the way because if somebody found her, she stood to inherit eight hundred thousand dollars that Asbery had mostly mislaid. I was in the way because when incompetent old Leo hired me they thought I would probably find her."

"You good at what you do, baby," Grab said, not smiling at all.

"The San Mateo sheriffs going to charge him on Tock Maranian first," I said. "The evidence for the rest is weak, but for Maranian they got a confession on tape and some tire tracks outside the greenhouse."

"Six to seven, man," Grab said, blowing smoke. His eyes had narrowed to black lines and his voice was chilly, without a trace of jivester patter. Behind his shoulder I could see the imposing shadow of the bald man who sometimes drove for him, sometimes did other things.

"Six to seven," he said. "Second degree homicide. Dude be out no later than that."

I pulled out one of my own cigarettes and lit it while Grab watched silently.

"They changed the law a year or two ago," I said quietly. "Homicide for pay gets the death penalty now in California."

Grab tapped ash into the metal saucer by the telephone and looked at me without speaking. In the hazy light of the bar his face was small and ashen, as empty of expression as a piece of slate.

"Phil says he never touched Leo Matz," I said.

Grab made a motion of some kind with his hand and the big bodyguard was suddenly there, filling the whole space between me and the rest of the room.

"You all through with the martini, Sherlock?" Grab said.

"The Nilssons liked to use sub-contractors," I said. "Piers told me he liked to spread the business around. He thought it was cheaper that way." The bodyguard raised his left fist to his right palm and flexed all the lateral muscles of his chest that I couldn't even move yet. "I did some asking on Eddy Street last night, Grab." He tapped ash that wasn't there. "I wondered all along why you were so eager to help me out. Lending me Charlie Sleeve. Coming out to the beach with your people. I wondered why you never sent around the bill you kept talking about. I wondered why you were willing to show up in the first place and tell me about Christie and never charged a penny." The bodyguard flexed again and looked down at him. "You took the contract on Leo, Grab."

There was a long pause while he picked up the glass of Chivas and drained it. Then he refolded the newspaper and slipped it under the telephone.

"I hope you don't figure you're in another moral dilemma, Haller baby," he said in a flat voice. I took one long drag on the cigarette and ground it out in the saucer. "'Cause if you are, you just might not walk out of here like you came in."

I reached slowly for my wallet, keeping my face as impassive as his, and laid a dollar bill beside the untouched martini. Grab didn't move. I stood up carefully and turned my back on him and started for the door.

"You got your redheaded girlfriend back," he said behind me.

I bowed my head and kept on going.

"It's from Sacramento," Dinah said.

I took the envelope and held it up without opening it. State of California. Bureau of Collection and Investigative Services.

"Did I tell you Mrs. Maranian is only giving Christie five thousand dollars from what would have been Muriel's inheritance? That and her hospital bills," I said. "Nobody can talk her into giving any more."

"There's nothing you can do," she said. "Things don't always come out neat-edged, Mike. You can't be bitter. You have to be philosophic."

I put down the envelope and picked up a cigarette from the coffee table. "Philosopher, kings filter best," I said and it didn't come out neat-edged and funny at all.

She put her arm through mine and stood beside me, looking out at the clear afternoon sunshine.

"You couldn't have turned Grab in," she said. "Even

Fred said so. You made your decision two days ago. Now live with it."

"I never had any evidence anyway, not courtroom evidence."

"You couldn't turn him in, morally. He paid you back. In his terms he paid you back."

I looked down at the top of her head, smelled the faint perfume she uses every day and felt the warm pressure of her breast on my chest as she shifted to watch a sailboat far out on the bay. In any terms at all he had paid me back.

She kissed me and pulled away to go into the kitchen.

"I heard something on the radio," she called as she left. "A man in Berkeley shot his neighbor for mowing his lawn too early in the morning."

"The coup de grass," I said, and this time she laughed and reappeared a minute later carrying two glasses of Château Kaplan.

"Aren't you going to open it?" she said.

I slipped one finger down the end of the envelope and after a moment showed her the letter from Henry Sampson. "Yetta kept his word," I said. "They withdrew all charges. Sampson is pleased to enclose my gun permit and my new license, number 0032-39-40."

"Does that give you a license . . . like James Bond?"

I pulled her close and kissed her ear and while her eyes widened I explained what kind of license it gave me. She put down the wine glasses and clasped both hands around the back of my neck, pressing her hips against mine and rocking gently back and forth.

She stood on her toes and nuzzled my neck as the blouse came free and my hands moved up to touch soft breasts, taut nipples.

"At two o'clock," she said, "I'll just send out for a pizza."

ABOUT THE AUTHOR

Max Byrd is the award-winning author of fourteen other books, including four bestselling historical novels and California Thriller, for which he received the Shamus Award. He was educated at Harvard and King's College Cambridge, England, and has taught at Yale, Stanford, and the University of California. Byrd is a Contributing Editor of *The Wilson Quarterly* and writes regularly for the *New York Times Book Review.* He lives in California.

Coming in October 2012

THE PARIS DEADLINE

A NOVEL

MAX BYRD

One

THE EIGHTH WINTER AFTER THE WAR, I was living in a one-room garret, a fourth-floor walk-up not much wider than a coat hanger, on the disreputable rue du Dragon.

And no, to get the question out of the way at once, I didn't know Hemingway, though it was Paris and the year was 1926 and every other expatriate American in the city seemed to trip over his feet or lend him money as a daily occurrence. (Years later I did stand behind him in the mail line at American Express and listen to him denounce Woodrow Wilson in very loud and Hemingwayesque French, which had the slow, clear, menacing cadence of a bull's hoof pawing the ground.)

The only literary person I actually did know, besides Gertrude Stein's landlord, was the journalist who sat on the other side of the desk we shared at the *Chicago Tribune* offices on the rue Lamartine.

He was a slender, amiable young man named Waverley Root. He was twenty-six that year, the same as the century, five years younger than I was, not quite old enough to have been in the army. Root was a remarkable person who wrote English like a puckish angel and spoke French as if he had a mouthful of cheese, and a decade or so later he was to find his true calling as a celebrated food critic for the *New York Herald*. The last time I saw him he wore nothing but yellow shirts and had gotten so fat he appeared to have inflated himself in one push of a button, like a rubber raft on a ship.

But in those days celebrity was far over the horizon, and Waverley Root was simply another vagabond reporter who had washed up on the cobblestoned shores of the Right Bank in search of a job. He had gone to Tufts. I had gone to Harvard. He had worked for the *New York World*. I had worked for the *Boston Globe*. He drank anisette and I drank Scotch, and this small divergence in personal character accounted for the fact that on the chilly, rainy Monday morning of December 7, he was leaning against my chair, nursing a French hangover (as he nicely put it), rigid, classical, and comprehensive.

"Toby," he said, "I will never drink alcohol again."

"I know it."

"An owl slept in my mouth last night. My teeth turned green. My poor eyes look like two bags of blood."

"They look like two bags of ink." I typed "30"—newspaperese for "The End"—on a sheet of yellow paper and swiveled to hand it through a hole in the wall—literally.

The Paris edition of the *Tribune* occupied the top three floors of a rambling nineteenth-century structure that had not been designed with modern journalism in mind. Apart from the Managing Editor's sanctum behind a frosted glass door, our editorial offices consisted of one long city room, which held a collection of sprung leather chairs, a long oval table covered with typewriters and ashtrays, and a string of smaller rewrite desks like ours, crammed off to the sides and in the corners. All practically deserted, of course, at this time of the morning. Bedlam arrived later, with the regular reporters, at the civilized hour of noon.

The composing rooms were downstairs (we lowered copy by force of gravity, through a chute in the middle of the floor) and the printing presses were in the basement. Our copyeditors had been banished to an interior room mysteriously inaccessible to us except by going down two flights of stairs and up again three, hence the hole in the wall. More than one visitor, seeing a disembodied hand waving vaguely through a slot in the plaster, had been put in mind of the House of Usher.

"And there is no health in me," Root said and sat down heavily on his side of the desk.

"It's nine thirty-one," I said. "She told us to be there at ten."

Our urchinish French copy boy plopped a thick stack of rubber composing mats on my blotter, murmured "Mon cher Papa," as he did every morning, and sidled away, smoking a torpedo-sized Gitane, to the dark little basement cubby he inhabited down among the rolls of newsprint. He called me "Old Dad," because even at thirty-one, my hair was mostly silver-gray, almost white, like a policeman's helmet. Many people, especially women, assumed sympathetically that something had turned it that way in the war, and if they were young and attractive, I had been known not to correct them. In fact, it had simply happened overnight when I was nineteen, and for some obscure reason, possibly modesty, probably vanity, I had never tried to dye it.

"Goddam 'The Gumps,'" Root said and picked up one of the composing mats.

I sighed and took it back. "The Gumps" had nothing to do with his hangover. They were the Paris edition's most popular comic strip (followed closely by "The Katzenjammer Kids" and "Gasoline Alley"). On Colonel McCormick's personal instructions, the comic strip mats were mailed to us from Chicago twice a month, filed in a cupboard behind the City Editor's desk, and delivered to me every Monday to be arranged in chronological order and chuted down to the printing room.

"She asked for both of us," I reminded him. "Tous les deux. Root and Keats, Keats and Root."

Root closed his eyes in anisette-induced meditation.

I sighed again like the Lady of Shalot and got to my feet. "Suite twenty-five, Hôtel Ritz, if you change your mind."

"Suites to the suite," Root said, with eyes still closed. And as I reached the door he added, sotto voce, "Lambs to the slaughter."

Outside on the rue Lamartine it was raining softly in the slow, sad Parisian winter way and the street was almost deserted: a few soggy shoppers, a gendarme in his cape, a pair of disheartened workmen on ladders stringing waterlogged loops of Christmas tinsel between the lampposts. Another crew was silently studying an enormous and inexplicable pit in the pavement, part of the endless cycle of street repair and excavations in post-war Paris.

I took thirty seconds to gulp a thimbleful of black coffee from the stall in front of our door, and another thirty seconds to frown at the cold gray sky and disapprove of our climate. Then I made my way around the pit and started out, an obedient lamb, for the Ritz.

The *Chicago Tribune* and its Paris subsidiary were owned at that time by Colonel Robert Rutherford McCormick, who had won the Medal of Honor at Cantigny (a battle I'd also attended, in a minor role), and who ran his newspaper along much the same military principles of fear and feudalism that he had evidently employed in the Army.

Fortunately for us, he managed the paper at a distance, coming to Paris only once or twice a year for what he jocularly called "little friendly look-sees," but which had the grim, white-gloved, pursed lips air of a regimental inspection. Like other monarchs he was invariably referred to by his title—in three years at the *Tribune* I had never heard him called anything except "the Colonel"—and like other monarchs as well, he was seriously burdened by family.

In his case, the burden was the Queen Mother, Mrs. Katherine Van Etta Medill McCormick, a grande dame about a hundred and fifty years old, daughter of the famous Civil War reporter Joseph Medill, eccentric even for a newspaper family, and much too fond (in the opinion of the *Tribune* staff) of visiting Paris. She called the Colonel "Bertie," which he hated, and had previously called him, against all evidence, "Katrina," until at the age of nine he rebelled.

Mrs. McCormick liked Root, as everybody did, and the Colonel liked me, because he thought I was a project in need of completing. When Mrs. McCormick had errands to be done in Paris, she summoned us both and reported the results, good or bad, directly back to Bertie.

I stopped at the corner of the rue de Provence and

watched a girl herding five or six goats down the street, still not an unusual sight in Paris in the twenties. An old man leaned out of a third-floor window and shouted to her, and while I crossed to the rue Rossini I could hear the goats' hoofs clattering as they went up the stairs to be milked.

I was a long way from Boston, I thought, or even Cantigny, and turned my gaze to the smallish blonde woman on the opposite sidewalk.

She was studying a tray of croissants in a bakery window, she had no herd of goats, and she was well worth looking at. She wore a nicely tailored green waterproof coat, which was beaded with rain and showed off her waist and her calves and her sensible brown brogues. Her hat was a blue trilby of a style I had never seen before and which, if I were not five thousand miles from home, I would have called foreign. And she had a brilliant red feather in the hatband, like a Christmas tree bulb.

In the buttery reflection of the shop window it was hard to see her face. She seemed to be counting coins in her palm. And despite the relative emptiness of the street, she also seemed completely unaware that she was being followed.

The follower in question was half a block down the sidewalk, a squat, broad-shouldered, gypsy-featured man about my age. He wore a dirty gray quilted jacket and a scowl, and carried a leather-covered billy in one hand, like a swagger stick, and moment by moment he was inching closer to her.

Up to no good. Obviously a pickpocket, I thought, and I took a step off the curb with the idea of making some sort of warning gesture to my fellow foreigner. The swarthy man transferred his scowl to me and then, to my utter astonishment, bared his teeth in a wolfish snarl.

At which precise moment the skies over Paris broke apart in a stupendous clap of thunder and a squall of freezing hard rain swept across the cobblestones with the rattling sound of coal going down a slide.

I don't mind rain. I grew up in New Mexico, where rain is so important that the Navajos have dozens of different names for it, the way Eskimos have for snow. But thunder and lightning are another story, another story for a soldier— ask Colonel McCormick about it. As the first boom rolled overhead I closed my eyes and clenched my fists as I always do, and counted silently till the last vibration had died away.

When I opened my eyes again both Red Feather and Dirty Jacket had vanished like a dream.